INTRODUCTION

All Done with the Dashing by Pamela Dowd
Maggie Mackenzie determines that a Thanksgiving cooking everyone else's favorite dish is holiday insanity—and she decides to transform this Christmas from work to worship. Is she really ready, though, to give up the longstanding traditions? And what will the change mean for her household—her husband, preschool son, teenaged daughter, and extended live-in family? Can the Mackenzies find a new method of celebrating—or will they lose Maggie to the Christmas craze?

No Holly, No Ivy by Wanda Luttrell
Alone for the first time at Christmas, Loraine is determined to enjoy it—no frenzied shopping and wrapping, no all-night cooking or decorating. She'll miss her distant family, of course, but feels she has the perfect recipe for a stress-free holiday. But mix in one feisty Jewish widow, a lonely Muslim shopkeeper, and an intriguing new minister. . .sprinkle everything with a little adventure. . .and Loraine's structured, peaceful Christmas might have more meaning than she ever imagined!

O Little Town of Progress by Wanda Luttrell
The town called Progress had made no progress, and octogenarian Mary Martha Sims is content to live out her days in her late husband's dark old house. Nearby Olde Towne, however, is changing rapidly—and journalist Charlie Justice, expecting her first child, worries over a transformation that will affect all of her plans. Can a Christmas encounter teach these two women to see beyond past hurts and present circumstances to what they can learn from each other?

My True Love Gave to Me. . . by Christine Lynxwiler
Penny Lassiter has the Christmas season down to an art, from tree trimming to cookie baking to all the endless parties. But when her husband takes her traditions for a ride, Penny's left to wonder, Where do we put the tree? More importantly, she'll ask herself where the Christmas spirit lives, and whether it's marked on a map. Penny's about to find exactly what true love gives to her, on and off the road. . . .

Simply Christmas

Published by Barbour Publishing, Inc., P.O. Box 719, Uhrichsville, Ohio 44683, www.barbourbooks.com

Our mission is to publish and distribute inspirational products offering exceptional value and biblical encouragement to the masses.

 Member of the
Evangelical Christian
Publishers Association

Printed in the United States of America.
5 4 3 2 1

Simply Christmas

TWO HUMOROUS MOTHERS,
TWO LONELY WIDOWS,
FOUR STORIES OF REGAINING
CHRISTMAS PEACE

PAMELA DOWD
WANDA LUTTRELL
CHRISTINE LYNXWILER

BARBOUR
PUBLISHING

All Done with the Dashing

by Pamela Dowd

Dedication

My Lord Jesus: I count it all joy to have Your encouragement as I walk this narrow writing path.

I'm not Maggie, nor is my family hers, but we can relate. To Rodney, my husband of a million miles, and to Abigail, Lindsay, Natalie, and Wade: You pray, believe, and encourage my stories into print.

To my critique group: Jeanne, Vickie, Ruth, Nancy, Shelley, and Paula. You keep me inspired. Smile when you read your suggestions in print.

To Deidre Knight, my agent: You help me believe I can write all things through Christ.

To Charles and Gloria Fletcher: Thanks for genetic creativity and generous applause.

To Shannon Hill, my editor: You have refreshed my heart.

To Susan Downs, my copy editor: Your suggestions were like cream added to smooth coffee.

Chapter 1

Maggie Mackenzie's slippers crunched into the predawn snow as she lifted the latch and pushed open the neighbor's gate. She felt vulnerable dressed in her bathrobe with flashlight in hand at 3:00 a.m. *How ironic! I look like a "cat" burglar.* She snickered, and her mouth curved into a smile. Her breath formed little puffs in the morning air. It was unusually cold for east Texas.

Who's insane enough to be slogging around in the middle of the night taking care of a furry little chore on her to-do list? She rolled her eyes. *I am.*

Maggie's every step shattered the layer of crust on the fragile, frosted ground. Icy crumbs lodged between her socks and fuzzy house shoes. She shivered.

She worked her way along the bushes to her neighbor's garage and felt for the hidden key above the door. Her fumbling, cold fingers bumped the key, and she listened as it glanced off the concrete into what sounded like leaves. *Great!*

She tightened the belt on her plaid flannel robe and dropped to her knees. She shined the light and felt along the wall, her fingers growing numb. She cringed at the thought of searching the sticky, damp leaf pile blown into the corner by the rainstorm before the snow. Maggie had a good mind to march home, sleep late, and tell her family there'd be no Thanksgiving dinner this year.

She could send the family to McDonald's. . .and ship Samson, the cat expecting breakfast, to join his owners on their cruise. No plunging her hand into Thanksgiving Tom with his innards wadded in paper. No stinky giblet gravy for lunch.

Had her husband, David, ever noticed no one else liked that kind of gravy? *I've pointed it out often enough. I can hear him now: "But, honey, it wouldn't be the holidays without giblets."* It wouldn't be the "holidays" without the stuff everybody else expected *her* to do.

Maggie hoped the twenty-pound bird back at the house had cooperated in the thawing process and wasn't as frozen as her tender feet. It'd be her luck, although she'd defrosted it according to the package directions.

On her second stab into the pile, her fingers seized the cold metal key. She fumbled with the lock and entered the darkened garage, her nose instantly assaulted by the disgusting odors of gas and motor oil.

"Here, kitty! Samson? You in here? I have breakfast. . .or a late midnight snack. . .whatever. I have food."

Metal pelted the concrete, startling Maggie. She yelped, spinning toward the clatter. Her light revealed the mystery— a toppled tin of scattered nails.

Samson stretched and mewed while she recovered. He rubbed against her pajamas.

Maggie placed the cat food on the hood of the Suburban. As the opener circled the can, she tried not to scratch the paint. Pervasive canned liver quickly overcame all garage smells, and

Samson jumped to attention beside her. She scratched his ear. "Watch your tongue on that sharp can," she warned as she left.

Picking her way home, she looked at the stars. *Well, Lord, here we are. Just the two of us. Another Thanksgiving. Another time to be thankful. Sorry, God, I hadn't noticed.* She checked her watch by the moonlight. *Off schedule already!*

Hadn't God set her up in this crazy life? A proverb came to mind. *"She looketh well to the ways of her household." And her neighbors' household, and her in-laws, and the cat's meals.* Maggie tapped the flickering flashlight and chuckled. " 'Her candle goeth not out by night,' " she whispered.

She hoped God understood all she had on her plate. Make that *platter.*

She tiptoed back into the house, careful not to disturb the cousins littering the den floor that adjoined her kitchen. Cooking by candlelight wasn't romantic. *Stupid is more like it, but it's a sacrifice I'll gladly make to keep them all sleeping and "relatively" happy.* Preparing turkey in the dark was likely to result in a missing giblet or two, but if they came out in the dressing, she'd claim she meant to do it, and David would be pleased.

Contemplating the turkey in the sink, she placed one arm across her middle. The robe was still cold from her trek. *I need coffee. Bad.* She'd wanted to avoid waking the family with the aroma but decided to forget it. Who would wake at this hour of night?

"Morning," she whispered, correcting her internal monitor. *It's morning, and I have a turkey to dress and bake. Why have I wasted all this time on a stupid cat when I have a houseful of people expecting a meal it will take me hours to prepare and them minutes to eat?*

Maggie inhaled the cold thought. She hadn't considered

how desperate she felt until she held the butcher knife over the turkey, ready to clip the plastic cord holding its wings. Standing alone in the candlelit kitchen, knife in hand. . .snoring relatives sprawled on the floor. Well, there was no telling what she might do—with the bird.

Chapter 2

Worn out, yet pleased with her sacrifice, Maggie looked at Thanksgiving Tom. He brought fresh meaning to "dressed for success." While the household slept, Maggie crept back to bed, savoring the mingled aromas of coffee and cinnamon. Her Twizzler-shaped pumpkin dough could rise undercover while she slept.

She situated her cold, socked feet along David's shins. His soft snoring ceased, then resumed when she grew still. As she collapsed into a deep sleep, no visions of holi-daze danced in *her* head.

In the way known only to sleeping mothers, Maggie sensed her three-year-old standing at her elbow. She cast a selfish prayer heavenward—*Lord, send him back to sleep*—before peeking to see if it'd worked. It hadn't.

Brophy nudged her arm. Then he patted her cheek.

Maggie rolled toward David, feigning sleep. David hadn't awakened and probably wouldn't.

Maybe ignoring him would send Brophy scurrying. Surely, he wouldn't find a sleeping mommy half as endearing as she found a sleeping boy. *I only need forty thousand more winks.* She remained still.

Brophy stroked her hair. "It's Pilgrim and Indian day, Mama," he said in his wake-up voice. "And somebody's been in the kitchen."

This wasn't news to Maggie. She'd already experienced a turkey baster full of fun. Maggie hoped her dreary attitude wasn't contagious. For fear of harming her offspring, she harrumphed without a sound. *Pilgrim and Indian Day! I'd like to scare up some pilgrims to help cook my feast.*

"I want break-a-fust. Come on." Brophy climbed onto the bed and tugged her shoulder.

Maggie rolled toward the boy perched on his knees. Behind one hand, she perfected a yawn.

Brophy reached down for a hug, then lunged for Maggie in giggles. He squeezed her cheeks between chubby little fists and laughed at her fish lips.

Maggie drank in his dimpled smile, his sleep-tousled hair; he looked so glad to see her. How could she resist such. . . Her eyelids grew heavy before she could finish the thought.

Brophy's tickling fingers reminded Maggie she was supposed to be awake. Brophy smelled like the dog he slept with. Maggie didn't know why she bothered to bathe him at night except to give Scruffy a clean boy to lick.

Brophy pried one of Maggie's eyes open with his icy little fingers. "Mama, wake up."

Maggie pulled away, shaking her head side to side. "Stop. What do you want?" She didn't mean to sound grouchy. She popped her eyes open before Brophy could and looked at his expectant face. Maggie heaved a sigh.

She threw back the comforter and edged her legs off the

bed while Brophy jumped to the floor. "Okay, son. Let me get my bearings." She clutched the nightstand. "Is the room spinning, or is it just my imagination? Give me a second. I have to find my robe."

Brophy darted to the bathroom, grabbed it off the linoleum, and returned.

"Why don't you ever wake your daddy?"

" 'Cause all Daddy gives me is Loops from the bottom shelf."

"Where you can reach them," she interjected.

"I want pannercakes." He took her hand and squeezed it tight.

She walked toward the kitchen, swinging his hand along in hers. "Not this morning, sweetie. Mommy's way too tired to remember how to make them."

What she saw jolted her as much as if she'd thrown the car into reverse expecting to go forward. Instantly awake, her eyes followed the floury cat tracks circling her navy tile floor. She gasped at the sight of paw prints marring her perfect rolls. Samson gazed at her with hooded lids, then returned to licking his paw. "This morning's breakfast might be your last supper!" She grabbed the cat under the belly and headed to the door where she dumped him into the cold. She turned on her son. "How'd he get in? Brophy, do you know anything about this?"

"The kitty was crying." Brophy had the pot drawer open.

"Don't you ever let that cat back in this house. You hear me?" Her voice conveyed the seriousness of his offense, but he looked so cute she almost laughed.

He dragged the big iron griddle across the floor, scraping the tile without repentance. She rescued the floor and sighed. "Go wake the family." *Maybe I'll get some help that way.* Maggie glanced at the kitchen clock. She'd slept only two hours. *There's got to be a better way than dashing through the snow.*

She heard her own miniature Paul Revere announce breakfast, "Come on, everybody! Pannercakes are coming."

Maggie dead-bolted the back door and hid the key. After cleaning Samson's mess, she selected four eggs, ticking off the number needed for the afternoon meal. *Two for each pumpkin and sweet potato pie.* She cracked an egg into the bowl. *Two— or was it four—for the pecan?* Another eggshell split with precision. *The gingerbread men for the non-pie eaters will take two. Thank goodness I bought two dozen.*

Maggie dipped into the Bisquick box and offered up a sigh of thanks for convenience foods about the time Brophy shuffled in with his Spiderman undies and pajamas down around his ankles. Maggie stared without compassion.

"Brophy, after Christmas, bud, we're tackling this problem. Your days of being catered to are over." Maggie blew the hair from her forehead and turned down the griddle.

The cousins laughed as Brophy waddled by.

Brophy puckered his bottom lip and stuck out his tongue.

"You see?" Maggie said to him. "You're too big for this. They won't even take you into Parents' Day Out until you learn to wipe yourself. You want to go to Parents' Day Out, don't you?" It was a conversation they oft repeated, but the adventure had not called Brophy's name, nor had he signed on the pottied line.

At the bathroom door, Maggie lost it. "How could one little boy make this big a mess?"

She surveyed the damage to her guest bathroom. The Golden Book, once perched on Brophy's lap, had fallen by the tub. A brown trail ran across the seat where he'd scooted to stand, and the toilet paper he'd tried to use littered the floor in stained wads. "Brophy Mackenzie!"

David came to the door.

"He's yours." Maggie walked passed him. "I splurged on Clorox wipes. They're under the sink."

David called after her, "It's about time you trained him."

Maggie stuffed a frustrated comeback aimed at the man bearing the initials H.U.S.B.A.N.D. She didn't have time to defend herself.

Chapter 3

Maggie stared at her brimming Thanksgiving plate and wondered if she would fall face-forward into the mashed potatoes, or if she'd still be awake when it came time to top the desserts with the fresh cream she'd whipped to perfection. She didn't have enough strength to lift the utensil in her hand, and she wasn't hungry.

Maggie twirled the fork though the green bean casserole and used it to slice a trench between several pecans atop the buttery warm sweet potato mountain next to her homemade cranberry sauce. She stabbed a mandarin orange—the ambrosia was about the only food she hadn't sampled—but she couldn't bring it to her mouth. Nothing looked tasty.

"Maggie, this is delicious. I don't know how you do it every year," her cousin said, lifting a forkful of green beans.

I don't either. Maggie gave a weak nod of thanks.

She knew the script. Next her father-in-law, Pop Mackenzie, would mention the close proximity of this holiday to Christmas and its do-again menu.

Pop didn't disappoint. He patted Maggie's hand and, like a coach wanting to inspire his best player, said, "Can hardly believe we get to do this all over again in four weeks."

She could have predicted the table conversation almost word for word. After a round of compliments, the football talk began. Maggie thought she might burst from the room with her ears covered. *Same. Same. Same. Always the same conversation.* She didn't care who carried the ball on the third down of the Cowboys game against the Dolphins in 1993, nor did she care who would play the Cowboys today—as un-Texan as that seemed. And she didn't want any more compliments.

Her quietness must have been misinterpreted, because her new sister-in-law, Charlie's wife, Jill, said, "Don't be so bashful. You could give us all cooking lessons. I know I'd sign up."

Charlie punched Jill in jest. "She needs some. I never knew water could burn until I married her."

"That was his fault." She addressed those listening.

He sent an inflated wink to his honeymoon cutie, causing her cheeks to splotch. "You're the one who lured me into the bedroom."

Maggie covered Brophy's ears for fear Charlie would elaborate.

Charlie received a swift kick under the table. David's brother needed someone to restrain him; it was nice to see he'd found a well-suited wife for the task.

Charlie held his shin with an exaggerated pout, a male-dominant Mackenzie trait.

Brophy imitated him.

Maggie rolled her eyes at Charlie. "Oh, sure, indoctrinate him early," she said, indicating Brophy with a nod as she cut a small bite of turkey and pushed it around in the gravy on her plate.

"What are you talking about?" Pop turned a bent lip south.

"That, that. . .that. . .that. . . ," Ma Mackenzie stammered, pointing at Pop's mouth.

"Frown," Maggie supplied the word Ma's dementia had stolen.

Ma grew serious. "I was going to say elephant." Her eyebrows pinched together as she considered her blunder.

Brophy whispered to Maggie while everyone could hear, "Did Ma get her words mixed up again?"

Maggie leaned close to his ear. "Shh. Eat your mac and cheese."

Brophy demonstrated the Mackenzie pout to perfection.

Maggie's sister, Anne, said, "As usual, Mags, you outdid yourself." She leaned back. "Do you know how much I look forward to this meal every year? And. . ." She looked around the table and included everybody in a self-tanned smile. ". . .to coming home?"

"Twice," Maggie said under breath.

"Excuse me?" Her sister missed the point.

"Twice. I cook this meal *twice* a year. And you come home twice." *And watch football. Twice. And compliment me. Twice. And fail to help. Twice.*

Anne looked for support. "Pop's already pointed that out. Haven't you, Pop?"

"Here. Here." David tapped on his glass of sparkling cider. The spoon-to-crystal sound drew everyone's attention. "I don't know how we'd manage without Maggie. Three cheers for Mags." He led the family in hip-hip-hoorays.

The eating began again after the prayer that someone remembered "because God deserved a 'big hooray' today, too." Second helpings, "pass this," and "pass that" followed. "Oohs" and "aahs" surrounded Maggie like echoes bouncing off a dry cavern wall.

"Every year is better than before," Aunt Minnie said. "And

the carrots are perfect, my dear."

"Yeah, Mom. It rocks." Samantha's dwindling portion should have made Maggie proud. Her sixteen-year-old finicky eater had no complaints at all. "Mom, you all right?"

Maggie sensed them all staring. Like a perfectly browned turkey, her juices ran near the surface. Tears threatened. She choked them down with a nibble of buttered bread.

"You should get more rest, dear," Aunt Minnie, who never lent a hand in the kitchen, said as she scooped a giant serving of sweet potatoes onto her plate, dropping a slippery pecan on the tablecloth.

David said, "Hey, Mags, I could Cajun-fry us a turkey for Christmas if it would help." He winked at Maggie. She turned down his offer every year.

"Eww." Samantha wrinkled her nose. "In grease? I don't think so. Uncle Earnest and I care about things like that, don't we? Yuck."

David pointed a fork at Samantha. "Don't knock it till you've tried it, Sammy."

Maggie laid her napkin on the table and rose. "I'm done. Through." The browned turkey image remained.

Pop tried to seat her with a restraining hand. "Why, you haven't eaten a thing. Don't leave yet. The dishes can wait."

"I mean I'm through with Thanksgiving, Pop." Maggie kept her voice steady though her knees quaked.

"Well, of course you are," Aunt Minnie said. "All the work's been done."

Maggie glanced around her family member's picked-over plates, a still life of Americans with eyes bigger than stomachs. Thanksgiving—a time to feast, to indulge, and to sacrifice the fatted cook.

Well, this cook's had it!

Maggie eyed the captive, overstuffed family lounging around her table. "I've roasted twenty-some-odd turkeys through the years; peeled and boiled no telling how many carrots; baked and mashed sweet potatoes till I'm pulp, made countless pies from scratch, and giblet gravy no one eats but David." She stopped to draw a breath.

"I'm sure the gravy's wonderful, Maggie," Aunt Minnie said. "You know we all love your cooking."

"You love it so much, you've come to expect it. Well, no more. I resign." Maggie fled the room, feeling like she'd just performed a scene from Turkey Bird's Nightmare on Maggie Street.

She cupped one ear at the kitchen door, hoping to hear them agree the holiday was too much for her. She envisioned a helpful family gathered around the kitchen sink instead of the usual: another miraculous dishrag touchdown for Maggie—38 dishes to ZERO help.

Everyone remained still until David said, in a voice that defied *her* reality *and* imagination, "O. . .kay. Can I interest anyone in some pie and football? I'm sure Maggie made coffee."

Chapter 4

Maggie pried and scraped at the crusted drippings that clung to the greasy roaster but only managed to splash filthy dishwater on her blouse. *Errrr!* She threw a discarded dryer sheet into the pan to loosen the mess—a trick she'd learned from a magazine at the pediatrician's office—unlocked the back door, and set the roaster in the slush on the porch. She'd dare anyone to bring the thing in before next year.

Back inside, Maggie drummed her fingers on the counter. Aunt Minnie would lie down to recuperate from "stuffing herself silly." Earnest would join David, Charlie, Pop, and the boys around the television to offer reverence and holy shouts of encouragement to the sports gods they loved. Samantha would amuse her young girl cousins with stories of guys and makeovers until she tired of their company. Brophy needed a nap.

So did Maggie. But she had a strict personal policy against rest. She poured herself a pick-me-up and sipped the hazelnut coffee with pleasure. With enough in her veins, she could maintain her ideal, taking-it-easy-is-for-wimps approach.

When no second-string dishwashers arrived, Maggie opened the back door and carefully stacked her dirty china on the wet porch. She hid the grimy silverware inside the roaster. *One must be practical when considering what people might steal.* Even in her frustration, she didn't want to tempt anyone.

Samson sauntered over. Maggie watched him lick the top plate. *Why did I agree to feed a stupid cat on top of everything else I have to do?* She couldn't help thinking where his tongue might have been. She bent down to retrieve the plates.

"Nice dishwasher you found." Humor lined Jill's voice.

Maggie stiffened.

Samson licked the gravy grease, avoiding tidbits left from Maggie's famous corn-pudding casserole.

Maggie felt her face grow pink before she turned around. "Uh. . ." How did one explain undisguised insanity to a new relative? "I was. . .ah. . .just. . .um. . .letting the cat have some leftovers. His owners are away on a cruise. This way I won't have to feed him later." She spit out the sentences much like her teenage daughter did when trying to cover her mischief. It never worked.

"You need to come with me." Jill's serious tone would have scared Maggie if she hadn't seen the sparkle in her sister-in-law's green eyes. Jill grinned as she held up twin cucumber slices, rescued from the dinner salad.

What in the world? Charlie married a live wire.

"I thought you'd have honeymoon-itis," Maggie said, hoping to divert the conversation away from her odd behavior. "The kind where you glue yourself to a silly football game to demonstrate your love." Maggie couldn't imagine what Jill must think, watching a cat lick her china.

"I gave that up when I got the ring." She flashed her left hand at Maggie.

Maggie whistled. She'd been so busy, she'd overlooked the gorgeous wedding set. "It's beautiful. Elegant." *Like you.*

Jill and Charlie had met and married in Hawaii. Maggie and David hadn't had the money to attend, so this was their first chance to meet the girl who'd converted the staunch bachelor of the family.

Maggie headed for familiar territory. "I've got to get these dishes done. If I wait any longer, I won't have the energy. Besides, if anyone else catches me out here with the dishes and the cat, they'll know the truth: Thanksgiving made me loopy."

"That's what these are for." Jill jiggled the cucumbers with a flick of her wrist. "Unlooping."

Maggie looked at Jill with visible doubt before shooing Samson away. When he meowed in protest, Maggie scraped some turkey scraps onto the sidewalk. Then she helped Jill cart things back inside.

Her sister-in-law began loading the dirty dishes into the dishwasher. But as soon as Jill put one in, Maggie took it out, dropping each into sudsy water where it belonged.

Jill stood to the side, observing, looking somewhat baffled. "What are you doing?"

"The dishes." Maggie didn't know what the fuss was about; she always did them this way.

"You don't have to do all that. That's what *dishwashers* are for. Have you got any more cucumber? I want a couple slices, too."

Maggie searched the refrigerator drawer and hunted down the one she'd partially cut for lunch. "Here it is, but I'm warning you; I don't eat cucumbers. The only cucumber I'm friendly with is Larry on the Veggie Tales videos." Maggie returned to scrubbing.

"Where's a knife? I'll cut us some. You're going to love this." Jill dumped the old slices into the trash. "They're better cold anyway."

Maggie's insides were already in an uproar from being caught outside. "I really can't eat them." *They hurt my stomach.* She offered Jill a knife.

"We're not going to." Jill peeled the skin away from the cucumber. "I couldn't eat another bite if I wanted to. Everything was *so* good. I'm stuffed."

Maggie dunked dishes in the soapy water, then rearranged them in the dishwasher. "So, how'd you like your first Mackenzie Thanksgiving?"

Maggie felt her sister-in-law's eyes boring into her. She turned to see her intuition was right. *"Apologize,"* commanded an inner voice. "Sorry I ruined it."

"I'm not." Jill chuckled, clearly amused. "Finding you outside with your china let me know we could be friends. Before that, you intimidated me. I'd never want to cook this much or clean it up. I don't know how you've done it so long." Jill leaned against the counter and scrutinized Maggie. "Do you really always do your dishes that way? Prewashing them instead of just rinsing them?"

Maggie nodded, tackling a handful of silverware with a scrub brush before loading it.

"I put my dishes in with crud all over them," Jill said.

"And they come out clean?"

"Every time."

"I find that hard to believe." Maggie transferred the silverware to the dishwasher basket.

"Charlie said you've been catering the holidays since Ma got sick." Jill finished slicing the cucumber, then rewrapped it in plastic wrap. "That's why I worked for a cruise line. They fed me. I'm hopeless in the kitchen." Jill opened the refrigerator and stored the leftover in the drawer. "Now that I'm landlocked, I don't know what Charlie will eat. We'll both probably starve."

"Don't let Charlie fool you; he can cook." *Unlike his mother.* Maggie began scrubbing pots. "Just before our first Thanksgiving, Ma lost her mother. David and I were only dating, yet somehow I wound up cooking his great-grandmother's recipes. I don't recall being asked. I just stepped in to fill a gap and wound up a permanent replacement. David says my cooking won his heart." Maggie smiled.

She pushed a bit of hair away from her eyes with her forearm. "I should be used to it by now. I don't know why I gave that selfish little speech. I love my family. I love serving others. I even *love* to cook." Maggie shook her head. "I don't want to be self-centered."

"Phooey." Jill held a thin cucumber sliver to the light. "These work better skinny. I've only known you for a day, but *you're* not selfish. Far from it."

Maggie watched, her curiosity growing. She preferred hers cut thick for salads, even though she couldn't eat them. She couldn't imagine what Jill wanted with cucumbers.

Jill's slender hands with the perfect French-tipped nails offered some slices to Maggie. "Here."

Maggie wiped her hands on a dish towel, folded it on the counter, and stacked the slices in her palm.

Jill pointed toward the door leading to the backyard. "We need a way out of here where we don't have to cross the goal line by the TV. Or I'll get suckered in by *love.*" Jill winked and laid the knife on the counter.

Maggie placed the knife in the sink. "It's cold outside, and Brophy might need me. I can't leave. Besides, I've hardly made a dent in the mess."

"The kitchen can wait. This can't. Brophy's with Uncle

Charlie. I told him to keep him busy playing horsey. He's a cute little cowboy."

Maggie tilted her head to inquire with a smile, "Charlie or Brophy?" She liked her sister-in-law already.

Jill wore the confident grin of a newlywed as she stepped outside. "I did marry a handsome cowboy, didn't I?" She motioned for Maggie to follow. "Stay close." Jill tiptoed off the porch to the sidewalk and looked both ways like a spy. She took an exaggerated step over a small puddle as if it were gigantic. With a finger pressed to her lips, she motioned for Maggie to follow.

They crept around the corner of the house, embellishing every step. Maggie kept shushing Jill. They couldn't quit laughing. Slipping in the front door, they tiptoed to the master bedroom.

Jill flopped across Maggie's bed sideways and slid two cucumber slices over her eyes. "Ahh."

Maggie joined her. The coolness felt wonderful to her tired eyelids. "This is amazing. Now I know what 'cool as a cucumber' means." She laughed way too loud over her lame pun. Maggie's long legs dangled off the bed. She pulled her feet up, knees bent. "Where'd you learn this?" She lifted one cucumber to peek at Jill.

Jill drew in a deep breath before answering, "Women's magazine. I may not cook, but I know how to use vegetables. Wait till you try the avocado facial I found."

As magnificent as the pampering felt, it didn't take long for Maggie to become restless. A thinly sliced opaque vegetable couldn't stop her from reading the family's needs listed inside her eyelids.

She sighed, knowing she should get back to work. *No rest for the mommy.*

Chapter 5

Maggie hauled herself out of bed at six the next morning, grateful for God's gift to women. *Coffee.* While it brewed, she glanced over her morning devotional and moved on to her to-do list. The detailed record in broad neat strokes included:

1. *Feed Samson.*
2. *Christmas shop—keep Samantha in a good mood; make her feel extra-special.*
3. *David take Brophy for haircut—tell Brophy pilgrims had short hair—then to Santa for photo.*
4. *Boil turkey bones—soup.*
5. *Make turkey spaghetti—dinner.*
6. *Start Christmas decorating.*

Taking a mug of coffee, she tiptoed past her sleeping husband and placed her mug on the bathroom counter. The coffee wouldn't cool in the time it took Maggie to shower and dress.

By her second cup, she'd already boxed most of her everyday knickknacks in preparation for the decorations David would haul from the attic—if she reminded him. The turkey bones

29

simmered on the back burner, filling the kitchen with lunch smells that made her crave leftovers. She cut a slice of pumpkin pie and topped it with whipped cream.

"Mornin', love. 'Tis the month before Christmas." David began pouring coffee.

A sharp intake of breath whistled through her clenched teeth. "Believe me, I know."

Jill walked in wearing a rosy-cheeked newlywed glow. "I usually try to get my shopping finished by August."

Maggie gave Jill a head-to-toe inspection. "Let me guess; a magazine article suggested you shop early." Jill looked like she'd just returned from the spa—shower-fresh and pretty, even in a pair of plaid sleeping pants and a yellow ducky T-shirt.

How long has it been since I glowed like that? I usually leave my prince in bed, as dead to love as an unkissed toad.

"You're going to love your Christmas present, Maggie." Jill splashed a dash of vanilla syrup into her coffee.

"David. . ." Maggie hesitated. Was it her imagination, or had a look passed between Jill and David—as if they shared a secret? "Could you. . .feed Samson for me?"

"I will. Later."

Maggie sighed. "Not later, David. Now. *Please.*"

David looked her in the eye. "It will be fine if I do it later."

"Morning, Mama." Samantha wore faded jeans and a cloud of Sun-Ripened Raspberry from Bath & Body Works, a beaded purse slung over one shoulder. "I figured the stores would open early. When're we going? I already know what I want."

Maggie rolled her eyes. "Figures. You started planning this trip last December."

"Did not." Samantha rolled her eyes in perfect imitation. "I waited until New Year's." She grinned.

Maggie opened the refrigerator and removed the 2 percent milk for Samantha's cereal. She popped off the plastic lid and said to Jill, "Today Sammy picks out and tries on everything she wants for Christmas. You're invited." Maggie reached for the Fruit Loops. "David keeps Brophy. Then, this afternoon, I go back to the mall without her to purchase as much as I can of her 'To Die For' list."

Maggie looked at her daughter with obvious pride. She enjoyed their annual shopping spree, even if it did wear her to a frazzle. The results were worth the effort: Samantha got what she wanted—her new clothes fit, the CDs were the latest, and the electronic equipment was always the right style and color. The thanks she received was the best of all. *Over the river and through the mall to the holiday I go!*

Jill whistled. "Sounds like tons of work. You're one lucky lady, Miss Samantha Jo. My mother always got me things I hid at the back of the closet." Jill poured eggnog into a glass decorated with a snowman.

Samantha gave Maggie a big hug. "Mom's pretty great." She plunged her spoon into the cereal Maggie provided.

Maggie brightened at the compliment, ready to buy Samantha the world. This day was known in the Mommy Manual as Samantha's Day, and there were many compliments ahead. Gifts spoke love to Samantha in a language she understood. Maggie turned to put the cereal away as David cleared his throat.

"Uh, I meant to tell you last night. . ."

Maggie straightened the pantry shelves, pretending they were messy. She didn't want to hear any excuses.

"I can't keep Brophy today. I promised the guys"—he meant the cousins—"I'd take them skeet shooting."

He moved to retrieve the cereal he liked from a shelf at Maggie's eye level.

They made eye contact.

She let her eyes communicate bitter disappointment. *For a man who works hard, you're a holiday goof-off.*

Maggie felt David's quick forgive-me hug and forced a pleasant smile. "Can't Brophy go along? I was counting on you." She remembered how the cousins had begged yesterday, but she hadn't figured he'd go along with their plans.

"It's too dangerous for a three-year-old."

"He needs a haircut." Maybe she could guilt him. "I needed your help with that, too."

"His hair's not in his eyes yet. Take him with you. He needs to see Santa."

Brophy entered as if on cue, his footed pajamas slapping the kitchen floor. Maggie hissed, "Shh!" at David.

"I don't wanna sit in Santy's lap." Brophy folded his arms and scowled.

Annoyed at David's insensitivity, Maggie cast him a warning glare. She'd hoped he would pick up the slack since Santa had scared the stuffings out of Brophy last year.

"You'll like Santa this year, son," David assured Brophy as he scooped him into his arms. "Hey! You're a big boy, aren't you?" David's nasty habit of mocking his children reared its head.

"I y'am." Brophy puckered his lips.

"You won't get any toys." Samantha liked nothing better than to frustrate Brophy. "You have to sit on Santa's lap to stay off the naughty list."

"I been good." Brophy kicked at her though David held him.

Maggie wrung out the sponge, frustrated that Jill had to witness all this.

"Why, you little. . ." Samantha leaned close enough to make Brophy cross-eyed and pinched his arm.

Brophy cried out, "She gave me an owie."

David dumped him into Maggie's arms. "Samantha Jo Mackenzie, you're way too old for that." He pointed toward her room.

"Me!" Indignation blossomed on her innocent face. "You're always sticking up for him like he's some kind of baby. Tell him, Mom. He bites when you're not around, Dad."

Maggie hated her children's bickering. "Don't say another word, or you'll be on my naughty list, and that doesn't bode well for a girl who wants to *see Santa today,* if you catch my drift." She hesitated long enough to compliment herself for the zinger she was about to deliver. "In fact, you're going to sit on Santa's opposite knee, holding your little brother's hand. I want a joint picture this year."

Samantha sputtered, "What? At the mall? But. . .my friends." Disbelief and humiliation mingled on her face.

David came to Maggie's defense. "Your mother said 'not another word.' Call it punishment or encouragement—whatever you like. But if you continue, I'll have Mom sign you up for a holiday job while you're at the mall." He paused—letting the initial threat sink in—and, winking at Maggie, added, "As an *elf.*"

Maggie knew that one stung. While Samantha morphed into a semipleasant teenager, David smiled at Maggie. She placed Brophy on the ground, thankful for her husband.

Jill drew the pumpkin pie across the counter and cut a slice with the knife propped on the rim. "I'll be ready as soon as I have some of this and throw on some clothes. I can apply my makeup in the car." Jill added a dollop of whipped cream, delaying Samantha's trip even longer. "I *want* this recipe." Jill hooked her pinky through the topping and dashed a streak on Maggie's forehead before she could protest.

Before Maggie knew what came over her, she'd poked Jill's pie and smeared pumpkin on Jill's cheek. She hardly recognized herself today.

Maggie glanced at Brophy. "Sorry, son. Mommy shouldn't have acted that way."

Jill rubbed the pie into her skin like moisturizer. "We'll see if this works as well as the forty-dollar stuff I bought last week." She laughed. "It's called Pumpkin-A-Peel. The enzymes remove dead skin cells and make your skin feel tingly."

Maggie opened the bottom bin of the fridge and tossed the leftover cucumber Jill's way. "Merry Christmas, facial girl."

"Merry to you, too." Jill faked a pout. "You *know* what your problem is, don't you?" Jill tossed the cucumber back in Maggie's direction while Brophy stared wide-eyed. "You don't subscribe to any magazines."

"That's not a problem," David said. "There's no money for extras." He opened a sales circular. He'd made it his job to find the best holiday buys, frequently telling Samantha she should get more for their money.

"Too bad," Jill said. "Magazines are the ticket to joining the Facial Girls' Sisterhood."

Maggie sighed. "David's right; I *don't* have the money. *Or* the time." She pitched Samantha's plastic cereal bowl into the dishwasher. "I can barely get my Bible reading done each morning; then it's go, go, go till bedtime." She indicated her open planner on the counter. "That thing has a life of its own. Pampering isn't for me."

Jill placed an encouraging hand on Maggie's shoulder. "*Your* choice."

Chapter 6

M om, you missed the turn. This isn't the way to the mall," Samantha called from behind her, having been relegated to the backseat of the minivan with Brophy due to Jill's riding shotgun.

Maggie glanced at Jill. Did she know what she'd started? The seedling had been planted by her random "your choice" comment and could only thrive without guilt, so Maggie drove without looking at Samantha.

"Mom, did you hear me? You went the wrong way."

Maggie stayed calm. "You're very observant."

"I'm *not* looking for clothes anywhere except the mall, no matter what Daddy says." Panic rose in the teenager's voice.

"I'm not asking you to." The scowl Maggie saw when she glanced in the rearview mirror almost turned the minivan around. She hated opposition.

Before she could renege, she said, "I'm looking for some magazine ideas to destress our holidays. It shouldn't take long. Maybe I'll even find something on how to change a sourpuss into a sugarplum." Maggie turned and smiled her brightest, hoping to transform the frown on Samantha's face.

"*Mom!*" Samantha moaned like a teenaged drama queen.

"This is *my* day, not yours."

"It's everybody's day, Sammy. Where's your Christmas spirit?" Maggie attempted to sound sunny, though a chill wind threatened to scatter her plans.

She parked the van in the nearest vacant space—a mile from Wal-Mart's front doors. Maggie unlatched Brophy's child restraint, then focused on her headstrong daughter. "I need a change, Samantha. I'm looking for a way to transform Christmas from 'gimme-gimme' to. . .oh. . .I don't know what. . . ." Despair and defeat landed with rock-solid footing. *Who am I trying to kid? I probably can't change, even if I want to.* Maggie heard the familiar tinkle of holiday bell ringers in the background. *Gimme—gimme—gimme,* they announced charity-style.

"This isn't fair!" Samantha looked at her aunt as they neared the store. "She and Dad dreamed this up." It was obvious Samantha wanted to draw her aunt into the argument, but Jill continued walking and sorting the contents of her purse. Samantha fumed. "I'll never buy clothes at Wal-Mart like Mom."

"This isn't about you." Maggie offered the stiff girl a one-armed hug. *Every time I try to do something for myself, my family goes ballistic.*

"My point exactly." Samantha pulled away. "You know you can't go in here without filling a basket." The automatic doors parted.

Maggie said, "I'm looking for a better way to manage Christmas." *Something has to change, and it had better be me.*

"I wanna see the toys," Brophy said, delighted by the prospects inside the stadium-sized store. Brophy yanked Samantha's hand, ready to run. "Come on, Sissy."

"Wait, Brophy." Maggie trudged behind, the energy

robbed from her heartfelt desire. How would she ever change Christmas if she couldn't even maneuver a stubborn teenager?

Jill accepted a shopping cart from the door greeter and turned it toward the magazine aisle as if she hadn't heard a single unpleasant thing. "What did we do before we could buy panties, hunting gear, and toys in the same store?" She didn't look at mother or daughter.

They moved past an in-house bank, a photo developer, and the optical department. Cashiers' machines *ka-chinged* all around them as shoppers prepared to depart with buggy loads of bulging blue plastic bags. They passed the Angel Tree, an evergreen decorated with the names and needs of impoverished children in the area.

Maggie slowed. *Perhaps we should shop for an Angel Tree child instead.* It would teach her children a valuable lesson about what the season was really all about—not mother or daughter, but a baby named Jesus. But before she could stop, Brophy darted for the toy section. "Samantha, keep an eye on your brother. And don't lose him."

Samantha followed at a calculated distance.

Jill chuckled. "Everything's so spread out, they ought to add aerobics to their advertising slogan. Falling prices and lower pounds *guaranteed.*"

Maggie eyed her thin companion, glad for the subject change. "I'm not sure about the pounds part, but there *is* one thing they don't advertise—the miscellaneous stuff we can hide in a grocery bill. It's dangerous when you can go in for a dozen eggs and come out with a TV." The children were many aisles away, and she felt the relief. "Here's what I need." Maggie reached for the magazine *Real Simple* from the abundant selection on the racks in front of them. She loved the photographs and features. "It's a bit pricey." She tossed it into the basket. "But it looks like a great way to simplify things."

Jill placed a hand on Maggie's arm. "I hope I haven't steered you in the wrong direction." Concern lined Jill's voice and wrinkled her brow. "Tackling the holidays in a different way could prove more stressful than doing things like you always have. And it might cost more money." Jill's mouth twisted with unease.

"You think I'm doing the wrong thing, too?" Maggie heaved a sigh as her mood swung from newly excited to typically discouraged. "I didn't think you'd disapprove." She groaned. "I should have gone shopping with Samantha as planned, shouldn't I? Let her have her way. I mean. . .day." Maggie squeezed her eyes shut and rubbed her temples. "How could I be *so* selfish?"

"Whoa. Slow down." Jill patted her firmly on the back as though she were a deflated exercise ball in need of a good pumping. "It's not like you're swearing off Christmas or anything. You're not trying to skip it. Just make it a little saner. Take a deep breath." Jill demonstrated.

Maggie followed.

"Good. And another." Jill breathed deep and exhaled through pursed lips. "Now let's see what we can find." Jill pointed to a teaser entitled "Diet Mistakes." "I don't need that one. I like Cheetos. Eat them every chance I get."

"That was *real simple*." Maggie snickered at her pun. She picked up a magazine on home decorating, easily discarding it. "I'd have to start from scratch. It'd be like redoing a bargain basement. Way off the stress charts."

"Your home is what I call homespun charming."

"Don't open any doors. I hid the junk in the closets."

"Here's an article you might like." Jill opened to a page

promising ways to unstuff Christmas.

Maggie glanced over her shoulder. "Hmm. How to get everyone involved in preparing the meal. Wouldn't that be something? Toss it in the basket." The next magazine promised "Homecomings to Remember," and she flipped it atop the other glossy covers in her cart. "Oh, and put in the one over there about simplifying stress. I've got to read that."

"This one includes make-ahead recipes, a Christmas countdown, and photos. See?" Jill held it out.

"I'll take it," Maggie said without looking. She began laughing. "Here's a quote from Franklin D. Roosevelt that fits the Mackenzie clan: 'Sometimes the best way to keep peace in the family is to keep the members of the family apart for a while.' "

Humor danced in Jill's eyes. "Are you asking me to go?" She tossed a cooking magazine in the general direction of the others. "I can't. You're stuck with me."

As newlyweds, Charlie and Jill were in the process of building their first home, Maggie knew, but all of a sudden Jill sounded like the other relatives. They all wanted to stay. With Maggie! "Maybe I should leave it open on the coffee table." Spite crossed Maggie's face, but then she looked at her feet as guilt snaked up her spineless back. "I shouldn't have said that. Sometimes I think I'll go nuts, but then I'm glad Sammy and Brophy get the chance to know their older relatives. Some kids don't. I try to count my blessings." She hoped she didn't sound like a martyr.

"Spoken like a true Thanksgiving Day leftover!" Jill smirked.

Whoops.

Jill picked up another magazine and started thumbing through. "Speak of the devil. Here's one with your name written all over it—'All You Need for Christmas is a Stress-Free Season.'"

"Hand it over." Maggie turned to an article titled "Managing Difficult Personalities."

"Speaking of the relatives—" Maggie began to skim. She'd needed this one yesterday!

"Definitely buy that one, and I'll read it, too." Jill took it from her and laid it on top of the others.

"Let's walk to the checkout counters. There're more up there. And we need to page Samantha." Maggie envisioned the loudspeaker summons and Samantha's unhappy response. *Another confrontation.* "She'll die a thousand deaths."

"Maybe we ought to page Brophy instead."

"Much better plan. Thanks." Maggie pushed the cart toward checkout. "How many articles do you think we've found?"

"Seven or eight."

"I want one for every day between now and Christmas—that makes twenty-eight. Oh, rats. I forgot. File folders to organize them." She turned the buggy toward stationery.

"Whoa. If you read them too close to Christmas, they won't do any good. I'm warning you. Choosing not to be like you've always been is like walking uphill backwards."

Maggie wished she'd taken her antacid. "Our Sunday school teacher claims, 'Choosing to do what you've always done while expecting different results is the equivalent of insanity.'"

Jill walked along, flipping pages. "I don't guess your teacher would like this one." She showed Maggie what she'd found— "Santa's Tavern: The Guide to Mixing the Perfect Holiday Drink."

With her conservative-evangelical roots exposed, the innocent comment pricked like a dart. Maggie stopped midaisle, causing the lady behind her to almost bump into them. She moved to let the woman pass, then asked Jill, "Do you think it's too worldly to try to change Christmas this way? I mean, these aren't exactly articles about the baby Jesus." She pointed to the top title on the stack, "Six Keys to a More Rambunctious Sex Life," and blushed. "They're not Christian magazines."

"So the real world has nothing to offer *Christians?*" Jill raised an eyebrow. "I think self-help articles are something Christians should approve of—part of finding an abundant life."

Maggie didn't have an argument for that, though she knew it wasn't what Christ meant. She didn't know her sister-in-law well. *I guess I shouldn't have assumed Jill was a Christian.*

Maggie turned toward the pharmacy. "I'm going to find some antacids. Then it's on to the mall."

Chapter 7

A t the mall, Brophy had screamed at Santa as Maggie predicted, and Samantha had shopped till Maggie dropped. But Maggie had caught holiday fever yesterday as surely as she'd catch the flu bug later this season. This morning she ached, and her bank account needed a pain reliever, but she was ready to decorate.

Yesterday's to-dos hadn't been done. The tree wasn't up, and they'd shared a bucket of Tasty Cluck for dinner instead of the turkey spaghetti she'd planned, but all in all, she'd accomplished a lot.

She poured a cup of coffee and grabbed her Bible and planner. Jill was convinced the magazine project would bring Maggie ready answers to de-stressing. But how could man-made advice bring joy to a holiday that revolved around the divine?

Maggie pushed the magazines aside, took her planner, and moved yesterday's to-dos to today's list. She read from the book of Psalms for a while, glad for the uninterrupted time, then went to find Mr. Claus.

She needed help with the tree—although trying to get David to fluff the smashed artificial branches would be equivalent to keeping Brophy's magnet letters on the refrigerator door when it slammed.

Maggie found David where she expected to, sitting in a recliner, listening to football on the radio. "Can't we do it later?" he asked between plays.

She posed like a referee—nonnegotiable with hands low on hips. "No," she said. And it worked.

David cheered the unseen football players on the radio. Though he ignored Maggie, he kept working, and she accepted it as a fair compromise. Every once in a while, as they sorted and inserted branches, she had to explain things like, "That branch doesn't work in that spot," or "Let's shove the tree six inches to the left."

And he would say, "Too bad we can't earn frequent flyer miles from all the talking you do. I can hardly listen to the game with all your chatter."

When it came time to add lights, he threw a penalty flag. "Who sees the back side anyway? The window faces the yard."

"You sound like Samantha, always trying to stop me from doing things right." It would take them both standing on separate ladders and cooperating to string lights around the tree. His attitude annoyed her, but she kept working.

"Speaking of Samantha, where is the princess?"

"I sent her to the store for more lights." Maggie stood back to survey the eight-foot tree. Thanks to her efforts, the top section was lit. Maggie climbed the ladder and leaned toward the tree, steadying herself with one hand against the wall. She balanced the wobbly angel. "Is it straight? . . . Honey? . . . David, did I get it straight?"

"Hmm?" He held the ladder with one hand, his eyes glued to the radio on the floor.

"Can you *see* them if you concentrate?" Maggie climbed

down one step and leaned back. She hoped David had hold of the ladder.

"Hmm? What? Did you say something?" David glanced up. "Careful, hon. Don't fall."

As if because of his prediction, Maggie tumbled into David's arms. She shut her eyes, expecting a sweet kiss of relief.

"No! Aw, come on!" David stomped his foot. He put her down with the gentleness of a linebacker. "I can't believe that ref."

She glared at him but he didn't notice. "It isn't like any of *this* matters." She indicated the light cords strewn around the den.

"Oh, honey, I'm so glad you understand." David gave her a genuine hug, then retreated with his game to the bedroom.

She glared after him. *I'd like to take that radio and punt it out of the stadium!* What was so hard about listening to something distracting *while* working? Mothers did it all the time.

Maggie plopped down on a kitchen chair and flipped through a magazine left on the table, anger washing over her. *How dare he? It isn't like I asked him for anything hard. Why does everyone treat me this way?*

She tore out articles whether she needed them or not. "Four Quick Cures for Stress"; "Creating a Day You'll Treasure"; "Homecomings to Remember"; "New Twists on Tradition"; "Make-Ahead Recipes"; and "Simplify Your Holidays." Maybe if she read them, she could ignore the stress.

Samantha fluttered in, dropped a Wal-Mart sack on the counter where it would stay until Maggie moved it, and opened the refrigerator door. "What's to eat?"

"Whatever you want." Maggie stapled an article into a folder.

"Thanks, Mom. I'll take grilled cheese."

"The pan's over there. It's time you put your home-economics skills to use."

"Mo—om," Samantha moaned as if Maggie had asked her to scoop doggy poop.

Before guilt could stop her, Maggie blurted, "I'm in the middle of a project here. The cheese is in the refrigerator drawer. You'll find the bread second shelf down in the pantry." Maggie pulled her Bible close. She hesitated before adding, "I'd like one, too." Maggie felt Samantha's astonishment before she looked. Samantha stood like a statue frozen by the escaping refrigerated air.

Maggie moved to the den, carrying her project along. A box of decorations awaited her attention. She ignored it as she folded herself onto the couch and reached for a magazine. She stopped and opened the Bible where she could glance over a verse or two. Multitasking made her feel better.

Jill surprised her by rounding the corner, and Maggie quickly covered her Bible with a magazine.

"Something to hide?" Jill asked.

"You startled me." Maggie cringed at the conviction she'd hidden her faith. "I was working on our project."

"Good. You need some veggie time."

The frying pan clanged against a burner, followed by the sizzling of melting butter. "I was going to ask Samantha to help me decorate, but I set her to making sandwiches instead. She has a bad habit of keeping me off track with questions like. . . ," Maggie mimicked, " 'Wouldn't this look better over there? Let's not do this now. We need some new decorations; let's go shopping. Do we have to put garlands everywhere? Can we take a break now? Who sees this anyway? Someone needs to if we're going to this much trouble. Why don't you throw *me* a party?' "

"Sounds like a decorating party pooper. I'll help. I can't wait till Charlie and I have a place of our own."

A spark in Maggie's mind burst into a flaming thought that made Maggie burn with guilt: *I can't wait till you move either.* The instantaneous wildfire turned her cheeks pink. *Lord, I'm sorry. I don't know where that thought came from. I want to be generous, especially at Christmastime.*

Jill picked a magazine, plopped down beside Maggie, and started turning pages at leisure. "I see you've made a good start on your project."

Maggie gathered the stapler, scissors, and scraps. She restacked the magazines and placed the clippings in folders.

Jill faked a cough. "You're kicking up dust. Tell your over-worked brain to be still." Jill's smile reached her eyes.

A glossy cover caught Maggie's attention. Rustling pages swished in Jill's hand. Butter sizzled in the kitchen as Samantha flipped a grilled-cheese sandwich.

Maggie moved Jill's feet off the coffee table. "It's time to tackle a *real* holiday project—making this place look like Christmas." She plucked thick white polyester batting from a plastic bag and formed fluffy hills and flatlands, then positioned a Christmas village on the "snow." She called to Samantha, "Put another grilled cheese on for Aunt Jill."

"There's nothing like the smell of burned cheese to make you hungry," Jill joked.

"I didn't want you to feel left out." The smile had returned to Maggie's voice.

Jill positioned the mirrored pond and skaters. "This is so pretty. Charlie and I don't have any decorations yet. What's next?"

"The manger scene." Maggie moved across the room toward the piano. "You almost done in there, Samantha?"

No answer.

"You want me to go see what's keeping her?" Jill asked.

"No, leave her alone. I haven't got time to eat anyway." Maggie cleared away Samantha's sheet music and replaced it with a doily. "There's one good thing about decorating. There's no room left for clutter when I get done." Maggie drew the Mary figurine from the box, followed by Joseph.

Jill looked into the deep cardboard box. "I can't believe you use all this."

"It's Christmas. This is how I help others celebrate." Maggie fingered the baby Jesus. "Everyone would be disappointed if I didn't. But. . ." Maggie hated feeling so downhearted.

Jill walked to the couch and brought back the magazines. She fanned them out with a raised brow. The covers practically twinkled with clever promises.

Maggie sighed. "It took designers and writers weeks to create those pages, and I'm only one person. I don't think that's the answer." She turned the baby figurine in her hand, then placed Jesus beneath Mary's and Joseph's watchful eyes. *This used to be the best part of Christmas.*

⌒

Something about setting out the manger scene yesterday had Maggie brooding this morning. She'd dreamed she'd lost the Christ child figurine, and no one in the family could find Him.

After a quick check over her planner and a final swig of coffee, Maggie reached for her Bible. Having been reminded by a Christian women's magazine article on holiday stress, she began reading about Martha and Mary, two of Jesus' friends. Martha cooked a meal all by herself while her sister, Mary, sat at Jesus' feet and worshiped Him. Martha complained and asked Jesus to make Mary help her.

It wasn't hard for Maggie to identify with Martha. *That's how my trouble began—by taking on too much responsibility. But You made me like Martha, God. You know that. You take pleasure in all I accomplish, don't You?*

She glanced back at the Bible. A verse flew off the page like a missile aimed for her heart. *"Martha, Martha, you are worried and upset about many things, but only one thing is needed. Mary has chosen what is better."*

God had gone to meddling. The verse might as well have read: Maggie, Maggie, you are worried and upset about many things. *Come on, God. You know I don't want to worry. I want to worship You. I'll get this under control, Lord, really I will.*

Resolved to get "Martha" some help, Maggie dragged out a notepad and wrote:

Dear Family,

As you know, Thanksgiving wore me to the wishbone. I will NOT be cooking the entire meal all by myself this Christmas.

Choose a casserole or gelatin salad to put in containers that can be thrown away. (Jill will tell you—this is for my sanity. She doesn't want to find me outside with dirty dishes again. Ask Jill—a funny story.) Only fix what the sixteen of us can eat. My waistline tells me we won't need leftovers.

While I enjoy rave reviews, I don't think the Lord deserves table-scrap thanks in a hasty prayer. Maybe this way God will get the praise He deserves, and we can

spread the compliments around to some other cooks.
Hip-hooray! Love,
Maggie (better known as Martha)

P.S. If you don't fix it, I guess we won't eat.

Now she had new worries. Should she include recipe cards for the family? Or let them figure out how to prepare everything without her input? She wondered if she'd enjoy relinquishing ownership and control of the fancy meal. But surely this would be her ticket to becoming more like Mary.

The phone rang.

"Maggie, it's Anne. Did I catch you at a bad time?"

My sister could bring the fruitcake and maybe some gourmet coffee since she's long distance. . . .

"Oh, Maggie. I'm glad you're home. The boys and I need. . . well, we'd like to come stay with you awhile. At least till Christmas, if that'd be all right."

"I'm afraid there's no room in the inn, Anne." Maggie finally had a reason to be thankful for her full house. "We're bursting at the seams." Anne's seven-year-old twins, Blake and Baxter, weren't the kind of angels Maggie wanted decking her halls.

"It'll only be a few weeks. Until. . .I just need some time away." Anne moved from ever-so-slight pleading to a cheerier tone. "Your house is always so fun over the holidays. We could call it an early Christmas present. Time together."

Maggie decided there must be a sign over her front door—Mackenzie Bed-and-Breakfast—full service, low rates, ten meals a day.

"I could help you cook."

Anne couldn't cook noodles without a recipe. A solid *no*

formed in Maggie's mind, but she heard herself say, "If you *really* need to. I guess we'll manage." Samantha would hate the couch, but something had to be wrong for Anne to return so suddenly.

"I knew you'd agree." Relief crossed the phone line, adding to Maggie's suspicion. "Our plane lands in two hours. Could you pick us up at the airport? Thanks, Maggie. Gotta go."

Maggie heard the flight attendant instruct those traveling with small children to board, right before the line went dead. She leapt from the couch, straightening pillows and magazines in a whirlwind. Here she'd been praying to become more like Mary, and now "Martha's" workload had suddenly tripled. She looked toward the ceiling. *Thanks a lot.*

Chapter 8

Maggie watched Anne enter the main terminal, a leopard-print tote slung over her shoulder, twin boys flanking her pencil-thin frame, and her blond hair swinging. With megabucks to spend, Anne's gift was shopping, not serving. Not once had she helped Maggie. She just arrived bearing gifts like some benevolent Mrs. Claus without the rosy cheeks or plump behind.

As she neared, Maggie noticed exhaustion in Anne's eyes. Anne, who usually offered a superficial peck and less than intimate hug, fell into Maggie's arms for several seconds. Then she reached for Samantha.

Samantha received her usual kiss-kiss. "Why'd you come so early?"

Anne looked at Maggie over Samantha's head. "I thought it'd be a nice surprise. I can help your mother with Christmas this way."

Tears shimmered on Anne's lashes. Blake and Baxter skittered to the nearest newspaper stand where they clamored over licorice and gummy worms.

"No need to pay inflated prices. We can stop for candy on the way home," Maggie offered.

"I'm sure you have better things to do with your time." Anne paid for the boys' candy.

Maggie bristled. "You have a nice flight? Samantha, take your aunt's bag."

Anne gave it over without argument. "The flight was fine. Good weather."

Maggie noticed the heavy coat over Anne's arm. "Was it cold at home this morning?"

"*Very* chilly," Anne answered, as if Maggie had posed a question with a double meaning.

"We had snow here last week. Not what *you'd* consider snow, but enough for Brophy to feel like he got to see some. It melted off by noon. Oh, I forgot." Maggie held her hand to her mouth. "You were here." She wasn't trying to be funny. The week seemed far away with Anne arriving off schedule.

"It's strange, isn't it?" Anne remained expressionless, staring across the terminal. "How things work out." She fished around in her red leather purse. "I miss my favorite niece and sister all year long; then I see them twice in a row." Anne smiled as if her emotions had returned to normal. She held up two baggage claim tickets stapled to an envelope.

Maggie could only stare.

Anne usually traveled with a stockpile of luggage, even if she only spent the night. Instead, she retrieved two slim bags and proclaimed, "I packed pretty quickly. We'll have to go shopping."

Samantha grinned at the suggestion, then asked what Maggie also wondered, "How long are you staying?"

"Till Christmas."

"What about Uncle John?"

"Has to work."

Maggie noticed she didn't say he'd join them for Christmas. Anne and John were obviously having marital problems. But it wasn't hard for Anne to avoid an answer since no one asked the question.

"Boys, don't run," Anne called the identical blond boys back to her side.

Samantha looked from boy to boy. "I still can't tell them apart."

⤸

When they arrived at Maggie's house, Jill threw the front door open. "Anne, it's good to see you." The aroma of gingerbread and sugar cookies greeted them. Jill had lit scented candles.

As Maggie passed by, Jill caught her arm and whispered, "Why is it when you decide to slow down, life accelerates? All the more reason you'll love your Christmas present."

"What is it?"

"You must have been pretty nice this year." Jill winked.

"I'm going to rest a bit." Anne announced, then headed for Samantha's room, entered, and closed the door as they watched.

"What if I need something?" Samantha asked, dismayed.

"You'll have to wait." Maggie lowered her voice. "She looks like she hasn't slept in a week."

Jill agreed. "She looks terrible. I think I'll grab a few winks myself."

Baxter tugged on Samantha's hand. "Where's your PlayStation?"

"You know we don't have one," Samantha said without hiding her irritation.

Blake frowned. "Then what are we supposed to do?"

Samantha flipped on the television and handed Baxter the remote. "We have cable. Knock yourself out."

Maggie rolled her eyes. *How am I supposed to monitor them and still get everything done?*

"Samantha, see that they don't watch the wrong channel."

"Why me?"

"Why not you?"

"They're not my responsibility."

"And they're mine?" Maggie whispered, hands on her hips. She glanced at Blake and Baxter to confirm they weren't listening. "They look content enough with the Disney Channel; just check on them now and then."

Samantha stormed toward her room, remembered Anne, then turned into the master suite—the only unoccupied room in the house.

In the kitchen, Samantha's dirty oatmeal bowl sat beside the remains of David's peanut butter-chocolate smoothie concoction, which had dried on the blender. Jill and Charlie had apparently gone shopping while she'd been at the airport, then returned with overflowing sacks and dropped them next to the unopened Christmas cards and winter garb littering the counter. Everyone had used two or three glasses or mugs and hadn't bothered to rinse them. Her kitchen resembled a yard sale.

In the living room, Maggie plopped down beside Baxter, grabbed a magazine, and started thumbing at speed-reader pace. The whole family expected her to clean, organize, dispense, and arrange their life. *Well, they can forget it. This elf's had it.*

⤸

"Looks like you need my favorite cure—a bubble bath," Jill said.

Maggie hadn't moved from the couch, and she'd grown drowsy from the effort of procrastinating.

"I'll go run the water. You got any bubble bath?"

Maggie yawned and stretched, sorry to be roused. "Brophy has some. Where is he, by the way? If he's quiet, he's probably in trouble." She started to stand.

"Stay seated. David said you needed a break. He and Charlie took Brophy fishing. I'll be right back."

Jill returned with three bottles, a green and pink tube of some unknown substance, and a lavender-scented candle. "Pick your favorite bubble-bath aroma: Sweet Attraction, Love Spoken, or Vanilla Romance." She squeezed each bottle under Maggie's nose.

Maggie took three luxurious whiffs. Her eyes closed as she compared the subtle floral selections against the decidedly vanilla fragrance. "I'll take Vanilla Romance." Maggie watched Jill scramble through the end table drawer, searching for something. *This is craziness.*

Jill held up a matchbook with a victorious grin. "I'll start the water."

Maggie panicked. She hadn't had time to clean her bathroom. She stood to intercept. "That's okay. I can run my own tub."

"Sit. I'm happy to do it for you." Jill headed toward the hall.

Maggie blocked Jill's path, reminding herself of a football player. "It's a mess. David leaves everything out."

Jill pushed past her. "It's not like I haven't seen underwear on the floor. I worked on a cruise ship. Remember?"

Maggie followed like a zombie. *A bubble bath in the middle of a day is a fantasy. I must be dreaming.*

In no time at all, Maggie found herself lounging amid popping, fragile bubbles with a gooey pink watermelon facial lathered across her cheeks, chin, and forehead. When the door burst open, she ducked for cover, expecting Brophy.

"Thought you might like some magazines." Jill laid them on the tub's edge. "Too bad you don't have a whirlpool," she said as she left.

Maggie leaned her neck against the cool tub rim and wiggled her toes through the bubbles. She had to admit it; pampering herself felt wonderful. The lavender candle, vanilla bubbles, and watermelon mask enveloped her in an aromatic cloud. But when she closed her eyes to savor the pleasure, her mind refused to relax.

She'd always organized her life around the family, so why the sudden need to change? And how much additional stress would accompany *not* being in charge? Maybe she should make a New Year's resolution to do Christmas different *next* year.

She piled bubbles on her stomach and chest, dipped her chin in the foam, and inhaled the sweet vanilla. Any peace she'd hoped to find had disappeared. She couldn't even hear the distant echo of her dreams.

The candle flickered. What did she want? Solitude. Time to relax. Time with David. And the children. The ability to say no. Clean closets. Neat drawers. A fully decorated house. Exercise. Money to eat out more. Without weight gain. Peace.

Maggie's to-do list appeared unbidden in her mind. The Christmas Day meal had been redistributed only to be replaced by an additional three mouths to feed. Brophy sang at church tonight.

She bolted upright. *Oh my!* Water sloshed over the edge of the tub to the floor.

Maggie bounded from the tub as though the water had scalded her. She checked the clock by the sink. Brophy's choir rehearsal began in twenty minutes! And she'd forgotten the cookies she'd promised to bake. She grabbed the first article of clothing she could put her hands on—her husband's threadbare bathrobe—and tied the sash as she rammed her feet into her fuzzy slippers.

Where had the afternoon gone? And where had David taken Brophy? Jill had only said "fishing."

Bubbles clung to the tips of her hair and ears as she ran toward the kitchen. "Jill, where did they go? Did they walk or drive?"

Jill stared at the holey bathrobe. "They walked. What's the big deal?"

"Go down the street, that way." Maggie pointed north. "Run to the end of the block and turn left. It's an emergency! At the second pasture, turn right and crawl over the locked gate. Then follow the road to the end, and you'll come to a big pond where you'll find them. Tell 'em to get home *right away.*"

"End of the street, left, up two pastures, then right over the gate."

Maggie nodded. "Hurry."

"What's the emergency?"

"Brophy needs to be at church in fifteen minutes with cookies in hand for his choir." Maggie flipped the oven to 350 degrees.

"So stop and buy cookies on the way. Or better yet, can't he miss it? It's only preschool choir."

"They're counting on him. He's one of the little lambs. Please hurry." Maggie wrung her hands. "I can't believe I forgot." *If Anne hadn't come home unexpectedly, I wouldn't have.*

Maggie checked the clock. It'd take Jill ten minutes to get there and back, just long enough to slice and bake the dough she'd bought for emergencies such as this. *Good planning.*

The self-proclaimed queen of fast mastered her element. Forget about frosting the cookies with white chocolate as planned. She could make three-circled snowmen faster than a blizzard could dump a foot of snow, then sprinkle them with powdered sugar with seconds to spare.

Anne emerged from a nap, looking somewhat refreshed. "What's the noise about? You could wake the dead. And what's that stuff smeared all over your face?"

"Watermelon facial Jill talked me into. There isn't time to wash it off. I forgot I've got to make cookies for Brophy's choir," Maggie said, breathless. "Hand me a cookie sheet from that cabinet." She pointed.

Anne did so, and Maggie practically threw the dough circles onto the pan. She joined each set of three into fat snowmen bound for the soon-to-be-fiery furnace. She rammed the cookie sheet into the oven before it could preheat, spinning the timer to nine. *Make that eight.* Then cranked the temperature up to 400 degrees.

If she made every traffic light between here and the church, she'd have half a minute to spare. Besides, everyone expected her to be late.

"Where are they?" Maggie fumed as she marched around the kitchen, throwing mugs and dirty dishes into the dishwasher without rinsing. When the bathrobe threatened to come loose, she cinched it tighter. "Jill should have found them by now."

Anne stared as if Maggie had lost her mind. Maggie knew Anne would never, ever leave the bathroom looking such a fright.

"Surely they took the four-wheelers. Come on. Come on." Maggie willed her son and husband toward the house as she pulled back the curtain.

Nowhere. They weren't anywhere in sight.

She ran to the front door to check. Behind her, she overheard Chevy Chase's voice. The twins had the television tuned to *National Lampoon's Christmas Vacation* where Chevy's character, Clark Griswold Jr. announced, "Nobody's walking out on this fun, old-fashioned family Christmas. No, no! We're all in this together. This is a full-blown, four-alarm holiday emergency here!"

A fitting description for a Mackenzie Christmas if Maggie had ever heard one. She looked back out the window and saw Jill sprinting toward the house. *Thank goodness.*

She readjusted the lapels of the bathrobe to cover her cleavage and stuck her facial-masked head out the door. "Did you find them?"

Huffing and panting, Jill bent over, her hands on her thighs. "Call 9-1-1!" She gasped for air.

"Who's hurt?"

"Just do it, Maggie. Hurry!"

Chapter 9

Maggie's hand trembled as she dialed 9-1-1. What should she tell the operator?

Jill yanked the phone from her hand. "Go get some clothes on, then go. . ." She pointed toward the door. "Yes, we need an ambulance," she told the operator, then told Maggie, "Go to the pond."

Maggie yanked her fake fur coat from the hall closet. Forcing her arms into the sleeves shoved David's robe into twin wads around her shoulders. Without stopping to adjust the uncomfortable mess, she raced out the door. She had to find out what happened.

Maggie ran. Her fuzzy slippers flapped. A brisk wind kicked up the front of the coat, reminding her she fled nearly naked.

Up the block. Around the bend. Her legs churned. Her head pounded. Her lungs burned. She threw herself over the fence like a Greek hurdler, then sprinted to the pond, clasping the robe and coat with one hand.

Her throat caught when she saw him on the ground. She forgot about her appearance.

David and Charlie surrounded Brophy like angels on bent

knee. "Don't move, son," she heard David caution. "Mommy's here." David looked at her in relief; then his brow rose as he surveyed her gooey pink face, bare legs, and *his* robe poking out beneath her coat.

"Brophy!" She collapsed beside him, then looked at David. "What happened?" Her hand on Brophy's chest assured her he was still breathing. As he lay pale and helpless, tears trickled down his cheeks onto the dry grass.

David answered, "We were wrestling, and I threw him over my shoulder. He landed on his back. At first, I thought he had the breath knocked out of him." David's mournful eyes communicated gut-wrenching fear.

Maggie focused on Brophy. "Tell Mommy what hurts."

"Nuttin'. I can't feel my legs." Her rambunctious little soldier wasn't moving.

"Can you wiggle your toes?" Maggie asked. She watched his feet. "I think I saw his big toe move, but I'm not sure. Did either of you see it?" She looked at David and Charlie.

"I might have," David said, but she could tell it was wishful thinking.

They could hear the ambulance in the distance, but she wasn't sure Brophy knew the siren sounded for him. "Everything's going to be okay. God sees you, Brophy, and He knows you're scared. He knows what *we* need." She looked at David and felt his concerned hand on her shoulder.

Brophy sniffled. "Why can't I move my legs?" Brophy tried to sit. "I wanna go home."

Maggie laid a tender yet firm hand on his chest. "Baby, Daddy would pick you up and carry you home if we thought that's what you needed, but you have to be a big boy and lie still. You're going to ride in an ambulance. What an adventure you'll have!" She created excitement with her voice while convincing herself not to fear. "I'll ride with you, okay?"

"Okay." His big eyes conveyed such trust, she almost moaned.

The siren's shrill approach made Maggie's skin crawl and the hair on her arms raise. "They're coming to help you, Brophy." She looked to David for comfort.

He held Brophy's hand. "The ambulance drivers will take good care of you."

Maggie nodded her head in agreement. "We can trust God. He knows what will happen next." *Even if we don't.*

The siren grew louder. How would she handle it if Brophy were paralyzed? She couldn't stand the thought. Her ninety-mile-a-minute, happy-go-lucky son in a wheelchair? Impossible!

"You're doing a good job of lying still." David's voice caught, a shadow of fear coloring his brow. "You're such a brave boy."

Charlie said, "When your daddy and I were little, we had a sledding accident."

"I'd forgotten about that," David said.

"I couldn't." Charlie stared across the pond at a distant memory. "Because it was my fault."

"That's right!" David slapped his knee, bringing Charlie's attention back to the present. "You finally admit it, you sorry louse."

"Focus, guys." Maggie had never heard this story. She continued to squat though her knees ached.

"Well, Brophy," Charlie said. "Your daddy couldn't move his legs either. But later on that night, he got all better."

"Me, too, Mommy?" Brophy looked at Maggie as if she knew the answer.

"Maybe." Maggie smoothed a wisp of hair away. She knelt down and kissed Brophy's cool forehead, praying it'd be so.

A frog croaked on the nearby bank, and a fish jumped in the water. The abandoned fishing poles lay nearby. The ambulance drew closer, winding through her neighborhood. Her mind recorded every detail—sights and sounds magnified.

Brown winterized grass waved in the light breeze around them like a halo. Brophy suddenly reminded her of the babe in the manger. How had His mother felt, looking at Jesus, knowing He'd give His life for people like Maggie?

Maggie couldn't imagine allowing her son to die for anyone, especially not a stranger. She leaned close to shield Brophy. *Lord, protect my son. Please don't let him be paralyzed. He's too little to bear such a burden. And so am I.*

Brophy's teeth chattered.

She warmed his hands in hers. "Don't be scared, baby," she said, attempting to quell her own fear. Her insides quaked. She willed the tears begging for release to stay put.

She heard the thunder of footsteps approaching and stood to see Jill leading two emergency medical technicians, as well as Anne, Baxter, Blake, and Samantha.

The EMTs went to work, strapping Brophy to a backboard, asking questions, and recording information. She recognized one of them from church, a man everyone called Ace.

Brophy's eyes grew as wide as the brown pond to his left. "I've got to go pee-pee." He whined, "I can't hold it."

Maggie hovered over him. "You'll have to wait. You can't go until you get to the hospital and see the doctor."

Brophy tried to lift his upper body off the board. "I've got to go pee-pee. Now!"

Watching Brophy struggle wrought agony. Maggie kissed her finger and, scooting around the EMTs, she placed it on Brophy's cheek.

"Just go in your underwear," Ace told him. "It'll be all right."

Brophy looked scandalized. This contradicted his whole life and upbringing.

Maggie could picture Brophy running through the house bare-bottomed because he'd had an accident, yet here he was, refusing to wet his pants. Pride showed itself in unusual ways.

Speaking of bare-bottomed. She wondered if Ace had noticed the bathrobe hem, blown against her legs by the winter breeze. She felt her watermelon mask turn hot pink. Maggie put on her stern expression, so Brophy would know she meant business. "Just wet your pants, soldier boy. Daddy'll get you some more."

Brophy started shouting, "I want to go in the woods! Let me up!"

"I can't believe this." Maggie placed her hands on her hips and threatened, "Wet your pants and get it over with."

Brophy started wiggling, and his legs moved, commanding everyone's attention.

Maggie noticed Ace watching Brophy intently. "Is he supposed to move like that?" she asked.

Ace said, "Looks like he's getting some feeling back. I think it'd be all right if he went."

Maggie couldn't believe it. "You're not going to let him up before he sees the doctor! What if it's a spinal cord injury?" She stared at Ace, incredulous, her knuckles white on her coat.

Ace began releasing the restraints.

"I want another opinion." David laid a firm hand on his arm. "Please, Ace, take him to the hospital. He can wait."

"I can not." Brophy's little cheeks puffed out from the strain. "Look." Brophy wiggled his newly freed right ankle, demonstrating the feeling had returned. Then he wiggled his left as best he could within the constraints.

"I think it would be fine," the other EMT agreed, unstrapping his other leg.

"Honey," Maggie asked Brophy, "can you really feel your feet and legs?"

Brophy nodded. "Yup."

"Just like before you fell?"

Brophy stood and darted toward the bushes before anyone could stop him.

Ace said, "It was probably just a pinched nerve. That happens sometimes."

"Maybe that's what happened when we were kids." David shrugged. Charlie nodded.

Ace wasn't finished. "You combine that with the fear of everyone telling him not to move, and you can cause a little guy to believe he can't feel a thing—kinda like hearing Santa on Christmas Eve. You guys still want me to take him in? It's a pricey sleigh ride."

"Guess not, Ace." David clapped him on the back. He turned to shake the other EMT's hand. "Thanks for coming."

"A Merry Christmas miracle to you, folks." Ace wore a smile as jolly as Santa's. "And, Mrs. Mackenzie, you go get yourself some hot chocolate. You deserve some after this scare."

Her body shivered beneath the fake fur. Maggie's self-conscious nakedness made an appearance on her stained cheeks. Her left hand remained locked on the coat.

After Ace and his partner left, David popped Maggie's bottom. "I can't believe you came dressed like that." He swiped a drip of facial threatening her eyelid. "Humm. . .makes me remember a certain carefree girl I married once." He winked.

"Oh, yeah. It was you, Maggie Mackenzie. I like you like this." He tweaked her nose.

Maggie let him smooth his robe's collar over her coat collar without protest. With David's arm around her and Brophy holding her hand, Maggie thanked God for her family. She hoped this close call would help keep their holidays in perspective, but she wasn't fooling herself. *It still won't be easy.*

Chapter 10

Maggie burst from several bubble baths without allowing the foam to fizzle before she learned to stay calm enough for a scented candle to burn down a quarter of an inch. It required robbing tiny bits of time from the family, but she'd accomplished the feat. Seven days after Brophy's accident, Maggie recorded her achievement in a newly purchased journal.

"What are you doing?" Samantha asked, finding Maggie in her new quiet spot. When Samantha lost her bedroom to Anne and started sleeping on the couch, Maggie had shoved a comfortable chair into the breakfast nook.

"Sitting, thinking, reading, and writing," Maggie answered without fretting. The Bible propped beneath the journal was open to Proverbs. She'd begun relying more heavily on Scripture for advice than the articles she'd clipped, but she hadn't found a bold dark line between the sacred and the secular as she'd expected. Truth, it'd turned out, showed up in unexpected places when she read God's Word daily. God reached Maggie in surprising ways when she stayed connected to Him in prayer.

"Why?" Samantha tilted her head. "Aren't you tempted to

homeschool me or order me to do something?"

"A little bit," Maggie admitted. She took a sip of hazelnut coffee. "Do you want me to?"

"Whoa. Mom, this is weird. This has been going on for a week now. You sure you don't want to teach me something?"

"Yes, but all lessons aren't in a textbook." Maggie replaced the china cup on the saucer and moved her journal aside. She flipped a page in the Bible.

Samantha moved across the kitchen, opened the cabinet, and grabbed a handful of Fruit Loops cereal. "Where's Brophy? Do I need to watch him?"

"Blake and Baxter are keeping him busy, but it'd be great if you checked on them now and then." Maggie glanced down and read, *"A kindhearted woman gains respect."*

Samantha popped the cereal into her mouth, one colorful loop at a time. "You mean we're on break?"

"I am." Maggie looked up and stifled a smile.

Samantha frowned. "Then. . .I am. . .too?" She sounded uncertain.

"If you like." Maggie resumed reading.

"Okay. So what are we doing today?"

Maggie smiled at her daughter. "I don't know. What are *you* doing?"

"Mom, come on. This is weird. It's like you've quit or something."

Maggie stretched. "Just taking a break to figure some things out."

"But the house isn't decorated yet, and Christmas is around the corner."

Maggie understood her daughter's tension but chose not to worry. "Feel free." Maggie fanned out a hand.

"Fine. I'm going to the pasture to look for some holly. The mantel's bare."

"Great." Maggie watched Samantha put on her coat and leave just as David rounded the corner.

"Where's she going?" David leaned down for a morning hug.

"To gather holly, wonder of wonders." Maggie couldn't believe she hadn't begged or bribed Samantha to help.

"What's for breakfast, Mags?" David had the day off, and she usually cooked something special.

"Whatever you want."

He ruffled her hair. "So, you're feeling more like yourself. I'm glad."

"Better than ever." Maggie couldn't believe how taking an intermission had settled her. She felt more prayerful. Stepping off the holiday treadmill hadn't hurt the family ecosystem. Anne had done the dinner dishes twice. Jill played with the kids and encouraged Maggie to relax. Pop's gallbladder hadn't acted up all week. Maggie suspected it might have something to do with the reduced stress around the house. Ma even seemed calm, her dementia less noticeable.

"I'll take two eggs over easy," David interrupted her reverie. The environmental changes hadn't improved his manners.

"The kitchen's in there." She pointed as though he were clueless.

David bristled. "Come on, Maggie. This is getting ridiculous. You're not doing anything you usually do. Do you need counseling?"

That hurt. She searched the Bible as if she'd lost her place. The pages blurred. *Did* she need a counselor? "Maybe."

"Our insurance covers it."

"Fine."

"Perhaps you're depressed."

She looked at him in horror. She bit her lip and shrugged. "Maybe I'm just changing."

"Why would you want to? You're perfect."

Maggie volleyed the question. "Why wouldn't I want to change?"

"I'm worried about you, Maggie. You're not yourself." He flicked a business card into her lap. "I made an appointment for you two weeks from Tuesday. Four o'clock. Promise you'll go?"

She looked at the psychologist's card. Maybe a shrink *could* explain how she felt. "Okay." She felt like a child.

"About those eggs. . ." David waited.

She couldn't believe he had signed her up for counseling. "Make them yourself, honey."

Chapter 11

Maggie stayed up half the night composing her speech, gathering thoughts from her previously drafted, yet unsent, letter. She hoped to end this before seeing the psychologist. But now, as she stood before her puzzled family, she thought she might need mental help if she confronted them.

Perhaps she should wait. Not invite trouble. Postpone the changes until next year. Hadn't they been through enough with the transformation she'd already accomplished? She silently recited the quote she'd taped to the bathroom mirror: *If this were easy, I would have done it long ago.* But she still couldn't find the courage to speak.

A twin twitched on each of Anne's knees. Pop and Ma Mackenzie claimed two recliners. Ma snored. Pop rocked. Samantha flopped onto her stomach, elbows bent. Beside her, David embraced their wiggly son. Jill stood next to Charlie, who drummed his fingers on the mantel.

Maggie swallowed what felt like a hard-boiled egg. She cleared her throat. "This Christmas we're going to. . ."

If this were a Hallmark commercial, everything would turn out fine and there'd be greeting-card emotions to commemorate the ending. *Wishful thinking.*

Maggie started over, "You know how frustrated I got this Thanksgiving? It wore me to the wishbone. Well, I don't want to be selfish at Christmas. I'm willing to share the fatigue and cooking chores." A high, nervous giggle erupted, but no one joined her.

She'd hoped to amuse them, not make herself sound like a hysterical martyr. Their awkward silence should have stifled her, but it made her laugh instead. She felt like an idiot. Her shoulders shook. Her nose ran. She hated being this nervous. *David already thinks I'm crazy. Now I'm confirming it.*

She forced herself to begin with him. "David, I'm taking you up on your Cajun-fried turkey. You and Pop can oversee the bird." Her voice raised an octave. Someone would think she'd consumed helium.

Pop said, "I can snap some beans. I know how to boil water." He'd caught on.

Maggie bit her lip. She preferred the green bean casserole seasoned with mushroom soup and Velveeta cheese to the boiled kind. "Uh. . .thanks, but the green beans go to Samantha." Maggie looked at her daughter. "I'll show you how. It's easy." Maggie felt her way forward. "Jill, how 'bout if you take the sweet potatoes, and Charlie, the pecan pie?"

They agreed.

"Anne, if you'll take the pump. . ."

"I hate that we repeat Thanksgiving. It's the same meal twice in a row." Samantha wrinkled her nose. "Can't we have something different for Christmas?"

Maggie thought a moment. "I guess so." She'd never thought of it.

David stood. "If we're going to implement change, dear, we

might as well really shake things up."

Maggie preferred control. "It's tradition. I use Ma's old recipes. Actually, they were her mother's." She glanced at Ma, asleep with her mouth agape.

Anne looked at Ma, too. "She'll never know. I have a great recipe for summer squash with Rotel tomatoes. It'll go perfect with the Cajun turkey."

"Okay." Maggie smiled, thankful for Anne's input. "Let's still do pumpkin pie."

"I'd prefer apple," Anne said.

Maggie frowned. "Christmas without pumpkin pie?"

"Sounds good to me," David said.

Charlie came to Maggie's rescue. "I'll make the pumpkin, or would everyone rather have pecan?"

"With my cholesterol, pumpkin's better for me," Pop said.

"Pumpkin it is. Who's going to buy the groceries?" Charlie asked.

"Let's see." Maggie hadn't thought of that. She looked at her mixed-up list. "So far we have Cajun-fried turkey."

"So much for my cholesterol," Pop said.

Maggie rolled her eyes. "We also have the green bean casserole. . . ."

"I hate those green beans." Samantha put one hand on her hip. "And I don't want fried turkey either." She frowned.

Pop leaned forward. "I'm not sure I can eat anything spicy, dear. Cajun turkey and Rotel squash sound like invitations to the emergency room. Though I'm sure your squash is real tasty, Anne." He smiled apologetically.

Maggie thought he should apologize to her. She scratched out the squash, then reconsidered. "Make it with less spice, Anne; then Pop can handle it. We need another vegetable if we eliminate the beans."

Ma stirred and opened her eyes. "Rots," she said.

"Rots?" Maggie asked.

"She's trying to say carrots," Pop explained.

Ma stuck out her tongue and licked her lips.

Maggie offered an encouraging smile to her mother-in-law. "I'm not sure it'd be Christmas without carrots or green bean casserole."

"How 'bout mashed potatoes? I wondered why we didn't have 'em with the dressing. Grandma always did," Charlie said.

"Yes. What about the dressing?" Anne asked.

"It's up for grabs," Maggie said, trying to distance herself.

"What are you making?" Samantha asked Maggie.

All eyes fell on her. Maggie swallowed another boiled egg. "I'm on cleanup crew. And I promise I won't put the dishes outside." She winked at Jill. "Other than that, you're on your own."

"How come you're getting outta cooking?" Samantha asked.

"It's somebody else's turn. Now, who will take the dressing?"

"No one makes it like you do," Pop prodded her with guilt.

"How do we know?" Maggie tapped her list with the pencil eraser. She watched it bounce without making eye contact with the family. "Jill, you want to tackle it?"

"If Charlie'll help, I'll try, but I'm not promising much. I'm no chef."

"Charlie?" Maggie looked at her brother-in-law.

"Gee-whiz! I got married so someone else would cook."

Jill chucked a pillow at him. "You married the wrong girl, buddy. Maggie told me you know how to cook. Your secret's out."

"A real manly man." David thumped his brother on the back.

Charlie burped, then sniggered with David.

Maggie ignored them. "I forgot you, Pop."

"I wondered. I can do more than watch David raise my cholesterol with his fried-up turkey." He sounded hurt.

Maggie checked her list. "Oversee the rolls. They'll need heating."

Pop looked at his daughter-in-law with concern. "Maggie, honey, have you not felt appreciated? Did we hurt your feelings?"

"You compliment me, Pop. You all do, but nobody helps."

David said, "You have impossibly high standards, Maggie. Admit it."

Maggie felt her throat constrict. "So? I want everything right. What's wrong with that?"

"You want everything *perfect.*" David stood and draped an arm around her shoulders. "You sure you're ready to give up the perfect Christmas?"

Chapter 12

"Charlie can't sleep," Jill told Maggie the following week. She rubbed her eyes. "The bed's too soft and it's getting worse. He kept me up half the night with back spasms. I'm not sure what we're going to do." She reached for the coffeepot.

Maggie sponged the kitchen sink. *A hotel comes to mind.* She moved to the den couch and folded her legs Indian-style.

Jill took the chair across from her, Santa mug in hand. She pulled her leg up and wrapped an arm around one knee. "Ma wouldn't know what to do in a new bed. . . . Maybe Anne and the boys could move. . . ." She massaged her temples with her free hand. "Does this couch fold out? Oh, that's right. Samantha's using it."

Maggie didn't want to think what the children might learn if the newlyweds moved to the den. "Our mattress is firm. I guess you could give our bed a try." *You'd give your life away if someone needed it, Maggie.*

David would disapprove. But maybe he'd remember what it felt like to be "in love." *If only!*

Jill's eyes blinked with hope. "Are you sure?" She held the steaming coffee mug to her forehead, closed her eyes, and sighed. "You give so much. I didn't want to ask."

"Let Charlie try it tonight and see if it helps. Then we'll decide." She'd tell David it was a temporary arrangement, though she doubted it. They had the most comfortable bed in the house.

Jill stood. "I'll take care of the sheets. You're great, Maggie. I owe you."

Big-time. "It's no problem." Maggie presented an article she'd clipped. "I thought we could make these cute ornaments with the kids today. Keep 'em busy awhile." *And get my mind off moving out of my own room.*

Jill looked at the photos of the tri-bead and candy cane ornaments. "I like today's 'de-stressing' plan."

"One a day—like vitamins." Maggie tried to stand, but her foot cramped. "Ouch." Maggie rubbed her aching instep, then her heel.

"Do your feet hurt?"

"Sometimes."

"I have the best cure for aching feet." Jill went to the kitchen cabinet where Maggie stored the pans. "Is this the biggest pot you have?" She indicated the stockpot.

"Yes, why?"

"You ask too many questions. Keep reading. I'll be right back."

Wanting to show Jill a good example of Christian living, Maggie opened her Bible. Her eyes roved down the page. *"Do not fret—it leads only to evil."* *Everywhere I turn, God sends the same message—don't worry.*

"Close your eyes." Jill inserted a pillow behind Maggie's neck, then tapped her forehead. "Lean back."

Maggie heard water running in the sink. She peeked.

Jill lifted a filled pot, sprinkled in something granular that sounded like rock salt, then swished it around with her hand. She tucked a hand towel under one arm, picked up the heavy pot, and walked toward Maggie. "No peeking."

Maggie shut her eyes. She felt the soft towel go under her bare feet, felt Jill lift her pant's leg, and guide her tired feet into hot water. She caught a whiff of peppermint. The water tingled against her skin.

Maggie curled her toes so they'd fit in the pot. The water rose ankle-height. Some splashed over the edge. "Why the princess treatment? You're the one who didn't sleep. I should be doing this for you." She eyed Jill. "This feels incredible." She stretched her toes.

"I wanted to do something nice for you. When you mentioned the candy cane ornaments, I thought of a peppermint footbath. Isn't it relaxing?" Jill tuned the radio to a Christmas station. She pulled one of Maggie's feet from the minty water. Jill massaged the tightness away. First the toes, then the foot, up to the ankle, and finally the calf.

"Oh, my goodness. This is wonderful. I can't believe you'd do this for me."

Jill sat back on her knees. "I can't believe you'd give up your bed. What're you reading?"

"Psalms." Maggie hadn't thought Jill would ask.

"I thought maybe you were reading the Christmas story." Jill glanced at the manger scene. "Read it to me?"

"Silent Night" played in the background as Maggie turned to Luke, chapter 2. She practically had to quote from memory because tears blocked her view.

Jill tenderly dried Maggie's feet and legs, then rubbed in lotion. "I love that story."

Before Maggie could steady her pounding heart enough to explain how Jill's actions had mirrored Christ's love, Jill said, "Let's tackle those ornaments. Where're the kids?"

"The twins and Brophy are outside. And Samantha's around here somewhere. I thought Ma could make the tri-bead wreaths with the boys; they're so easy. The rest of us can make the peppermint hearts. This way we can decorate the tree without unpacking any more boxes." She grinned.

"Aha! Ulterior motive." Jill poured the footbath into the sink while Maggie found the glue gun. "Show me first how to melt the white chocolate; then you round up the family," Jill said.

❧

Snap. Another peppermint stick fractured, frustrating the perfectionist in Maggie. "The article didn't say it'd be hard to unwrap these." Maggie surveyed the split canes. "You can't make hearts with pieces."

"Let's make whatever shapes we can using the broken ones and hearts from the ones that don't break." Jill glued candy cane pieces together, creating a snowflake.

"The melted chocolate will hold the hearts together, even if they're broken." Anne poured white chocolate into the center of two canes facing each other on waxed paper and decorated the surface with crushed peppermint.

"That looks just like the article." Jill unwrapped a cane with success.

Maggie bent more pipe cleaners at the end, so Ma and the boys could continue their tri-bead project. "Remember, red, then white. Red, then white."

Bing Crosby crooned "White Christmas."

Brophy slid his hand up the pipe cleaner with force, sending little beads spewing across the table toward Blake. Brophy pointed. "He took my beads." He looked like he couldn't figure out how Blake got his beads. "He took my beads," he repeated, frustrated.

"You knocked your own beads off," Blake said with seven-year-old superiority.

"Blake didn't take your beads," Samantha explained, placing Brophy on her lap. "Here, help me make a chocolate heart." She offered an unwrapped cane to Brophy. When he tucked it in his mouth, she didn't complain.

Maggie noticed Samantha's attitude had changed toward her little brother, and she attributed it to the accident at the pond. *Thank You, God, for peace in my family.*

That afternoon they baked and decorated homemade sugar cookies for the neighbors. In the evening, David and Charlie took them all caroling and "cookie-ing," as Maggie liked to call it. They drove around the neighborhood in the back of a pickup truck, singing and taking turns distributing cookies. Even Anne had fun, and it seemed some of her worry had lifted.

After David and the family went to bed, Maggie stayed up to read the story of Jesus washing his disciples' feet. Not wanting to disturb Samantha, she dimmed the lights and curled into her cozy chair.

Maggie considered her new sister-in-law. It was Jill's gentle acceptance of her that allowed Maggie to discover something likable inside herself. Maggie didn't feel the need to be perfect with Jill around. The Bible said Christ showed His friends "the full extent of his love" by washing their feet. Jesus said, "I have set you an example that you should do as I have done for you." Did Jill realize the significance of her gift?

Christ had washed Judas's feet, too—the one who in a matter of hours betrayed Him, leading to His death on the cross. How could Christ accept someone who would betray Him? *Someone like me.*

Tears welled in her eyes and slid down her cheeks. She was Judas. She was the overworked Martha. She was the believer who worried and fretted her way through life. Not just at Christmastime. And Christ. Who was He to her? She pictured Him washing her feet as tenderly as Jill had. She slipped off her fuzzy slippers as if her feet rested on holy ground. He'd done it for her today. Through Jill.

Maggie dropped her head. She clasped her hands over her heart. God didn't need her to be perfect. He accepted her. When she acted like Judas and betrayed Him. Or, like Martha, failed to recognize Him. And now, like Mary, as she worshiped Him! Christ accepted her as she was!

Oh, come let us adore Him. The familiar hymn matched her heart's song.

Jesus didn't love her any more or any less because of her failings. Suddenly, His love felt deep and wide, broader than she'd ever imagined. Jesus had delivered Christmas to her doorstep. Like a baby's gentle coo, it had awakened her slumbering blindness. A deep bubbling laughter welled up inside, a heartfelt joy and freedom she'd rarely experienced before.

"Mom?" Samantha called from the adjoining den, having awakened to Maggie's mirth.

"I'm fine." Maggie quieted her joy. "Go back to sleep." She leaned her head back, intending to pray, but dropped off to sleep instead.

Maggie awoke around 2:00 a.m., dazed and disoriented. She rubbed the stiffness from her neck, unplugged the tree, and performed a routine check of locks and lights. She turned left into her bedroom, entered the bathroom, and closed the door so as not to wake David.

She washed her face, brushed her teeth, and put on her pajamas. Flipping the light switch off, she made her way to the bed, avoiding the chair that had relentlessly stubbed her toe on many occasions.

Maggie pulled back the comforter and slid between the cool sheets. She rolled toward David and threw her arm around his middle.

A female scream pierced her eardrums.

Maggie rolled off the bed's edge onto the floor.

"Holy smoke!" a male voice yelled, confusing her even more. It didn't belong to David.

Maggie squealed, trying to make sense of the situation.

The male voice in bed moaned. "Ack! Ouch. Ouch. My back," he said.

The woman giggled.

The voices finally registered as Charlie's and Jill's.

David burst into the room. "What's going on in here?" He switched on the lights, bathing his nearly naked brother and sister-in-law in brightness.

The newlyweds fought for cover beneath the tangled sheets. "Cut the lights!" Charlie yelled.

A bomb of nervous relief and gut-wrenching hilarity exploded in the room. Pop ran in, armed with a fire extinguisher. And before they could stop him, he doused them all.

Ma held a flashlight backward, illuminating her flannel gown. She shouted without a hint of dementia, "Someone yelled fire! Someone yelled fire!"

Maggie sounded like an inexperienced trombone player, spewing laughter through her pinched lips. She collapsed on the bed next to Jill.

"Ow." Charlie slid from the bed, claiming the sheet.

Jill grabbed the comforter in hysterics.

Charlie danced a crippled jig. "My back. Gee-whiz! Have some respect next time, Maggie. Holy smoke!"

"That's what you heard, Pop," Maggie managed to say between giggles. "Charlie yelled smoke, not fire."

Chapter 13

Anne knocked on Brophy's door early the next morning with the leopard-print traveling tote over her shoulder. "Maggie, I'm going home."

Maggie sat up in bed. "Why? We were finally starting to have some fun." She grabbed her robe and belted it as they moved toward the kitchen.

Anne's suitcases waited beside the door. "I talked to John last night. All the fun we've been having around here, and Brophy's accident last week, well. . .I've seen what's missing in our family." Anne dashed away the sadness. "John's not so bad. . .oh, he can be difficult, but so can David. I've seen that. I thought you had the perfect marriage."

Maggie stopped and faced her. "Me? You've *got* to be kidding." She snickered. "I thought *you* did."

"Clearly, we need to spend more time together."

As they neared Samantha, asleep on the couch, Maggie lowered her voice, "Want some hot chocolate?"

"Like we used to? Sure."

Many sister secrets had been shared over mugs of steaming cocoa. Maggie put the water on to boil. She removed a canister of homemade hot chocolate mix and a bag of mini marshmallows from the cabinet.

"John wants me to bring the boys home. He says he's going to take some time off."

Maggie turned toward Anne. "Will you come back for Christmas?" She set two Christmas mugs on the counter.

"I don't think so. We need time alone. Baxter and Blake hardly know their dad."

Maggie couldn't say the same for David's relationship with her children. "I know what you mean about needing time with your husband. I hope everything will be all right between you and John. I've been praying for you." Maggie laid a hand on Anne's arm.

Tears leapt to Anne's lashes. She blinked. "I have to believe it's going to be. That's why I'm going home. I was running when I came here. Now I'm ready to face the hard stuff. Thanks, Maggie."

"For what?"

"For showing me life can swirl around you, and you don't have to cave in. You stay sane in craziness."

"I'm not so sure I'm sane." Maggie thought of the counselor David wanted her to see.

"Oh, you are. You might be a pushover with a big heart, but you haven't lost your ability to connect with people around you."

Maggie frowned, trying to sort the compliment from the way it made her feel. *Pushover* wasn't her favorite trait.

"You know what I mean. You want to please people so much that you ignore your own needs. Jill and I talked about it."

Maggie scrubbed chocolate powder from the countertop, uncomfortable knowing she'd been the topic of their conversation.

"I've been watching how you take care of everyone.

Noticing how generous you are. To a fault."

Maggie felt her eyebrows rise. Was Anne complimenting her or being critical?

"Then when I saw you run out the door, looking such a fright, unafraid to meet the challenge ahead no matter how you looked or what else you had to do—I got the cookies out of the oven, by the way. Well. . .I felt small and shallow. No matter who was hurt, I wouldn't have run from the house half-naked with that goop smeared all over my face, not even for my boys or John. I would have thought of myself, my needs, my image. I would have been wearing a carefully applied mask—one that says everything's okay—not a drippy facial, daring the world to see me come undone. I want to be a mom and wife like you."

Like me? Maggie stood a little taller.

"Mom and Dad would have been proud. You behave more like an older sister than I do. You've made a good life for yourself, Magpie." Anne used her pet childhood name.

"I don't know what to say." She looked at Anne—her flawless skin, hair, and makeup. Her perfect life wasn't flawless beneath the surface.

Anne interrupted Maggie's thoughts. "Tell me you love me, and you'll pray for me as I go. The challenges back home won't be easy to fix."

Maggie opened the canister of mix. "Is there any way I can help?"

Anne smiled. "Yes."

"How?" Maggie spooned hot chocolate mix into Anne's mug, then hers.

"By continuing to find ways to pamper and care for yourself. I like my less-stressed little sis." She offered Maggie a hug.

Maggie welcomed the hug, glad for sister-love.

"I'll call you later when you're not so overwhelmed."

Maggie rolled her eyes. "And when might that be?" She poured hot water over the chocolate and stirred.

"Sooner than you might think," Jill said as she entered the room with Charlie right behind her. "We're going apartment hunting."

Charlie put his arms around Jill's waist and leaned his chin on her head. "Don't worry. We'll move back in February." He winked at Anne.

Maggie's eyebrows arched in surprise. *Why?* The question formed in her mind but never reached her lips because life distracted her. She reached for two more mugs, scooped in cocoa and water, then stirred. Maggie topped the four mugs with marshmallows.

Anne accepted a reindeer mug from Maggie. "You know Ma will need a nursing home soon."

"I couldn't do that to her." Maggie offered a Santa mug to Jill and an elf mug to Charlie.

Jill blew on the top of her chocolate to cool it. "You might not have to. Charlie and David have been talking to Pop about retirement centers."

As usual, God had a plan. "David and I need some time alone. Actually, I've been thinking we need to get away." Maggie's deepest need lay bare and exposed.

"Such a perfect lead-in." Anne held her mug in both hands and took a careful sip. "Charlie, go get David and Pop."

"Lead-in to what?" Maggie asked.

Jill stirred more of the extra-rich chocolate into her mug. "You'll see. Just remember, I told you you'd love your Christmas present." She popped a marshmallow into her mouth.

While Charlie went to wake David, Anne reached into her

leopard-print tote and withdrew an envelope. She set it on the counter.

Maggie eyed it as she put more water on to boil. "I can't imagine what that is. Is it for me?"

Neither woman answered.

"You knew about this?" Maggie asked Jill.

Jill nodded. "Anne and I talked about it at Thanksgiving. I thought we'd have to wait till Christmas; then Anne pulled us aside last night and said we should do it today." Her eyes crinkled with delight.

David, Pop, and Charlie walked in.

"Drum roll, please," Anne said.

Charlie tapped a cadence of beats on the counter.

"Maggie. David." Anne acted as master of ceremonies. "This is for you two." She presented the envelope like an Oscar.

David sniffed it, held it up to the light, and shook it.

"Open it, silly." Maggie punched his arm. "Don't keep me in suspense any longer."

David looked at his brother. "I don't know if we can afford to open it, Mags. It might be a gag gift. Charlie, did you have anything to do with this? There aren't any snakes in here that'll jump out at me, are there?"

Charlie gave a wry smile. "Maybe."

"No way. I don't trust him." David laid it on the counter.

Maggie grabbed the envelope and tore the seal. "I don't care what you say."

"A truer word was never spoken," David shot back.

Everyone laughed at the couple's banter.

After giving Maggie and David a chance to review the information inside, Anne said, "They're reservations to John's and my time-share lodge. It comes available in February. By then your schedule should be less crazy."

Maggie looked into Anne's sparkling eyes. "You're the best sister in the world. How can we ever thank you?" Maggie hugged Anne close and whispered, "Are you sure about this? If you and John have issues to tackle, don't you need this vacation more than we do?"

Anne whispered back, "No. That's what we need to work on—how to become a family like you. Appreciating each other won't come from getting away from the boys; for us it will happen by staying home."

Anne pulled back and announced, "John plans to take the rest of December off—until the boys go back to school. Maggie's shown me how important family is."

Amazement spread across Maggie's face. Her eyes widened. "In all this craziness? With me throwing the meal back in everyone's face—and staging my own sit-in? No way."

"Yes, way!" Anne said. "Grabbing for sanity in the middle of an overworked holiday is acceptable, little sis. I could tell you set your boundaries with God's help. I felt proud when you *finally* stood up for yourself. But since doing less is rarely an option with you. . ." Anne indicated with her hand that Jill should take the next part.

"Yes." Jill repeated, "Since doing less is rarely an option for you, Maggie, we wanted to give you something more to do— pack for a ski trip. And you don't have to look at a magazine to enjoy this kink in your schedule."

Anne smiled her biggest. "Skiing is perfectly self-indulgent. And the lodge is *so* romantic."

David wrapped an arm around Maggie's waist.

Jill opened the drawer and handed Maggie another envelope. "Where'd that come from?"

"Oh, we keep our secrets well hidden." Jill sipped her chocolate.

Maggie opened the envelope.

Jill said in childlike excitement, "We put enough money in here to foot the bill for eating out all week, and Charlie and I threw in a couple's massage package I found online. You're going to join the facial sisterhood, David."

"Fat chance," he said.

"Y'all are incredible," Maggie said. She swallowed hard. "You've given me a gift I didn't deserve and couldn't afford."

"Kinda like our Savior," Jill said to Maggie's amazement. "It's beginning to feel a lot like Christmas around here."

After Anne and the boys left for the airport with Charlie and Jill, David said, "Samantha's on the phone. Let's go see if we still have a bedroom of our own."

They sat on the bed with the tousled sheets left by the honeymooners. For some reason, the mess didn't bother Maggie. She snuggled into David's embrace considering the gift, not expecting another one.

David spoke into her hair, "I thought you might like to finish decorating the tree tonight, with just our family. I'll get the rest of the boxes from the attic and send the lovers out with Ma and Pop." David took her hand. "I miss family time."

She stroked her favorite sheets. "I miss our bed."

"Charlie and I are going apartment hunting today. I think you scared the wits out of them last night."

They shared a hearty laugh. David took her hand and stroked her knuckles. "I'm sorry I haven't been much help lately."

She snickered. "When have you *ever* been a big help, sir?"

"I'm trying to apologize here, Mags." He removed his arm from her shoulder and cupped his hands in his lap.

She sobered, anticipating an oft-ignored apology.

He bit his lip and looked toward the ceiling.

She gave him time.

"I didn't realize how you felt until Thanksgiving. But I didn't pay attention until you called the family meeting. Then after Brophy's accident. . ." He swallowed hard. "God's been dealing with me, Mags."

She knew he meant it. "Anne mentioned the accident."

"You wearing my bathrobe was a turn-on, in case you didn't know." His eyes crinkled playfully.

He couldn't stay serious, but that was okay. Maggie felt herself go warm inside. She burrowed her hand in his. Apologies by David were so rare she gravitated toward humor, as well. "You're just suffering from holiday celibacy." She touched his hair with her fingertips. Sleeping with Brophy had more disadvantages than elbows in the cheek.

"Another reason for Jill and Charlie to get out." He patted the mattress.

"Amen." She let him pull her downward despite the unmade bed. His shoulder formed a pillow.

He cupped her chin like she was the dearest, most precious woman in the world. "At Thanksgiving, I wanted life to go on as it always had. And I was mad at you. But watching you last week, I knew I needed to adjust, or you'd break." He kissed her neck. "I rode you pretty hard about all the changes you were making."

"Uh-huh." She relished the answer to her prayers.

"I don't like change, Maggie, but I realized something incredible. You're *not* the one changing. Not really."

She leaned up on one elbow to see what he meant. "You'd better explain that one."

"You are more like the girl I married now—relaxed, playful, happy." He enfolded her with his arms.

Her cheek found a resting place near his heart.

He rubbed her shoulder in rhythmic circles. "You're self-sufficient. You're beautiful."

Her heart leapt. *He thinks I'm beautiful.*

"You're Christ-centered, Maggie—more now than ever."

Wow! She couldn't believe what she was hearing.

David wasn't finished. "You take care of a jillion things at once, yet stay focused and determined. You *are* the girl I married. You never were a pushover, Mags." He kissed the top of her head.

Maggie cocked her head, considering. Something didn't make sense. "But what about the counselor you said I needed?"

He rubbed her shoulder. "I canceled the appointment."

Maggie kept her eyes on him. She didn't understand.

His lip twitched, a sure sign of discomfort. "Charlie said *I* needed to go. Said *you* had your life under control. Maybe he's right, but I'd feel more comfortable if you went with me."

"We both have things to work on," she offered. "We could go to marriage counseling if you think it would help." She didn't know how he'd respond.

He looked embarrassed as he gazed toward the ceiling. "I want to become the man you should've married, Maggie." Their eyes met in an intimate exchange. "One who'll make things easier on you around here, not harder. You don't deserve how childish I am sometimes." He reached for her left hand and fingered her wedding band.

Maggie studied the man she'd fallen in love with so long ago.

He gave a sheepish grin. "Maggie Mackenzie, you didn't know it when you resigned at Thanksgiving, but you set some powerful changes in motion. You showed us that while 'it's more blessed to give than receive,' it works best when everyone shares the giving. When you slammed the door on the familiar, you forced us all to find another way. A better way."

Maggie chuckled inside. *Now that's something worth giving thanks for.*

PAMELA DOWD

Pamela lives in east Texas with her husband, Rodney. They have three daughters and one son-in-law. Pamela enjoys creating strong stories with characters who display candid, growing relationships with God. She has published short stories, devotionals, magazine articles, and greeting cards, including her own line, Cookie Jar Greetings, published by Warner Press. Besides writing, Pamela has been a private school principal, a preschool director, a kindergarten teacher, a legal secretary, and a children's clothing designer. On street or treadmill she enjoys reading and walking simultaneously! Pamela loves to hear from her readers. E-mail: grammargurl@hotmail.com.

No Holly, No Ivy

by Wanda Luttrell

Chapter 1

The bright red cardinals scattered across the snowy branches of the crabapple tree gave it the look of a flocked white Christmas tree decorated with red velvet bows.

"The only Christmas tree I'll have this year!" Loraine vowed. There would be no draping of pine rope or holly, no dragging out of time-honored decorations, no baking, no shopping, no wrapping, no cards. She had absolutely no interest in a traditional Christmas this year. *With no one to share it, why should I?* she thought.

She did enjoy the cardinals, though. In fact, she enjoyed all the little birds that came to the redwood feeder hanging from the crab apple limb just outside the patio fence—the tufted titmice, the juncos, the shy little wrens, even the rascally blue jays that scared away the smaller birds as they swooped down to take over the feeder.

"The crab apple my only Christmas tree and the birds my only Christmas company," she said firmly, pulling on her boots and parka and reaching for the bucket of seed beside the kitchen door. She would spend the usually frantic holiday serenely, alone in the big, old two-story house where she and

Jack had raised their three children. *And I will enjoy it!* she thought determinedly as she opened the door and stepped cautiously onto the icy stoop.

The birds' food supply replenished, she went back inside and lit the fire in the kitchen fireplace. Tigger, the plump, old tiger-striped tomcat she let stay in the house for company now that Jack was gone, was stretched out on the couch like he owned the place, already full of milk and his favorite tuna-flavored cat food.

Loraine plumped the pillows on the love seat, refolded the quilted throw, and draped it over the back of the recliner, then looked around for whatever she needed to do next. But the house was neat, vacuumed, and dusted. Both bathrooms were spotless, and the refrigerator and the oven had been cleaned just two days ago.

She took a deep breath and let it out in a long sigh. *Two days before Christmas, and I have nothing to do!* she thought in amazement. *I should be making Susan's favorite potato salad or little Jack's chocolate cake,* she thought. *I should be frantically trying to take in or hem up some new outfit to fit Beth's tiny frame. I should be wrapping stocking stuffers or letting Jack catch me under the mistletoe.*

She pushed away the loneliness that threatened the thin veneer of contentment she had built so carefully. "Nothing to do? Good for me!" she said aloud as she looked around for that John Grisham book she had bought yesterday evening at Wal-Mart. *Skipping Christmas.* It fit her mood perfectly.

Well, she wasn't really skipping Christmas. She had hung a beautiful Douglas fir wreath on the front door and put up both nativity scenes—the traditional one with the stable, shepherds, wise men, and camels, as well as the one with Mary and Joseph, the babe, and anything else she fancied.

Who's to say there weren't birds, geese, mice, a cat, and a sweet little chipmunk nestled in the hay of that stable? And if Saint Nicholas had been there, he certainly would have knelt to worship at the manger, she thought firmly. She looked around for the book, found it, and settled into her recliner.

No, she thought, opening the book, *I won't skip the honoring of the advent of the Savior into the world. I'll be at the midnight service tomorrow night.* Loraine loved the praise and worship, the communion service, the carols, the bells, the candles raised high in recognition of Jesus—the Light—coming into the world at Christmas.

I'm just skipping all the man-made folderol and hoopla that has grown around Christmas, she thought, feeling deliciously rebellious.

It had been a long time since she had wondered what it was that made her children such rebels. She knew it was in their DNA, and most of it, she admitted honestly, didn't come from Jack. She sighed, remembering that rebellion was what got Eve into trouble in the first place. She wanted to be her own god.

Well, I don't want that! she thought. *I'm glad there's Someone up there to direct my steps, as it says in Proverbs 3:5 and 6.* She had tried to live by those verses most of her life, trusting in the Lord, acknowledging him, sharing her faith without forcing it on others. *I try to obey the Lord and the laws of my country,* she defended herself, *but I do enjoy, on occasion, breaking a musty, old rule or defying some demanding tradition!*

When Jack was still alive and the children were home, she had done it all—weeks of cleaning and sewing, hours of shopping and wrapping, days of baking, all-night cooking before Christmas Eve. Many times, after their family dinner, after Jack and little Jack had gone to bed, she had attended the midnight service. By that time, she was so tired that she often placed Beth on one side of her and Susan on the other to prevent her from falling off the pew if she went to sleep.

This year, Loraine's fourth without Jack, Beth was in Italy, and six-foot-one "little" Jack was somewhere in the Middle East with his army unit. She had sent their cookies and stuffed stockings weeks ago. Susan was visiting her new husband's family in Maine. There were no grandchildren, so she need not slip outside to ring sleigh bells or leave a snack for Santa.

I'll miss the children, she thought, flipping the page in her book. *And I'll miss Jack whether anyone else is here or not. But I'm sure going to enjoy having a hassle-free holiday for the first time in thirty-five years,* she told herself firmly.

"How long has it been since I actually sat down to read a book two days before Christmas?" she asked herself happily.

She was chuckling over the third chapter when the phone's shrill ring cut into her concentration. She picked up the receiver and said, "Hello."

"Merry Christmas!" the cheery voice at the other end sang out. "It's Peggy!"

"Peggy?" Eleanor repeated, unable to keep an edge of displeasure at being interrupted from showing in her tone. "Peggy who?"

"You know," the voice insisted, "Peggy. Down at the Coalition."

Loraine recognized the voice as that of the coordinator of activities down at the Coalition of Committed Christians, where she had volunteered three or four times with some of her church group. She didn't know the woman's last name, barely knew her at all, but she had a sinking feeling that "Peggy" was calling to snatch up some of her peaceful Christmas time.

"I'm calling to see if you could help us out with the Christmas dinner we're serving here at the shelter today at noon. We are holding it on the twenty-third so our people can spend Christmas Eve and Christmas Day with their families. With your family away, I thought you might be free to lend us a hand. I know it's short notice, but I've had three of my servers call in sick this morning."

"I'm sorry," Loraine broke into the woman's spate of words. "I have plans. Maybe some other time. Thanks for calling." She hung up the phone, wondering how this very casual acquaintance had found out about her family being away. *Someone at church must have told her,* she decided.

Loraine tried to settle back into her book, but the mood had been broken. And, to tell the truth, she felt a bit selfish. It would only take a couple of hours, maybe three, from her day, and she still would have this evening, as well as Christmas Eve and Christmas Day, to herself.

Sighing, she closed the book and laid it on the table beside her recliner. Then she found the last number on the caller ID and dialed it.

"Peggy," she said when the woman answered, "I find I can make it after all. When should I be there?"

"Thank God!" Peggy breathed. "As soon as possible. People are already coming in, and it's more than an hour till noon."

"I'll be there in twenty minutes," Loraine promised, hanging up the phone and hurrying to the closet to pull on a Christmassy green sweat suit with a jolly snowman on the shirt. Straightening it, she noted with satisfaction that it was a little big now that she had lost that last twenty pounds that had weighed her down and plagued her arthritis.

She went into the bathroom and brushed her teeth, ran a

comb through her short hair, and lightly touched her lips with lipstick. "Who are you?" she asked the impudent, green-eyed, silver-haired image staring back at her from the mirror. It was a private joke she had developed to keep from being depressed when she encountered more and more evidence of the passing years.

Back in the family room, she perched on the edge of the recliner to pull on ankle socks and walking shoes. She knew from experience that she would be on her feet the entire time she was at the soup kitchen.

"Tigger, I'm going out for a while," she told the cat, rubbing his broad, striped head and scratching a little behind his ears. The cat looked up at her, yawned, and blinked sleepy yellow eyes before tucking his head between his front paws and settling in for a winter's nap. "I can tell you'll miss me!" she laughed wryly, reaching for her coat, wallet, and car keys.

"See you later," she promised both Tigger and John Grisham.

Chapter 2

Loraine eased her small green Honda into one of the few remaining parking spaces, locked the door, and made her way carefully down the sidewalk that had been cleared of snow then dusted lightly by the wind. She certainly didn't want to spend Christmas—or any other time, for that matter—lying in some hospital with a broken bone!

"Thank you for coming!" Peggy greeted her earnestly as she entered the big lobby of the sprawling building that housed both the city's soup kitchen and the Senior Citizens' Center.

"You're welcome," Loraine answered, looking around the room. Already the faux leather couches and chairs were filled with people watching TV, playing checkers, and reading. Many simply stood against the wall, staring at the floor, waiting. Loraine knew that all of them had one thing in common—the desire for a good hot meal. She nodded a general greeting as she followed Peggy's short, stocky figure in tight jeans and bright red sweater to the serving area.

"Honey, am I glad to see you!" Gloria, the head server, exclaimed, a huge white-toothed grin splitting her dark face. "I've only got one other server and two cooks here today, and none of us is an octopus! Here, put on this apron and slap some turkey, dressing, and cranberry sauce on these plates! Oh, and add one of those hot rolls."

Loraine hung her coat on one of the pegs in the hallway and slipped the straps of the big white coverall apron over her neck. She had just finished tying its strings behind her waist when Peggy hollered to the crowd, "Come and get it!"

Slipping on the required latex gloves, Loraine took the first plate from Gloria—already bearing green beans and mashed potatoes—slapped a piece of turkey on it, and added a scoop of dressing and a slice of jellied cranberry sauce. She tossed a hot roll on it and looked up to hand it to the first in line.

The man in front of her reached out stained hands with dirty fingernails to take the plate, his eyes on the food, never meeting hers. Loraine noted that his thin, gray hair straggled over the collar of his oversized Columbo raincoat, and the ripe odor of unwashed flesh wafted through the pleasant aroma of dressing and freshly baked rolls. She held her breath and swallowed hard as he shuffled off to sit at one of the many tables set around the dining room.

Gloria shoved the next plate into Loraine's hands. She glanced up at the woman who took the filled plate from her. The woman's watery eyes were full of gratitude and hunger. Loraine noticed that her worn, dark red coat was fastened across her bony chest with twine. The woman smiled weakly and blinked hard.

"Don't let it get to you, honey," Gloria advised. "Jesus said we would have the poor with us always. Just be glad you're helping feed 'em the only decent meal they get."

Vowing not to look up again, Loraine concentrated on filling plates. Soon her movements became routine—slap a generous slice of turkey on the plate, add a scoop of dressing and a slice of jellied cranberry sauce. Keep your eyes off the pitiful line of humanity winding its way past. Play a game with the round clock on the wall across the room to see how many plates you can fill in five minutes.

"Oh, Mama, it smells so good!" she heard a child exclaim. Involuntarily, she looked up, straight into the sad, tired eyes of a woman standing in line behind three children—a three- or four-year-old boy and two little girls of elementary school age. The children were scrubbed, their hair shiny clean, their mismatched, obviously hand-me-down clothing washed, pressed, and mended. Loraine smiled as the mother and her children passed by, and received an apologetic smile that did not reach the mother's despairing eyes.

What circumstances have caused this woman to seek food from the soup kitchen? Loraine wondered. *Where does she live with her small brood?* Surely they weren't one of the homeless families she had read about who lived under a bridge or in a cardboard box somewhere! Loraine felt her throat tighten and tears sting her eyes. *And here I am with an all-but-empty two-story house,* she thought guiltily. She wasn't ready to take in strangers yet, but. . .

"You do the turkey and dressing. I'll add the sauce and roll," a deep voice suggested beside her. The voice belonged to a man she'd never seen before who was wearing an apron like hers, smiling a wide smile that spilled over from dark brown eyes. She noted the turned-up corners of a generous mouth.

"I'm Ted," he added, taking the first plate from her, "new associate pastor at the church down the street."

"I'm Loraine," she answered, returning his smile gratefully as she struggled to regain the rhythm of her interrupted routine. *I don't care what weird denomination he represents,* she thought, recalling stories she had heard about that congregation, *so long as he helps serve this food!*

"God bless you, sir," she heard Ted say beside her as he handed the filled plate into the trembling hands of a red-faced man smelling of stale alcohol.

At least he will be drinking only tea or coffee with this meal, Loraine thought, pushing her hair back from her damp forehead with her right wrist and reaching for another plate with her left hand. Again, she glanced at the clock. She'd been serving for more than an hour, and the shuffling line still stretched halfway around the big room.

"There's no rest for the weary," Ted breathed beside her. She threw him a tired grimace and reached for another plate.

Finally, Ted was placing the last plate into the hands of an elderly man who let go of his grip on the counter to take it, then nearly dropped it as he clutched the counter again for support.

She saw Ted quickly come around the counter, take the plate in one hand and the elbow of the old man in the other. As he guided the man to the last empty place at one of the tables, Loraine leaned wearily against the wall behind her.

"Could you give us a hand with the cleanup?" Gloria asked hopefully.

Loraine thought longingly of her clean, quiet house, with Tigger asleep on the sofa and John Grisham waiting on the table. *I have the evening before me,* she reminded herself. *I have no all-night cooking, wrapping, or decorating to do. I am free to spend this time as I please, since I'm not really "doing" Christmas this year.* Looking into Gloria's tired, hopeful eyes, she knew she really couldn't refuse. She took a deep breath. "Sure," she agreed, glad to see that her answer brought some relief and a broad grin back to the woman's face.

Loraine removed the stainless steel pans from the heating elements on the counter and carried them to the big sinks in the back room. They had two automatic dishwashers back there, but the pans were done by hand. She placed one into the sink, turned on hot water, squirted soap into it, picked up a sponge, and began to scrub.

The two cooks, who had been there since 5:00 a.m., left, but Gloria was hard at work cleaning the stoves, and Peggy was in her office busy with paperwork. As Loraine went back and forth to gather soiled utensils, she could see Ted out in the dining room busily wiping tables, straightening chairs, and picking up trash.

When the cleanup was finished, Gloria handed her a filled plate. "Enjoy!" she ordered. "You've earned it."

"Thank you," she said, feeling her empty stomach rumble. It had been a long time since breakfast.

Gloria held a plate out to Ted, but he shook his head. "Thanks, but I've got to run," he said, taking off his apron and shrugging into the overcoat he had retrieved from one of the hooks in the hallway. "The men at church are delivering Angel Tree gifts later this evening," he explained to Loraine, "and I promised to coordinate our efforts. I enjoy that duty, though," he added. "It's such a joy to see little eyes light up at a special gift supposedly from a dad or a mom who is in prison. Most of them couldn't give their children anything for Christmas without the assistance of some program like Angel Tree, and many of them really do care."

She nodded. She had heard of the program on TV and among the many solicitations she received each week in the mail. Angel Tree was an outgrowth of Chuck Colson's Prison Fellowship, and she was sure it was a good cause. There were just so many appeals, and she couldn't help them all on retirement income—even though hers now seemed relatively comfortable after seeing the needy people here today. She threw loose change into the Salvation Army kettles each time she passed them, donated to the food pantry through her church, and sent small checks here and there for special needs.

"It's men only for the deliveries," Ted said, pulling on leather driving gloves, "but there is a get-together at the church afterward—a chance to fortify ourselves with some refreshment. You'd be more than welcome to join us," he offered.

Loraine shook her head. "I'm pretty well worn-out," she said with a smile, "and I have a good cat and a good book waiting for me at home."

"No family you need to prepare Christmas for?" he asked, his dark eyes searching hers. "No last-minute shopping, wrapping, cooking? My wife used to be up nearly all night sometimes these last two days before Christmas."

Again, she smiled and shook her head. "Been there and done that!" she replied. "But my son's in the Middle East this year, and my two daughters are—" She stopped, suddenly irritated at the man's prying. "They're away," she finished abruptly, removing her apron and tossing it in the bin for washing.

"No husband eagerly awaiting your return?" he probed.

"My husband is dead," she snapped, "and I'm spending Christmas alone for once. I plan to enjoy every quiet, peaceful moment of it!"

"I'm sorry," he said sincerely. "I didn't mean to pry. Maybe you can join us some other time." And giving her a wide, apologetic smile, he was gone.

A strange man, Loraine thought, digging into her turkey and dressing. *It depresses me to think of how many pitiful specimens of humanity have passed through this line today,* she thought. *Drug addicts, alcoholics, the homeless, the down-and-out, and the downright ornery, as Jack used to put it.*

She knew that Jack would have given the shirt off his back to someone who truly needed it, but he had little patience with those who wouldn't try to help themselves. This Ted had shown equal courtesy and kindness to even the most repulsive of their guests, sharing that wonderful smile with each of them, and walking away with his apparently natural cheerfulness intact.

A strange man, she repeated, taking her keys from her coat pocket and heading for the door.

Chapter 3

B ack home Loraine took a hot shower followed by a short nap in the recliner between favorite segments of *Fox News*. Then she got out the popcorn popper, the jar of popcorn, and a bottle of vegetable oil. The lunch she had eaten down at the center was long gone, and it was time for a snack, she decided. One of her favorites was plain old-fashioned popcorn popped in hot oil and covered with salt. She didn't care what *anybody* said about it being bad for her cholesterol or her blood pressure or her triglycerides.

"If it tastes good, spit it out immediately!" her doctor had joked at her last visit, recommending a bland, low-fat diet. *Well, let young Dr. Spencer eat Styrofoam popcorn and soy burgers,* she thought defiantly. *I will eat what I please!*

Of course, as Dr. Spencer had reminded her, she didn't want to have a stroke or a heart attack and be an invalid, and generally she ate a fairly healthy diet. *But if I want a bowl of oil-popped popcorn covered in salt once in a while,* she thought, *I'll have it!*

She plugged in the popper and poured in oil and popcorn. Then she virtuously sliced a Granny Smith apple into a saucer and looked around for that John Grisham book, *Skipping*

Christmas. She found it just in time to rescue the popcorn before it scorched.

Comfortably ensconced in the recliner, munching on popcorn and apple slices, she tried to settle down with her book again. As much as she enjoyed Grisham's writing, though, she couldn't focus on the story. Something was nagging at her— like the time she forgot to make Susan's potato salad, or the time she neglected to buy candy and trinkets for the stockings and had to send Jack out to buy what he could find at the last minute.

"It's just that it's the evening before Christmas Eve, and there's nothing that I have to do," she told herself smugly.

She got up and went through the house switching on lights. With the clocks back on standard time for the winter months, it was dark outside by six o'clock.

Usually, this was the day she and Jack had made an evening of last-minute shopping and a quick dinner together amid the crowds. It was a ritual they had both looked forward to and insisted on keeping, even when they had to hire a babysitter because the children were not yet old enough to stay alone. Then she had stayed home on Christmas Eve to put the finishing touches on packages and food for that night's dinner and gift opening.

What is it like downtown tonight? she wondered, entertaining the thought of walking the three blocks to the shopping district to experience the small-town Christmas atmosphere without any personal urgency and watch the frantic crowds of shoppers without the stress of having anything to do to complete her own celebrations. *It would be a first!* she thought, the idea suddenly sounding appealing to her.

Loraine put on her coat and boots, wrapped a jaunty red scarf around her neck, and pulled on gloves to match. She was on the front stoop when it occurred to her that she should ask her next-door neighbor to accompany her. Esther surely had no last-minute Christmas duties to perform.

She glanced at the neat brick house next door. *Esther Cohen doesn't "do" Christmas*, she thought. *She keeps Hanukkah.* Each year, Loraine saw her lighting the eight-branched candelabra called a menorah on the table in her front window. She would add a candle each night until she reached the eighth one. This ritual commemorated the great miracle God had performed in keeping the temple menorah burning for eight days until more oil could be brought through enemy lines.

The year after Jack died, Esther, who had been a widow when she moved here, had invited Loraine over for latkes, delicious shredded potato pancakes eaten with sour cream and jellies. Then, while the menorah candles burned low, they had sung Hanukkah songs and played games with the little top Esther called a dreidel. They ate home-baked cookies in the shapes of menorahs, dreidels, and the six-sided Star of David, which Esther called the "Mogen David." Before Loraine had left, Esther had given her the recipe for latkes. Loraine still made them during Hanukkah when the holiday did not fall on the same busy days as Christmas.

She recalled the time she had asked at the Christian book-store if they had Hanukkah cards, thinking she would send one to Esther. The horrified clerk had responded, "Certainly not!" She supposed she should have enlightened him that the Jewish holiday was simply the commemoration of a great miracle God had performed. It was no more anti-Christian than the parting of the Red Sea, the manna in the desert, or the providing of oil and flour for the widow in Elijah's time.

"O Hanukkah, O Hanukkah! Come light the menorah!" She sang softly the happy little song Esther had taught her and that she had passed on to her own children. What were the next lines? *"Dum de dum dum dum, de, dum, dum dum dum dum,"* she hummed as she went back inside and pulled off her gloves. "There'll be dreidels to play with and latkes to eat," she remembered. Then came her favorite part of the song, where the tempo slowed and the words became nostalgic: "And while we are playing, the candles are burning low. One for each night, they shed a sweet light to remind us of days long ago," she sang.

She might not have all the words right. Her children had often teased her about making up her own words to songs she couldn't remember, and sometimes even her own tune. But it was a nice little song for a beautiful holiday. "The Festival of Lights" Esther called it.

And Esther is a beautiful lady, Loraine thought warmly. They weren't "bosom buddies," just friendly neighbors who had shared many things over the years. She enjoyed having her as a next-door neighbor, the kind with whom she could exchange cookies and new recipes, who would lend her a cup of sugar if she ran out in the midst of her usual frantic baking splurge before Christmas or give her a ride to the supermarket if her car was in the shop.

Loraine turned and looked out the window to her right. The Mitchells' house next door was temporarily empty because they had gone to visit their daughter and new grandson in Colorado for the holidays. Beyond that, twenty years ago, Mr. Feroz and his quiet little wife had built a small stone house to resemble the houses of their native Iraq. The son they raised there had now grown up and moved away.

Esther was convinced that the Feroz's son had gone back to

the Middle East to become a suicide bomber. She spat on the ground whenever Loraine mentioned the family. Although there was no reason to believe that the Feroz boy had done any such thing, she knew that Esther's anger arose from the loss of an uncle and his family killed in a suicide bombing in Tel Aviv.

Mrs. Feroz had died last year of cancer. Loraine could almost see her now, creeping out of the house behind her husband, only her beautiful dark eyes visible above the scarf tucked securely around her hair and face. She had never seen the woman's face, never known her first name. On those rare occasions when she met up with her, Loraine had simply addressed her as Mrs. Feroz.

Mr. Feroz, of course, did not keep Christmas, either. He kept Ramadan, fasting all day and feasting all night, or at least that was what she had heard. His Islamic beliefs were not something Loraine could share. His Allah was not the same God she and Esther worshiped. However, as an American, she respected his right to believe as he chose, and they exchanged friendly conversation when they met on evening walks or when she shopped at his little market a couple of blocks away.

As far as she could tell, Mr. Feroz had no family or friends here. Like Esther, he attended worship services in a larger nearby town.

Loraine laid down her gloves and picked up the phone. "Esther!" she said when her friend answered. "Would you be interested in a walk downtown to watch the crowds tonight, and perhaps a little something at the tea shop?"

"Loraine? Aren't you frantically into your Christmas preparations? Oh, I'm sorry," she said. "I forgot that this year you are as alone as I am." She hesitated then said, "Of course. I'd love to go with you, so long as you don't expect me to celebrate the birth of Yeshua. You know I don't believe—"

"I know, Esther. I may disagree with you on Jesus being the Messiah, but I promise not to bring that up tonight. I'm sure we'll see more of Santa Claus than Jesus, anyway. Come and go with me. It will be fun!"

"All right. Just let me put on my coat and boots. I'll meet you out front in five minutes," she promised.

Esther always makes my five-foot-three seem tall, Loraine thought as her diminutive neighbor joined her on the sidewalk, merry brown eyes peering out from the fur-lined hood of a warm parka.

"Oiy, what a night!" Esther exclaimed as they set off briskly toward the center of town, their breath forming frosty, cartoon-like blurbs on the air in front of them. "We could surely reach out and touch that evening star!"

Loraine looked up. "I believe we could, Esther," she agreed, wondering if it had looked that way on the night the angels appeared to the shepherds to announce the good news of the Savior's birth. Still, she was sure the supernova hanging over the manger in Bethlehem that night had been bigger than this ordinary evening star.

She took a deep breath, feeling the invigorating sting of the crisp, cold air in her nostrils then traveling down into her lungs. She noted the fuzzy glow of streetlights outlined against the nearly black velvet sky, and all around them the decorations of the season—gaily blinking multicolored lights, Santa scenes on the rooftops and lawns. Here and there a lighted crèche depicted the birth of Jesus, or Yeshua, as Esther called him.

Loraine wanted to say, "This really is what Christmas is all about, Esther, 'that white-hot moment when eternity melted into time,' as her pastor had described it. It was the moment when God sent his Son to become Emmanuel, God with us." But she had promised Esther not to talk about such things.

In minutes they were at the edge of the shopping district. They slowed their steps, enjoying the brightly lit shop windows, the gaiety of Christmas tunes blaring from loudspeakers, the spicy scent of evergreen, and the festive air of small-town Christmas.

In front of Hale's Department Store, Loraine saw the familiar red kettle of the Salvation Army hanging from its tripod. She dug in her pockets for something to contribute, but Esther turned away and peered into the shop window where a miniature train wailed through a Christmas village.

I suppose she has her own charities and doesn't want to contribute to anything having to do with the scorned Yeshua, Loraine thought, pulling out a crumpled dollar bill and reaching out to drop it into the kettle.

Suddenly, she recognized the figure standing beside the kettle. Wearing a red and white Santa hat and vigorously ringing his bell was the pastor she had met earlier at the soup kitchen.

"Thank you," he said with that infectious grin. "Merry Christmas!"

She grinned back. "Merry Christmas, yourself," she answered. "But what are you doing here? I thought you were out delivering Angel Tree gifts."

"It's our church's day to help the Army with its annual drive," he explained. "It's my first year, but I understand they have done it for several years now. We're doing Angel Tree later. The gifts all are wrapped, tagged, and ready, but, you know, Santa always comes after the children are 'snug in their beds.'"

"Of course," she said. "Well, you look very chic in your fur hat," she added, trying unsuccessfully to picture her own pastor in the ridiculous getup.

"Thank you," he said primly, his eyes twinkling as a full-fledged grin took over.

Loraine became aware of Esther's questioning glance. "I've got to go," she whispered. "I'm giving my Jewish neighbor a small taste of our Christian Christmas."

"Really?" His eyebrows rose. "I'm surprised that she's willing. I mean, I'm aware that our Christian faith is built on a firm foundation of Judaism, but doesn't she believe the Messiah is yet to come?"

"Yes," Loraine answered, "but other than that, our beliefs are almost exactly the same. And I enjoy her company," she added.

"Oh, there's nothing wrong with being friends," he agreed. Then a frown wrinkled his forehead. "But if a person is wrong about Jesus Christ, it doesn't really matter what else he is right about," he said. "Your friend needs to know the Savior, Loraine." Coins rattled into the kettle, and he turned to acknowledge the contribution with a "Thank you. Merry Christmas!"

Loraine sensed that he turned back immediately to say something else to her, but she had already moved over to join Esther at the shop window.

"I give to Coats for Kids and Feed the Children," Esther explained defensively.

"Good for you," Loraine answered. "Let's go inside out of the cold."

They let the crowd carry them through a swinging shop door into the milling throng snatching last-minute bargains from the scrambled mess on the counters inside. Loraine took in the ropes of holly, ivy, and pine, with their red velvet bows and brightly colored ornaments, suspended from the walls and ceiling and twined around every post. *I guess I really have missed my decorations this year,* she admitted to herself, *though I haven't missed all this frantic hullabaloo.*

Above the din of voices, a fat man in a red and white suit sitting on a throne at the center of the store boomed, "Ho! Ho! Ho! Merry Christmas! Merry Christmas!" A throng of children waited to climb onto his knee and whisper their requests, while parents and grandparents strained to hear so they could ensure the granting of those requests.

Gradually, Loraine became aware of the scowling expressions of irritated shoppers and the sheer exhaustion in the faces of harassed clerks. She winced at the jab of a heedless elbow and the crunch of a heavy shoe on her left foot. When she was assaulted by a spate of vulgar language from the lips of a pretty young girl standing beside them, she threw an apologetic glance at Esther, who was hunched defensively against a post studying a poster advertising a brand of alcohol as the perfect "spirit of Christmas."

"See, Esther," she pointed out, "the modern Christmas is mostly Santa Claus, presents, food, and alcohol."

Esther gave her a wry grin. "They don't carry Hanukkah cards, either," she said sympathetically.

Loraine grinned back. "Let's get out of here and go to the tea shop," she suggested.

"Whew!" Esther breathed, removing her furry hood and then her coat when they finally were seated at a small round table in the back. "I think I'm glad I only have to buy a few presents and make some latkes and cookies for Hanukkah. I'd never make it through one of your Christmases!"

"I think you're right!" Loraine sighed, massaging the boot over her injured foot. "I've forgotten how bad it can be out there! Jack and I used to enjoy this last night of shopping, but now I wonder why. It must have been just the fact that it was time we always spent together."

Esther nodded. "It's been nearly twenty years, and I still miss Jacob." She pronounced it "Ya-a-cov." "Zal," she added. Then seeing Loraine's puzzled look, she translated, "May he rest in peace."

Loraine patted the older woman's hand, then took the menu a waitress extended. "I think I'll have spiced tea and a couple of those wonderful raisin cookies they make here," she said. "What's for you, Esther?"

Esther ran her gaze over the small menu. "I'll have the carrot cake and plain tea," she decided, handing back the menu.

As they waited for their orders, Loraine said, "I'm sorry, Esther. I guess this nostalgic visit downtown at the peak of the Christmas frenzy wasn't such a good idea after all."

Esther nodded in agreement, then smiled. "I guess you needed to get it out of your system," she said. "I don't regret trying it once. We just won't do it again soon!"

When their food came, Esther was telling a story about one of her children wanting to become a Christian one year just so she could share in her friends' Christmas. "She wanted to be Jewish for Hanukkah and just convert to Christianity for the Christmas season!" she explained.

Loraine laughed, breaking off a piece of cookie to dip into her tea. Then she said seriously, "Maybe your daughter had the right idea, Esther. We have so much in common. It's a shame we can't just share the best of our beliefs and not squabble over the differences."

She remembered Ted's comment earlier, "If a person is wrong about Jesus Christ, it doesn't really matter what else he is right about." She knew that in the eternal scheme of things that was true, but she had told Esther what she believed. She couldn't force her to accept it.

Esther looked up from her cake. "Our own little 'road map to peace'?" she said with a grin. "Now, if we can just get America and all the countries of the Middle East to accept it—shalom!"

They were laughing as they left the shop and made their way home, going a couple of blocks out of their way to avoid the downtown mob.

When Loraine left Esther at her front door, she automatically called out, "Merry Christmas!"

"Laylah tov! Good night!" Esther responded with a twinkle in her eye. Then she added, "Happy Hanukkah!"

Laughing, Loraine let herself into her house. She undressed and put on her gown and robe. Finally, slipping her tired feet into soft, warm slippers, she picked up John Grisham's book.

"I've put the ghost of December twenty-third to rest," she told Tigger, satisfied that she truly had. The big cat looked at her as though he understood and came over to nestle beside her in the recliner where she could scratch his ears while she read more about skipping Christmas.

Chapter 4

Loraine was up and dressed by seven, as had become her custom as she had grown older. She might take a small nap in the recliner in the afternoon, but she generally could not lie in bed after seven in the morning.

She filled Tigger's water bowl and warmed him a small bowl of milk in the microwave. It was a habit she had developed while caring for the small, orphaned kitten. Tigger had been the last of a litter of kittens being given away in the Wal-Mart parking lot. She couldn't bear to think of that small, striped ball of fur with the frightened yellow eyes being taken off to the pound. Immediately he had claimed her for his own. *That's what Tiggers do best!* she remembered thinking.

While the house was so full of Jack and the children and their possessions, Tigger lived on the back porch. But now that she was alone, Loraine let him share the big empty house, grateful for his companionship. "And you expect warm milk in your bowl every morning, don't you, old buddy?" she said, reaching down to pat him on his broad, striped head. He purred an "uh huh" and went right on lapping up warm milk.

Loraine filled the teakettle with cold water, set it on the burner, and turned on the stove. Then she took her favorite

Christmas mug down from the cupboard and dropped a teabag into it. Next, she sliced a piece of date bread, placed it on a small paper plate, and carried it to the table. It wasn't that she particularly wanted date bread, though she did like it. She was just determined not to cook today.

As she ate and sipped her tea, she read about the Savior's birth in the second chapter of Luke. Closing her eyes, she remembered back to Christmas Eves past—once the family was finished with dinner and before any gifts were opened, they always took turns reading that chapter.

She could almost hear Beth lisping through missing teeth, "And there were in that thame country, shepheths abiding in the field. . . ." She could picture Susan sitting primly in her small rocking chair awaiting her turn and little Jack, still too young to read, squirming impatiently on the hearth. He was always eager to get to the presents they would be allowed to open before going to bed. Contributions left by "Santa" in the night—those mysterious packages that appeared on the hearth and the stuffed stockings hanging from the mantel—were dealt with on Christmas morning.

After throwing her empty plate in the trash and rinsing the tea mug at the sink, Loraine looked around for something to do. The bird feeders looked nearly full from the kitchen window, but she put on her coat and boots and went out to replenish them anyway.

A fresh snow had fallen during the night. *It's a beautiful Christmas Eve day,* Loraine thought, *clear and crisp, with the sun's rays picking out diamonds in the grass and along the tree limbs, and the bright red cardinals completing the picture. Beth would be out here with her camera. Little Jack would be begging to go sledding. Susan would be wanting to make snow cream, and*

Jack would be shaking his head, saying he couldn't understand how they could fool their stomachs that way. She smiled at the fond memories and felt a wave of longing wash over her.

She was confident that she knew where Jack was, but what was he doing up there in heaven this very moment? Could he see her down here feeding the birds, spending Christmas alone for the first time in all these years? After all the laments he had heard her make about not having enough time, was he laughing at her efforts to find ways to fill the hours this year?

What were her children doing? Was little Jack sweltering in the Middle Eastern sun? Was he in some kind of danger? She said a quick prayer for his protection, then realized that it likely was evening over there, with the hot sun sinking into the desert. Perhaps he and his buddies were playing cards or resting for the night. Susan was probably visiting with yet another group of new in-laws, and Beth surely was out somewhere exploring Italy with her ever-present camera. In her last telephone call, she had mentioned someone named Roberto, more than once.

Anyway, Loraine felt sure that none of her family members were alone this Christmas. *I'm the only one alone this year, rattling around this big old house, trying to find something to occupy my time,* she thought. *But I'm not having a pity party here,* she reminded herself. *I'm enjoying the peace of a stress-free holiday for the first time in thirty-five years!*

Her thoughts went to Esther Cohen next door. Last night Esther had asked her not to talk about her belief that the Old Testament's promised Messiah had come. Loraine knew that Pastor Ted was right. Esther, like everybody else, needed the Savior. They had discussed this before, more than once, and Loraine knew that no matter how convinced she was that her beliefs were right, she could not force them on her friend. They had enjoyed a pleasant evening together in spite of that one major difference in their beliefs and the mayhem they had encountered downtown.

She could not see the front of Esther's house from here, but she knew there were no Christmas lights outlining its eaves and windows. In contrast, the Mitchells' house on the other side of hers was lit by a string of Christmas lights that they had programmed to come on with the house lights to convince would-be robbers they were not out in Colorado visiting their children for the holidays.

Beyond that, the Feroz place would be dark. Mr. Feroz certainly did not decorate for the Christian holiday. How did he handle this time that so absorbed most of his neighbors, those his Qur'an called "infidels"? Did he just retreat inside his house until the commotion was over, going out only to run his shop or to visit his place of worship in the next town?

The question Loraine had to deal with, however, was not what Mr. Feroz or Esther Cohen did while the whole town, the nation, most of the world was caught up in celebrating some version of the birth of Jesus Christ. The question was what she was going to do today to pass the time until the midnight service at church tonight. *It's unbelievable that I have absolutely nothing to do on Christmas Eve!* she marveled.

Loraine sat down at her desk in the family room and pulled out some notepaper. She wrote notes to some out-of-town friends and one to her Aunt Caroline in Georgia, addressed the envelopes, stamped them, and laid them by her purse to mail the next time she was out.

Now what? she thought. *Should I make some more date bread?* No, she decided. In addition to the one she had cut, there was another fresh loaf wrapped in foil in the cupboard. It wasn't likely she would finish both of them before they molded. Should she prepare something for her own quiet dinner tonight or for lunch tomorrow? She had baked a small country ham and made a fruit salad two days ago that she hadn't touched yet.

She threw a small load of laundry into the washer, added detergent, and turned it on. She ran the dust mop over the polished hardwood floors and a wet mop over the linoleum in the kitchen area. She wiped off the counter and the stove-top. She watered the vines in the window over the sink. Then she wandered through the house straightening pictures and lamp shades that were already straight.

At noon, Loraine fixed a ham sandwich and ate it with a small helping of fruit salad and a glass of iced tea. Then she puttered around the house rearranging the figures in both nativity scenes, making a new street of shops and houses in the Dickens village, which she kept year-round on the top shelves of her grandmother's poplar cupboard in the living room.

She glanced at the bare mantel, debating whether or not to hang stockings from it just for old-times' sake. *That would be foolish,* she decided at last. It could only serve as a painful reminder that her loved ones weren't here to take them down and exclaim excitedly over the contents that always had appeared in them "magically" during the night, even in the years long after Santa was expected. She remembered fondly that it had been her last chore—putting candies and small treasures into the stockings before falling into bed for a couple of hours of exhausted sleep before the early risers were up.

It was nearly dark now, she noted, flipping on the light. Only a few more hours and it would be time to get dressed for the midnight service. She went to the closet and rummaged through it, trying to decide what to wear. *Something appropriately red or green,* she thought, shoving the hangers and their contents back and forth on the rod. Maybe she would wear the red velvet pantsuit since she wore it only during the Christmas season.

Suddenly, she heard carolers out front begin a joyful, if not so melodious, rendition of "It Came upon a Midnight Clear." *I'm not going to invite them in for hot chocolate!* she promised herself, stifling a twinge of guilt as she peered out from behind the living room draperies.

The streetlight at the corner revealed that they were not from her church, but from various congregations around town. She recognized Bessie Adams, Maude Simpson, and Bill Thomas. And there were Sam Curtis and Alma Tate. There were a few faces she did not recognize scattered through the impromptu choir. *Must be a group of volunteers from the Senior Citizens' Center,* she decided, noting that all of them appeared to be her age or older.

I've always wanted to go caroling, she thought wistfully, *but there just never was enough time.*

"Time is something I have plenty of this year," she reminded herself.

Smiling, she put on her boots and her coat, pulled the front door shut behind her, and dropped the key into her pocket.

Chapter 5

"Welcome!" Sam Curtis called as Loraine came down the sidewalk toward the group. "Come share my songbook!"

Loraine wondered if she had made a mistake in joining the group. Sam was a widower who had retired from his hardware business a couple of years ago. She had known him all her life, had gone to grade school with him. She knew that he and his wife had raised six children, who, with their families, were scattered all over the country. His wife had died suddenly last year of a heart attack. Not wanting to hurt his feelings, she accepted half of his offered songbook and began to fit her husky alto into the so-called harmony of the carolers.

Having thoroughly serenaded Loraine's street, the group moved on to another block. There had been no sign of Esther or Mr. Feroz, but she had not expected them to appear. The Christian carols probably did little more than irritate them.

She thought their singing was getting better, but maybe it was just her imagination, an illusion created by being part of the singers rather than a captive listener. She hoped they were a blessing to those who heard them and not an irritant.

Sam smiled at her warmly, showing yellowed teeth with a

gap where he had lost a couple right in the front bottom half of his mouth. *Is he too tight to get a bridge put in?* she wondered, recalling stories she had heard over the years of his stinginess with his wife and children. *Or maybe he's just wrapped up in a deluded notion of his own attractiveness.* Loraine remembered that he had been that way even as a child. *Maybe he doesn't think we'll notice,* she thought, smiling at the few long, gray hairs combed across his extensive bald spot.

Sam hooked his left arm through her right elbow and gave her a suggestive leer from under slightly raised eyebrows. Loraine shuddered involuntarily and carefully removed her arm from his grasp. As casually as possible, she eased over to stand between Sophia Carter and Ilene Tussey, hardly missing a word of "—and loud and deep, their words repeat of peace on Earth, goodwill to men."

A little later, she threw a sideways glance at Sam and saw that he was sharing his book with Alma Tate, who seemed delighted by the attention. Loraine sighed in relief and entered wholeheartedly into the singing in front of the apartments for the elderly and then the Senior Citizens' Center, where lonely people had gathered for a pleasant evening of board games and cookies and punch.

Suddenly, Loraine heard a new, deep baritone voice bolster the weak contributions of the men around her. She looked around to see Ted, the new associate pastor she had met in the food line at the soup kitchen and downtown ringing his bell for the Salvation Army. He was standing in the back row singing with gusto, though slightly off-key. He gave her a warm smile that lit up his dark eyes. So what if Ted was a pastor and married. She had no designs on him, and she was sure he had none on her, except as a potential convert for his church, perhaps. She returned the smile.

As they trudged along the street to the next residential neighborhood, Loraine found Ted beside her.

"Did you get the Angel Tree gifts delivered last night?" she asked.

"We did!" he affirmed, blowing absently on cold and reddened hands. "Those children were so excited! Three of them were in the food line yesterday with their mother. She was so overwhelmed by her kids getting gifts that she cried. It was a very gratifying experience." He ended quickly as the group took up its next song.

All at once, Loraine noticed that he was wearing only a thin jacket and his hands were gloveless. If she remembered correctly, Ted had worn an overcoat and gloves when he left the soup kitchen yesterday afternoon. Last night, too, he had worn them, along with his furry Santa Claus hat, as he rang his bell over the Salvation Army kettle. She couldn't remember if he had worn a hat before, but his head was bare now, the streetlight overhead picking up silver highlights in his thick, dark hair.

She glanced around. All the other men wore overcoats and gloves, and most of them had on sock caps or hats of some kind. "Where are your overcoat and gloves?" she whispered between verses of "O Little Town of Bethlehem." She was surprised to see a flush creep over his face as he stuffed his hands into the pockets of his inadequate jacket.

The woman standing on the other side of the pastor leaned toward Loraine. "He probably gave them to some homeless man on the street," she whispered. "We can't keep warm clothes on the man. He's always giving them away!"

"Now, Shirley!" Ted admonished. "Anyway, he was wearing

some thin old cast-off suit coat and shivering. I've got more clothes at home. I just didn't have time to go get them."

"Yeah, right!" the woman answered sarcastically. "Pastor Hammons, I just don't know what we're going to do with you!" But Loraine noticed that she smiled up at him fondly and patted him on the arm.

Loraine thought of her own pastor, so dignified in his tailored suits and designer ties. She respected the man. He was an excellent speaker and had been faithful to visit, or to send someone else to visit, two or three times a week during Jack's illness. But lately she had become a little disenchanted with his politically correct sermons. When she asked him to have the congregation participate in the day of prayer for Israel this past October, he had nodded agreeably but done nothing. The day had passed without notice so far as her congregation was concerned.

She had grown very interested in the plight of Israelis because of Esther. Born in Tel Aviv, Esther had relatives and friends there still. After every bombing, Loraine grieved with her friend for those killed, for the orphans left behind, for parents deprived of their children, for the maimed who could no longer earn a living or take care of themselves.

Whenever she could, Loraine sent small contributions to help the survivors of this never-ending struggle with those who were determined to drive the Jews from their tiny piece of land.

Her thoughts went back to the Old Testament story of Abraham and his two sons, Ishmael and Isaac. *How sad,* she thought, *that Abraham's giving in to his childless wife's pleading to have a son by her handmaid has resulted in centuries of bitter hatred between the descendants of two half brothers.*

Loraine felt that she could understand Ishmael's resentment at being cast out into the desert by his father as a result of the strife between his mother, the gloating handmaid, and her vengeful mistress, Sarah. She could understand how that resentment had been passed down for generations. And she could understand why the descendants of Sarah's son, Isaac, clung so desperately to the little country called Israel that they had carved out of a small portion of the land given to them by God through Abraham so long ago.

What a mess we make of things, she thought, *when we try to "help" God fulfill His promises!* She had thought the least her church could do was join in the international prayers for the "peace of Jerusalem" planned for that one day.

Only twice in the seven years that he has been my pastor have I asked him to do something special, she thought with a twinge of resentment, *and both times he either forgot or decided to ignore my request. Perhaps it's time I found another place of worship.* Loraine couldn't help but feel envious as she watched the warmth and camaraderie between Ted and Shirley.

Instantly, she was contrite and asked God to forgive her for envy and harboring a grudge against her pastor. What was it the angel had said to the shepherds? "On earth, peace to men of goodwill," she believed one version put it. Where was her goodwill?

"Come on, slowpoke," Ted joked, reaching out one bare hand to pull her from her disturbing thoughts back into the group. They were heading up a walk to the front door of the house they had just serenaded. "The Nelsons have invited us in for coffee and hot chocolate."

Loraine hesitated, then took his cold hand and let him lead her past a life-sized Santa and sleigh pulled by all eight reindeer and Rudolph—complete with a blinking red nose. The front door was outlined by multicolored lights and decorated with a huge wreath of real candy canes.

"Coffee or chocolate?" Ted asked when they were inside. Lights and ornaments dangled from a vaulted ceiling, and a twelve-foot pine tree glowed regally in one corner.

"Oh, I've always felt that sleigh riding and caroling call for hot chocolate," she said. She took the mug he handed her from the table in the center of the room and stirred the miniature marshmallows with a plastic spoon. Gingerly sipping the hot liquid, she walked around exploring the whimsical displays on every available surface. She couldn't help but think of her own decorations still packed away in boxes in the attic. *But I won't be up all night New Year's Eve packing them away again,* she thought smugly.

"You're grinning like the proverbial cat that swallowed the canary," Ted said, coming up beside her. He held a cup of coffee in one hand and a large brownie in the other. "What's so satisfying?"

"I was just thinking of my uncluttered Christmas this year," she answered. Then, suddenly wanting to be at home enjoying it, she added, "I need to get home."

"I'll walk you back," he offered instantly. "Where do you live?" When she told him, he said, "We're about four blocks from there. Are you too tired to walk?"

She shook her head. "No, I'm fine, and you don't need to—"

"It's dark out there, and walking home alone is not a good idea," he said firmly. "Criminals take advantage of times like this when people are so absorbed in their celebrations."

"But it's cold out there, and you don't even have an overcoat!" she protested.

"I've got to go that way, or part of it, anyway. Come on,"

he said, "time's a wastin'!"

Loraine let him take her by the elbow and steer her out-side, both of them murmuring thanks to their host and host-ess and saying good night to their fellow carolers on the way.

As they walked through the frosty night, Loraine found herself laughing at Ted's comical stories of his own childhood Christmases and those when his two children, both grown now, had been at home.

"Those were good days," he sighed. "Hectic, but good."

She nodded, recalling those boisterous Christmases when Jack and all three children were home. She could almost see the lights on the tree, smell the turkey and dressing baking in the oven, hear the happy voices raised in excitement. "Yes, I know what you mean," she agreed. "I was exhausted by the time Christmas Day got here, but those were good days."

"I miss Regina and the boys," he said then, "sometimes so badly I can hardly stand it. But I know Randy and Craig are busy with their own lives now, and Regina is in a much better place."

"Your wife is—" she began in surprise.

"—in heaven," he finished with surety. "If anybody's there, Regina is."

"I'm sorry," Loraine blurted. She had assumed that he had a wife. Hadn't he said she stayed up all night getting ready for Christmas like she had for so many years? "I mean, I'm not sorry she's in heaven," she stammered. "I'm just—"

"I know," he rushed to her rescue, "you're sorry for my loss. So am I, but how was it Edna St. Vincent Millay put it? 'Life must go on, though good men die,'" he quoted. "'Life must go on; I forget just why.'"

"My husband was a good man who loved the Lord with all

his heart, though he had his own way of showing it," she broke in. "But he was a pillar of our church, a good role model for the children, a strong arm for me to lean on. He never met a stranger, and he never hesitated to say exactly what he thought. He had a sarcastic sense of humor that sometimes made me laugh, sometimes embarrassed me, and sometimes irritated me. I miss him terribly at times," she added softly.

He nodded. "Yes, I know what you mean, but life does go on, and it doesn't do any good to sit around moping over what we've lost. At least we've had something really special and good, something some people never experience." He smiled that contagious smile. "Your husband and my wife are up there somewhere together tonight, and here we are."

She smiled up at him, then looked away, suddenly uncomfortable. "Here's my house," she said, fumbling in her coat pocket for the key.

His hand on her arm stopped her flight. "It's been a nice evening, Loraine," he said seriously, looking her straight in the eyes. "You don't mind if I call you Loraine, do you?"

She shook her head. "Of course not." She grasped the key and held it up, feeling relieved without quite knowing why. "Well, it's been a long day, and I can't wait to sit down with a good book and relax. Good night," she added.

"Merry Christmas," he answered, his eyes studying hers for a moment. Then he turned and walked away, back in the direction from which they had come.

Loraine went into the house and quickly locked the door behind her, as though something threatening might be lurking outside. She took a deep, steadying breath and bent to remove her boots. Her feet were nearly frozen, she realized, but she had a warm feeling inside.

My first caroling venture was a totally satisfying experience even if I did have to fend off the attentions of Sam Curtis, she thought, removing her coat and scarf. She was even less interested in some lonely old widower with missing teeth and hair combed carefully over his bald spot than she was in a traditional Christmas celebration.

The warm brown eyes and wide, friendly smile of the associate pastor came into her thoughts, but she pushed them away. *He's just interested in a new convert for his church, and I have no interest in any man.*

"It's you and me against the world, Tigger, and I like it that way," she vowed, stroking the cat, who purred his agreement.

She ate a bowl of fruit salad, smiling over the efforts of John Grisham's hero to skip Christmas by taking his wife on a cruise. *I've been more successful than he has,* she thought smugly. To be honest, though, she had done more Christmassy things than she ever had intended. *But after the candlelight service tonight,* she promised herself, *I'm going to do absolutely nothing until December twenty-sixth, if then.*

She read awhile longer, then took a shower and dressed in the red velvet pantsuit. At exactly 10:30 p.m., she was backing the car out of the driveway on her way to the church.

This ancient English-style church is beautiful any time, Loraine thought as she walked through the tall, double doors into the sanctuary, *but it always looks its best at Christmas with candles burning under hurricane lamps nestled in holly on the wide stone windowsills and greenery entwining its posts and altar rails.*

Taking a small white candle in its paper skirt from the usher, she chose a pew about halfway down the middle aisle. She sat there enjoying the ambiance of history and tradition until the robed choir members and pastors came down the aisle, two by two, carrying lighted candles and singing "Ring Out, Wild Bells!" Rising with the congregation to join in the last verse, she gasped as Ted Hammons appeared beside her.

"What are you doing here?" she whispered, moving over to make room on the pew.

"We don't have a midnight service, so I decided to join yours," he whispered back, taking the left side of her hymnal and adding his off-key baritone to the chorus.

Loraine was a little aggravated by his presence. She had looked forward to this quiet time of worship just between herself and God, but she guessed it would be selfish to deny someone else the same blessing. *This is my favorite service of the entire year, and nobody is going to destroy my delight in it,* she told herself firmly.

Loraine couldn't help being conscious of Ted there beside her, though, as they sang the familiar carols, listened to the minister's perfectly planned and executed message, and walked down the aisle to the altar to take part in communion. Back in the pew, she joined in singing "Silent Night," while Ted dipped his candlewick into the flame of the usher's candle. Then, lighting her candle from his, she held it high overhead as the service ended with the usual rousing "Joy to the World!"

I'm not going anywhere for coffee or tea or anything, so don't ask! she told him silently as he waited for the crowd to thin so they could ease into the aisle.

He moved ahead of her to the front entry, dropped his candle into the box on the table, and shook the minister's hand. Outside on the steps, he turned to her. "Well, it's officially here," he said. "Merry Christmas!"

"Merry Christmas," she answered. She watched as he disappeared into the crowd, leaving her only the memory of his grin. *No, thank you, I didn't want to go for coffee,* she thought, *but I might have liked to be asked so I could refuse!*

Laughing at her childish response, she headed home, exulting in a Christmas Eve with no last-minute presents to wrap, no stockings to fill, no food to prepare. It was an unheard-of phenomenon—*one I look forward to with great pleasure,* she told herself firmly.

Chapter 6

*I*t's raining! Loraine thought, stretching luxuriously under the covers. *There's nothing I like better than rain on the roof while I sleep. It will wash away our Christmas snow, but at least we had it for Christmas Eve.*

She glanced at the clock. "Seven-thirty!" she gasped. "On Christmas Day? It's time to get up!" She threw off the covers and searched for her slippers with bare feet reluctant to touch the cold floor. Then, slowly, she sank back onto the edge of the bed. It was Christmas Day, all right, but she had absolutely nothing to do.

"Incredible!" she breathed. Back when the kids were home, there would have been paper knee-deep in the living room and cast-off ribbon tangling around her ankles as she tried to escape to the kitchen to put Jack's scalloped oysters in the oven and to start their traditional sausage and scrambled eggs. And if, like this year, the day didn't fall on a Sunday, the children would have spent the rest of the day divesting the stockings of their treasures, eating leftovers, and sitting around fingering their new possessions with glazed, satiated expressions on their faces.

In those days, she wouldn't have imagined being alone on Christmas Day. She sighed, feeling a little hollow inside as she slipped on a pair of faded jeans and a blue sweatshirt sporting a scene of evergreens in the snow. She added socks and loafers before going to the bathroom mirror to run a comb through her hair.

The green-eyed image of an aging woman stared back at her. She studied it for a moment, then stuck out her tongue. "You can get old if you want to," she told the reflection, "but I'm going to go right on enjoying life as long as I have it! So there!" *And I'm going to enjoy this peaceful Christmas Day if it's the last thing I do!* she vowed.

Loraine sliced off a piece of the date bread and turned on the teakettle, looking out the window, where a few small birds braved the rain to feast at the half-empty bird feeders. There was no need to venture out into the wet to refill them yet.

She went to the refrigerator to get Tigger's milk, but when she picked up the jug, she could tell it was nearly empty. She removed the cap and turned the jug upside down, but only a trickle of milk ran out into the bowl. She warmed it in the microwave, anyway, and set it down for the cat.

Tigger lapped up the meager offering and looked up at her reproachfully. *"Meow?"* he questioned.

"I'm sorry, old buddy, that's all I've got. I'll have to go to the—" She stopped. Even the supermarket, which stayed open day and night, would be closed today. Why hadn't she thought to replenish the milk yesterday while she was out running around doing everything else?

Then she thought of Mr. Feroz's market a couple of streets over. Surely he wouldn't be closed for the Christian holiday!

"I'll get you some milk in a little while, Tigger," she promised, opening a small can of tuna and spooning it into his bowl to compensate. The cat sniffed at it disdainfully, sampled a bite or two, then jumped up onto the couch. He turned his back and began taking an elaborate spit bath, giving her an unmistakable cold shoulder.

Loraine laughed and sat down at the table with her date bread and tea. She picked up her much worn NIV Bible, and it fell open to her favorite book, Isaiah. Chapter 58. Her eyes fell on verse 10. "If you spend yourselves in behalf of the hungry and satisfy the needs of the oppressed, then your light will rise in the darkness, and your night will become like the noonday." *Should I take these words as a commendation for my work at the soup kitchen the other day or an admonishment to do something more today?* she wondered.

She got up, threw away her empty paper plate, and rinsed out her cup. "Might as well get that trip to the market over with," she said aloud, going to the hall closet for her coat, scarf, and boots.

As she passed the phone, she hesitated. *Should I call Esther to see if she needs anything?* she wondered. Then she remembered Esther's feelings for Mr. Feroz. She absolutely refused to have anything to do with him—that included using anything from his market.

Loraine grabbed her purse and keys and headed for the garage. She got into the car, started it, and gave it a few moments to warm up. *If that were snow drifting down out there instead of heavy rain, I'd have walked,* she thought, putting the car into gear and backing slowly out onto the pavement. Actually, she liked walking in the rain, too, but not in a soaking downpour on a cold day.

She maneuvered the car onto the street and drove carefully to the market, where she was surprised to find a parking place right out front. Then she remembered that it was Christmas Day. Everyone was shut inside four warm, safe walls with their loved ones. A wave of longing swept over her.

"Nonsense!" she scolded. "My living room is straight, my dishes are clean, and I have had seven or eight hours of sleep." Beth and Susan both had called the night before, and maybe even little Jack would be able to get a line out sometime today or tomorrow. "What more could I want?" she asked, chuckling as she parked and headed into the market.

The small dark man behind the cash register looked up as the bell over the door announced her presence. "Good morning, dear lady," he greeted her in his usual way, but his lips did not bear his customary smile, and his eyes seemed troubled.

"What's wrong, Mr. Feroz?" she asked, without thinking that he might find the question an intrusion into his privacy.

He sighed, then gave that typical Middle Eastern shrug. "Ah, nothing to worry your head about, dear lady," he replied in perfect English, but with a thick accent that had not lessened during his many years in America. "The question is, what are you doing here on your busy holiday? Ah, I suspect that you have run out of something you need to prepare the meal for your family. No?"

"Yes and no," she laughed. "I've run out of milk, but only the cat is disturbed by it." She explained about her Christmas this year, and he chuckled with her.

"Today, then, you can be like me," he said, "alone in a big, empty house while everybody else celebrates their biggest holiday of the year. Perhaps you can stay here with me for a while. We can speak of our families who are not with us this year," he offered, but she caught his furtive glance at the front window. Was he afraid of something, of someone?

143

"Mr. Feroz, I can tell that something is wrong. Can I help you. . . ?" she began.

He shook his head, refusing to look her in the eyes. "I will be all right, I think. They told me not to open the store on Christmas Day, but I do not believe they will come back today. Such a busy day for most."

"Come back?" she repeated. "Who, Mr. Feroz?" Then, before he answered, she knew. Someone had threatened him because of his faith and his birthplace. "It's the trouble in the Middle East, isn't it?" she asked. "Someone has taken out his frustrations on you."

He nodded, still not looking at her. "I understand their frustrations," he said then. "But I have done nothing. I came to America to escape the bitter struggle in my homeland. This country has been good to me. Why would I send money to help destroy it? Why would my son, Said, leave his nice job at the university to become a suicide bomber? My family has never agreed with such violence!"

"Mr. Feroz, I am so sorry!" Loraine said. "Did they threaten to hurt you? Perhaps you should call the police."

He shook his head. "They have threatened to burn down the store if I do, to harm my son and his family. They said they know where he lives. I cannot take the risk."

"Who are these people, Mr. Feroz?"

Again, he shook his head. "I do not know, dear lady. There were three of them. They do not live in this neighborhood. They had never been in my shop until two days ago."

They both looked up in alarm as the bell tinkled over the door. Loraine was relieved to see it was Pastor Ted Hammons.

"May I help you?" Mr. Feroz asked, still a little wary of the visitor.

"It's all right," Loraine whispered. "I know this man."

Ted appeared a little uncomfortable, she thought. Had he given away his winter clothing again? But that couldn't be the reason for his embarrassment. His jeans were topped with a warm, waterproof jacket, and he was wearing gloves. He even had a sock cap perched on his head.

"Hello," he greeted both of them. "What are you doing here on Christmas Day?" he asked Loraine.

"I might ask you the same thing," she countered.

He hesitated. "I guess I might as well confess," he said then, "since you've caught me literally in the act. I'm worried about that mother with the three children who were in the food line the other day. We took Angel Tree gifts to the children and found that they are living in a house the mother inherited from her parents. The good news is that they aren't homeless. But I'm afraid they don't have food. The kids have those big hungry eyes. You know, like you see in those Feed the Children ads on TV."

Loraine felt her heart contract. She and Jack had known some lean years in the early days of their marriage, but their children had never gone hungry. "Can we take them some food?" she asked, already part of the venture in her own mind. Then she felt her face flush as Ted's smile spilled from warm brown eyes to the corners of his mouth.

"Well, I came here to do a little shopping for them. You're welcome to help," he said.

In answer, she grabbed a shopping basket and handed one to him. Quickly, they moved through the market, filling the baskets with potatoes, fruit, cans of vegetables, cereal, and bread. Loraine had thought to add a small ham to the pile, but looking at the meat in its glass case, she realized that Mr. Feroz did not sell the meat of hogs.

Loraine chose the biggest chicken she could find and placed it in her basket. She saw Ted pick up hamburger and a hefty beef roast.

"There," he said, with satisfaction, adding a large bag of cookies to his gleanings. "I think that's all the money I have," he said apologetically.

"Oh, I'll get these," she offered, indicating her own basket. "I just need to add some milk and get some for myself. I almost forgot why I came in here today."

At the register, Mr. Feroz quickly ran the total, then cut it in half. "I, too, will feed the children," he said.

"You don't have to do that, Mr. Feroz!" Loraine exclaimed.

Ted looked at her, then at the shopkeeper. Loraine saw some kind of understanding pass between them. "Thank you," Ted said. He turned back to add more meat and another bag of cookies to their purchases. Then, picking up two of the grocery bags, he walked out of the store.

Loraine picked up two more and followed him. He placed his bags in the back of a van parked behind her car, then turned for hers. She handed him the sacks, which he placed in the van before going back into the market. She followed, seeing him pick up two more bags and carry them outside.

"Call the police, Mr. Feroz," Loraine urged as she left the market with the last bag and her own jug of milk.

"Come with me. We'll take these to the Perkins family together," Ted invited when they had finished loading the van. "It won't take long. They live just five or six blocks over on the north side of town."

Loraine knew the area, a run-down section of houses. The inhabitants either could not afford to fix them up or were too lazy to do so.

She hesitated. "My son may call from overseas," she began, "and my cat will be missing me, or rather, missing his milk," she added honestly. *Where has my quiet, peaceful Christmas Day gone?* she wondered. Then she realized that the day was still young.

"Put your milk in your car, and get in the van," he insisted. "You're in this deep; you might as well see it through."

Knowing that she really had nothing more important to do, she obeyed.

Chapter 7

As they careened through the wet streets, Loraine held tightly to the armrest. *He drives just like Jack used to*, she thought. She remembered how scared she had been at times, sliding around curves on the wrong side, praying the brakes wouldn't fail when he tailgated, gritting her teeth and hanging on, determined not to admit her fear.

I haven't been in a car alone with a man since Jack died, she realized suddenly, *except for my son and my son-in-law. Relatives.*

"Do you have many relatives in town?" Ted asked, seemingly reading her mind.

"No, I don't have any close relatives left, other than my three children," she answered, eyeing a lamppost flashing by only inches from her face. "I have some cousins in Maine and an aunt in Georgia," she added through clenched teeth. "Slow down!" she cried as the van fishtailed, then righted itself.

"I'm sorry!" he said, easing his foot off the accelerator. "I didn't realize I was scaring you."

"My husband drove just like you when we were teenagers," she said, laughing shakily. "I wouldn't tell him I was scared then, but after we had kids, I learned to speak up for their safety."

"So you're saying I drive like an irresponsible teenager?" he asked indignantly.

"Well. . ."

He burst into laughter. "Don't worry, I'm used to it. My wife used to tell me that all the time. I've tried to do better. Guess I just needed someone to remind me."

"Do you have anyone besides the two sons you mentioned the other night?" she asked, able to concentrate on conversation now that the van was moving steadily at a reasonable speed.

"My dad lives in Oregon with my brother," he said.

"Do you ever visit?" she asked, wondering why he hadn't spent Christmas with some of them.

"Sometimes, but having just taken this new position at the church in October, I didn't want to leave right now," he explained. "My son Craig and his wife are expecting a baby in February, so I'll probably go out then."

"Are both of your sons in Oregon?"

"No, Randy's a geologist working with an oil company in Alaska. But Craig lives in our old house. After Regina died, I felt I had to go where the memories weren't so painful. When this position opened up, I jumped at the chance."

She nodded. "I thought about selling our house when Jack died. I didn't think I could live in that house without him, but my daughters and my son wanted me to keep it. They had never lived anywhere else. Now they only use it as a stopping-off place between travels, and I'm there alone. But I'm glad they talked me out of selling it. I'm content there. It's home. And I like being there when one of them wants to stop off for a while."

"It's time you made a life for yourself, Loraine," he said abruptly, wheeling the van into a driveway, putting it in park, and turning off the motor.

She considered his words, trying to decide whether she should appreciate his concern or resent his meddling.

"I don't mean to meddle," he said then, again uncannily in sync with her thoughts. "But from my own experience, it helps to find closure to that past chapter of life and get on with the next chapter. In our old house, I kept running into ghosts of Regina. Not literally, of course, but I'd walk into the kitchen and see her stirring something on the stove, or setting the table, or perched on her favorite stool at the cooking bar, leafing through a catalog. I'd see her in the hallway, going into the bathroom or the bedroom, smiling back at me."

At the break in his flow of words, Loraine looked at him and found that he was struggling with emotions the memories had evoked. "I know what you mean," she said gently. "The painful memories mellow over time, but sometimes I still 'see' Jack turning to give some sarcastic comment on the news, looking up at me from the recliner—" Overcome with emotion, she also stopped.

Ted laughed then. "Aren't we a pair, sitting here conjuring up ghosts! Let's go feed these children."

For the first time, Loraine noticed the house in front of them. It was a small brick bungalow. The trim had not been painted in a long time, and a shutter hung crazily from one hinge. The yard had been cleared of fallen leaves, though, and the front stoop was clean-swept, with a pot of frostbitten petunias sitting in one corner. A crayoned wreath of green with red holly berries colored into it hung on the door.

Ted got out of the car, went to the door, and knocked. Ted spoke to the child who answered, and then he waited as she vanished inside the house, leaving the door ajar. Soon a woman appeared in the doorway. Then Loraine saw her open the storm door and come outside to throw both arms around the pastor. She seemed to be crying.

Ted came back to the van and began to unload groceries. Loraine got out to help him. The woman held the door open for them as they carried the bags inside, and the three small children watched wide-eyed.

One of them, a curly haired little blond, reminded her of Beth when she was about six or seven years old—full of curious questions and trusting acceptance of everything from fairy tales to miracles. The other two children might have been her practical ladylike Susan and her impetuous little Jack, who never waited patiently for anything, including food.

Beth, Susan, and Jack, she thought fondly, *not one of them ever went hungry, unless Jack was hungry over there in the desert.* She turned away from her memories of those long-ago children and focused instead on those in front of her. Ted offered them cookies, which the girls took politely and began to munch. The little boy stuffed both of his into his mouth and held out his hand for another.

"Ted," Loraine admonished, "these children may not have had breakfast yet!" She looked around the kitchen, glad to see that, like the children, it, too, was scrubbed clean. There was no evidence that any food had been prepared or eaten there recently.

"Oh, it's okay," the woman said hurriedly. "They're hungry. With the soup kitchen closed yesterday and today, they haven't had much since the day you saw us there, and certainly no cookies. I'm so grateful for all this," she said then, indicating the bags sitting on her kitchen table. "I don't know how I can ever repay you." The tears began again, and Ted gave her a quick hug.

"Don't worry about it," he said. "Look, I'm putting you on our church's list to receive groceries each week until we can get you some regular assistance. You should have asked long ago."

She nodded. "I suppose I should have, but we've gotten by until recently. My husband's been—" She hesitated, glancing at the children. "—away for a year now," she finished. "Drugs, you know. I've used up what little savings we had. I've even tried to work, but good jobs are scarce, and everyone wants somebody with computer skills that I just don't have. Being a waitress doesn't pay much, and with Calvin only four and no one here to babysit, I've had to pay child care. Dana's very responsible, but I just can't see leaving an eight-year-old in charge of two smaller children."

Ted nodded in agreement. "Can you go back to wherever you came from, Mrs. Perkins?" he asked. "Are there grandparents? Do you have siblings who would help?"

The woman dropped her gaze. "I'm ashamed to go back to Memphis where they all know what's happened," she almost whispered. Again, Loraine saw tears gathering in her eyes.

"It's going to get better now," Ted promised, patting the woman reassuringly on the shoulder. "We have a daycare program at the church. Maybe Calvin could come there if you're working in the daytime. I'm sure we could arrange a 'scholarship' for him. And maybe we can find you some training so you can get a steady job. Oh, by the way, I'd be glad to have the church bus stop by for the children, and you, too, if you wish. I'm sure the girls would like Missionettes on Wednesday nights and our Super Church on Sunday mornings. Calvin will soon be old enough for Royal Rangers, and—"

"We'll let you know," the woman broke into his words.

Loraine felt that Mrs. Perkins was a bit overwhelmed by

Ted's many suggestions. *Men can be so insensitive sometimes!* she thought. She supposed he meant well, but the woman might be thinking that the pastor was helping them just to gain members for his church. *Is he?* she wondered, studying him.

"I hope you don't think you have to come just because we've brought you a few groceries!" Ted said then, with that knack he had for reading thoughts. "These things did not come from the church, and you should not feel obligated at all!" he insisted. "Of course, we'd love to have you in our services, but only if you and the children want to come."

"Mama," the dark-haired little girl asked tentatively, "could we? I'd take good care of Calvin and Megan if you can't go with us. Please? Could we go sometime?"

The mother studied the child. "We'll see, Dana," she promised vaguely, then turned back to Ted. "Well, as I said, we'll let you know." Loraine wondered if she was unfamiliar with the church's denomination and wanted to check into it before letting her children get involved. It was something Loraine would have done in similar circumstances.

Suddenly, she saw a wry grin touch Ted's face. "I understand," he said. "But let me assure you, despite what you may have heard, we don't jump over benches or swing from the chandeliers. And we definitely don't handle any snakes!" he added. "I'd be the first one out of there if that happened!"

The woman smiled, but Loraine detected a deep weariness in her eyes. "Thank you, again, for all you've done," she said, "for this wonderful food and for the toys the other night. My children would have had a slim Christmas without them."

"And you need to be putting some of this food into the refrigerator," Loraine put in quickly. "It was nice meeting you." She gave Ted a warning glance and turned to leave.

"I'll be in touch," he promised the woman. "See you, kids!" he added. Loraine was relieved to see that he was following her to the door.

Back inside the van, he turned to her. "You think I came on a little too strong, don't you?" he asked.

Suddenly, Loraine's doubts fled. This man was exactly what he had appeared to be since the day she met him—a warm, caring individual who was rebuilding his own shattered life by helping others rebuild theirs.

"Merry Christmas, Ted," she said, with a smile that said all the nice things she was thinking. "Now take me to my car so I can get home with Tigger's milk and ask him to forgive me for neglecting him."

He returned her smile, started the van, and put it into reverse.

Chapter 8

As they pulled into the parking space behind her Honda, Loraine gasped. Mr. Feroz's front glass had been broken out, and some of the contents of his market lay scattered over the sidewalk.

"Oh, Ted, look!" she exclaimed. "Those men came back to carry out their threats!"

"What threats?" he asked. "Who?"

Suddenly, she saw a flicker of flame back inside the building. "I'll explain later!" she cried. "Do you have a cell phone?" At his nod, she ordered, "Call the police. And the fire department! Call 911!"

As Ted punched in the numbers, Loraine ran into the store. "Mr. Feroz!" she called, dreading what she might find. "Where are you?" There was no answer, and her heart pounded in concern for her neighbor's safety. Had they killed the gentle old man and set the building on fire to cover their crime? She moved frantically through the aisles, calling his name, begging him to answer.

"Loraine?" she heard Ted call from the front of the market. "Where are you? What's going on?"

She ran into the center aisle where she could see the pastor standing in front of the cash register. "Are they coming?" she asked. "The police? The firemen? The EMTs?"

"They're on the way," he assured her. "Have you found him? Is he alive?"

"No. I mean, I don't know. I can't find him!"

She saw Ted tear a fire extinguisher from the wall and begin spraying foam onto the flames that licked greedily at the well-oiled wooden floor.

A groan came from somewhere in the back of the market, and Loraine ran toward it.

"Mr. Feroz!" she cried, discovering the small figure crumpled in a heap behind the meat counter, blood pouring from a gash in his forehead. "Thank God, you're alive!"

"Praise be to Allah!" he said weakly, trying to rise from the floor.

Quickly, she bent to help him, but the old man shrank back from her. She thought she had read somewhere that his religion discouraged close contact with a woman, especially an "infidel." Then Ted was on the other side, guiding him to a seat on a small bench behind the counter. She grabbed a hand towel from the counter and passed it to Ted. "Here," she said, "see if you can stop the bleeding. Is the fire out?" she added.

"No," Ted answered, dabbing at the wound. "But I think it's contained. And help is almost here."

Loraine could hear the distinctive sounds of the emergency vehicles as they turned onto the street and screeched to a halt outside the store. Uniformed men and women raced inside and spread throughout the room. The firemen pulled a hose near the smoldering fire and doused the fire while Ted led the EMTs to Mr. Feroz. Immediately they began to check his vital signs and treat his wounds, while the policemen, with guns drawn, searched the premises.

Soon the officers came to the little huddle of people around Mr. Feroz. Answering the officers' request for information, Loraine informed them of the threats Mr. Feroz had related to her earlier.

"I begged him to call the police," she said, "but he was afraid of what they might do."

"Well, it looks like they did it anyway," one officer remarked. "He should have known not to give in to terrorists!"

Terrorists! The word rang in Loraine's mind like an alarm. She had just thought of them as thugs, not terrorists. But she supposed that was what they were, no matter what country they came from or what motivated them. They certainly had succeeded in striking terror into Mr. Feroz's heart and, consequently, into her own.

"They try to burn my market!" Mr. Feroz exclaimed. "They threaten to harm my son! Please, don't let them harm my Said!" he begged, clutching at the jacket of an EMT who was bent over him putting a bandage over the gash in his head. "Please! He is a good boy, a good husband, a good professor at the university. He's done nothing wrong!"

"It's all right, sir," the female EMT soothed, reaching to prepare his arm for a shot.

"Could the male EMT do that?" Loraine questioned. "His religion—"

"Oh, yes. I'd forgotten," the woman said, handing the swab and the needle to the EMT beside her. "The shot will relax him," she explained to Loraine. "He will be okay. His vitals are strong, and he only has the one cut."

"Thank God!" Loraine breathed again.

The woman nodded. "It could have been much worse. But you're a tough one, aren't you, old fellow?" she said to Mr. Feroz. "It takes more than a blow over the head to take you out!"

"Please!" he begged again, looking at the man. "Send someone to protect my Said!"

"We will send word to the police department in that city, sir," an officer promised. "You just relax and let us get you to the hospital."

"No!" the old man protested. "No hospital! I want to go home."

"But, sir, you really should be checked out by a doctor. You might have other injuries," the woman EMT insisted. "We think you're okay, but our resources are limited."

"No hospital!" Mr. Feroz repeated. "I want to go home!"

The woman exchanged glances with Loraine. "I live a couple of doors from him. I can check on him," Loraine offered.

"I can drive him home and check in on him later," Ted added.

The technician nodded. "All right. I suppose that will be okay. Just let us get him to sign this release form, and you can take him home."

"I want everything in here photographed and fingerprinted, and I want a guard posted here until that window can be boarded up," Loraine heard one of the policemen order as she left the market behind Ted and Mr. Feroz.

She watched Ted help the old man into the front seat of the van, noting that the rain had stopped and a weak sun was trying to shine through the clouds that still hung over the town. She got into her own car, grateful that it had not been harmed. She reached over and touched the jug of milk, satisfied that it was still cold and unspoiled. Tigger would be happy.

So much for an uneventful Christmas Day! she thought wryly as she put the car in gear, eased out of the parking place, and followed Ted's van down the street. She glanced at the clock on the dash. *Oh, well, it's just past noon. I still have time to enjoy a few hours of unmitigated idleness,* she thought, pulling into her own driveway and turning off the motor.

She could see Ted helping Mr. Feroz from the van two houses down the street and hurried to help.

Mr. Feroz pulled a large, old-fashioned key on a leather cord from inside his loose shirt. He slipped the cord over his head and held the key out to her, dangling from its cord safely above her hand.

Loraine grasped the key and inserted it into the lock on the front door. It turned easily, and the door swung open on silent hinges.

As Ted eased the old man down into the deep sofa cushions, she said, "Point me to the kitchen, and I'll fix you a cup of strong, hot tea." Then she added, "You do drink tea, don't you?"

Mr. Feroz nodded. "But just a glass of water right now, please, dear lady," he said, pointing toward the kitchen. "It is in the refrigerator. I will fix some tea after I rest for a small time." With that, he sank back against the pillow Ted placed behind his head and shoulders. Ted took a brightly colored woven throw from the back of the couch and spread it over him.

Loraine found a glass in the kitchen. She took the bottle of water from the refrigerator and filled the glass slowly, her fascinated glance taking in the Middle-Eastern design of the room and its furnishings. *Casablanca,* she thought. *That's it. This could be a room straight out of Rick's Café Americaine. I wouldn't be surprised if Humphrey Bogart or Ingrid Bergman walked right through the beaded curtain covering that door back there.*

Isn't Casablanca in Morocco? she asked herself then. *I'm pretty sure that Mr. Feroz is from Iraq. Oh, well.* She shrugged, picking up the glass of water and heading back to the living room. *I don't know one Middle Eastern design from another. Maybe I just think it looks like Casablanca. Or maybe his wife was from Morocco.* Maybe someday she would ask him, but this didn't seem like the right time for idle questions.

She held out the glass, and Mr. Feroz struggled to sit up. Ted raised him gently from the pillows and held the glass so he could drink from it.

"I am eternally indebted to each of you," Mr. Feroz said, handing the glass back to Ted, who set it in a small crystal dish on a low table in front of the couch. "My life's blood might have seeped completely away from me there on the floor of my market had you not come along and rescued me."

"I doubt that you would have bled to death, Mr. Feroz," Ted assured him. "But it certainly was better to get you patched up quickly and the police started on an investigation to unearth the culprits who did this to you and your store."

"I pray to Allah that the police will find them soon and put them away where they cannot harm me or my son," the old man said fervently. He sank back against the pillows again and closed his eyes.

"Do you have a pen, Ted?" Loraine asked, picking up a phone book from a nearby table. She took the pen he held out and wrote her phone number on the back of the book. "I'm just two doors away, Mr. Feroz," she reminded him. "If you need me, all you have to do is call."

"Will you call Said and tell him what has happened?" the old man asked. "Tell him I don't want him to come. I just want him to be warned."

"The police said—" she began, but Ted interrupted.

"What is his number?" he asked. "I will call him." He took the pen back and wrote the number Mr. Feroz repeated in a small notebook from his shirt pocket. "We'll get out of here and let you rest now. But I'll be back very soon to check on you," he promised, heading for the door.

Outside, Loraine turned to face the pastor. "Do you think he will be all right here alone?" she asked. "Do you think those men will come back?"

"I'm going to pray hard that they don't," he answered, "but you keep a lookout, and if you notice anything suspicious over here, give me a call." He took a wallet from his back pocket, extracted a business card from it, and held it out to her.

"After I call 911!" she laughed, tucking the card into her jacket pocket.

As Ted drove away, leaving one of those infectious grins behind him like a disappearing Cheshire cat, she suddenly realized how empty the space was where he had been.

"Nonsense!" she told herself, retrieving the jug of milk from her car and carrying it inside. "I'm just tired. I haven't kept a single Christmas tradition, yet I'm as tired as though I'd been up all night cooking and wrapping presents."

She poured milk into Tigger's bowl, set it in the microwave, and punched the buttons.

He came over to watch with wide yellow eyes as the timer clicked off the seconds. *"Maalk!"* he reminded her when the buzzer went off.

She set the bowl on the floor and ran her hand over his soft fur. "Sometimes I almost believe you can talk," she told him fondly.

Sinking into the recliner, Loraine pulled her quilted throw over her. "It's time for that long winter's nap, Tigger," she sighed, already half asleep.

The phone's shrill ring jarred her awake.

"What's going on down at the old Arab's place?" Esther demanded when she answered.

"Oh, Esther, I'm glad you called," she said. "We need to keep an eye out for Mr. Feroz. He was attacked by terrorists. They roughed him up and tried to burn his market!"

"Oh my!" Esther exclaimed. "Terrorists attacking terrorists! What is this world coming to?"

"Esther!" Loraine scolded. "Mr. Feroz has never hurt anyone, at least not in the past twenty years that I've known him. He came here to get away from terrorism, to make a better life for himself and his family, just as my ancestors did at some point in history, and just as you did!"

"Harrumph!" Esther objected in disdain. "His son—"

"His son is a professor at some university out West. He's not in training to be a suicide bomber."

"How do you know, Loraine?" Esther asked seriously. "And if he's not, he may be one of those professors the universities seem so intent on coddling these days—the ones who tell their students, 'Kill the infidels!' and raise money for Hamas or Hizballah, or maybe even al-Qaida."

"I know, Esther," Loraine agreed. "Since 9/11 we've all had our suspicions of everything and everybody with any connection to the Middle East. But old Mr. Feroz—" She stopped, suddenly too tired to continue.

"You sound like you need some rest," Esther picked up astutely. "I'll keep an eye out down that way," she promised. "The last thing we need in this neighborhood is an 'incident' over some old Arab. Wouldn't the media love it!" With that, she hung up.

Loraine replaced the receiver on its base and pushed back the recliner. Within minutes she was asleep.

Chapter 9

Loraine struggled upward through the clinging fog of a dream. She was running from a terrorist who was threatening to blow up himself and the soup kitchen. The phone was ringing, and she snatched it up, unsure whether it was real or part of her dream.

"Hello?" she said, her voice thick with sleep.

"Hey! Are you okay?" queried the voice on the other end.

"Jack?" Had the bomber succeeded in blowing her straight into heaven where her husband waited? Then she realized that the voice did not belong to her deceased husband, but to their son. "Jack!" she repeated. "You sound just like your father. Are you all right?"

"I'm fine, Mom," he assured her. "I just wanted to wish you 'Merry Christmas.' I've had a time getting a phone line out of here."

"Oh, Jack, it's so good to hear your voice!" she said, feeling a lump gathering at the base of her throat. She swallowed hard.

"Thanks for the gigantic stocking," he said. "Everything is appreciated and will be put to good use," he promised, "especially the thick, warm socks and the chocolate that only requires hot water. You know how I hate cold feet and love hot chocolate!"

"I wasn't sure if you needed warm socks or hot drinks over there in the desert," she confessed, glad that she had sent them anyway.

"In the daytime, when that merciless desert sun beams down, we swelter and hunt for shade, but when old Sol sinks into the sea, it gets right chilly. These boots sweat, and when it turns cold, I hunt for dry socks!"

Loraine chuckled, remembering their sledding days. Little Jack—always the first to pull on warm winter clothing and head outside when it snowed—was always the first to retreat inside to sip hot chocolate and toast his nearly frozen feet by the fire.

"Are the girls there?" Jack asked. "I got a package from Susan and a card with photos from Beth, but I haven't talked with either one of them lately."

"No, son," she replied, explaining where they were, and telling him a little about her own futile plans for a quiet Christmas.

He laughed. "Well, you know, Mom, about those 'best-laid plans of mice and men.' I guess that applies to ladies, too."

He sounds like he's right here in the room. If only I could put my arms around him and hold him close for a moment! she yearned. *If only I could keep him safe from any kind of danger!*

"Is it—?" she began, but her voice caught on that lump in her throat. She swallowed and started over. "Is it really bad there, son? Are you in as much danger as the news makes it seem?"

"We never know what to expect," he evaded, "but, hey, don't worry about me, Mom! Just keep praying and trust in the Lord the way you and Pop always taught us to do."

"I pray for you constantly!" she assured him.

"Gotta go," he said then. "Some of the guys are still waiting for their turn on the phone."

Her mind searched for some way to hold him, to keep from breaking this thin connection between them. "I love you, Jack!" she said, wanting at least to touch him with that.

"Love you, too, Mom. Bye," he said and that quickly was gone.

Loraine sat cradling the receiver against her, as though it were her youngest child she was holding against her heart. She breathed a prayer for his safety.

A nasal voice demanded, "If you would like to make a call, please hang up and—"

She placed the receiver back on its base and untangled herself from the throw. *What time is it?* she wondered, noting the darkness outside the patio door.

She moved over to the window and looked out toward Esther's. The lights were on over there, and she could see Esther standing at her window peering out. She waved, then without waiting to see if she waved back, Loraine moved to a window on the other side of the house. *I promised to check on Mr. Feroz,* she recalled, the day's events flooding back into her mind.

The Mitchell place next door was brightly lit, giving its false impression of occupancy and making it almost impossible to see beyond into the darkness. So far as she could tell, there were no lights on in the Feroz house.

Loraine went out onto her front porch and peered into the darkness. *What's going on down there?* she wondered. Were those shadowy outlines people moving around in the Feroz front yard?

Now she could see moving lights, flashlights, she guessed, as newcomers joined the small group. She could hear some shouting, words she couldn't understand. Then she saw a man step up onto the front stoop and begin to paint something on the polished wood of Mr. Feroz's front door.

Loraine left her porch and moved across the yard. She could hear angry voices chanting, and now she could make out the words: "Go back to Iraq! Go back to Iraq! We don't want you here!" As she neared the house, she could read the words splashed across the dark wood in vivid yellow paint: "Arab pig! Get out!"

There was no sign of the old man as the growing crowd trampled his neat front yard and marred his front door. The house was dark, as it was much of the time during the Christmas holidays, the very absence of lights and decorations calling attention to the fact that this was the home of someone different. Suspect.

But he's been here twenty years! she protested silently. *We know him! He brought his wife and child here when his hair and beard were thick and black, and now they are as white as the snow you have trampled into the mud of his yard. He is not a terrorist! He runs the little grocery over on Fourth Street. His son is not a terrorist! He lives in Michigan or Wisconsin or somewhere, teaching mathematics at the university.*

"Go home, Arab pig!" someone shouted.

"Get out, or we'll drag you out!" another voice threatened. "We'll cut you into pieces like your cousins and friends do to our boys in your godforsaken country!"

Suddenly, Loraine recognized the angry man as the brother of a young man who had been in Susan's high school graduating class. She remembered reading in the paper that the young man had been killed in Iraq. Now this brother had turned his grief and frustration toward this innocent man simply because he was an Arab and followed the Muslim religion. And he had persuaded others to join him. She couldn't be certain in the dim light, but the men gave the impression that they had been drinking alcohol.

Loraine felt the viscous fog of their irrational hatred swirling around her. Fear lumped in the pit of her stomach like cold oatmeal. She had to do something.

Suddenly, without being aware that she had moved, she was standing on the front stoop of Mr. Feroz's home facing the mob. "Go home, yourselves!" she cried. "Leave this poor old man alone! He's done nothing to you!" She grabbed the rag dangling from the back pocket of the painter and began to scrub at the hateful words, smearing the ugly yellow across the once-beautiful polished wood, blurring the words into something as incomprehensible as the mob's unwarranted fury.

The painter snatched the rag from her hands and slapped her across the face with the paintbrush, leaving a wide streak of yellow from her left earlobe to the corner of her mouth. "Arab lover!" he hissed.

The mob cheered and milled about in the yard, as though ready to do something but not yet sure what.

Loraine put her hand to her cheek, feeling the thick paint coagulating there like blood. Fear spread through her. She wasn't an "Arab lover." Nor was she an Arab hater. She simply believed in freedom for everybody. It was what her son was committed to fight for even now. But what could she do against so many?

Then she heard the welcome sirens and saw the flashing lights advancing down the street. Loraine sank down weakly on Mr. Feroz's top step and put both hands over her face, paint and all. When she looked up, the mob had melted away like snowflakes on a warm surface.

She turned to face the old man standing behind her, searching for words to erase the pain the lights from the police cars revealed in his dark eyes, to somehow make amends for what her misguided countrymen had done tonight. "I am so sorry, Mr. Feroz!" she began.

"Praise be to Allah that someone called the police!" the old man said. "I don't know what might have happened if they had not come."

She looked around, wondering what *had* brought the police here just in the nick of time.

A van screeched to a stop behind the police cars, and Ted Hammons got out. *It couldn't have been Ted who called them,* she thought. *It looks like he just found out what was going on over here, or perhaps he has just come by to keep his promise to check on Mr. Feroz.*

Then she saw Esther Cohen standing on the Mitchell's illuminated porch, her cell phone in her hand. Esther's bright brown eyes returned her gaze for several seconds, then she gave a half smile and turned back toward her home.

Epilogue

The idea was born and grew without any encouragement from Loraine. In fact, she resisted it at first. Then, reluctantly, she let go of her last dreams of an idle Christmas and, glancing at the clock, reached for the phone. She would extend her invitations for tomorrow evening, she decided, her excitement growing. What did it matter to any of them that it would be the day after Christmas?

I can put on a pot of green beans and whip up a gelatin salad and a cake tonight, she planned, *and I can bake a sweet potato casserole and some of those rolls from the freezer just before dinner. But what can I do about meat?* There was nothing big enough in her freezer. She had baked that small ham for her own use, but she knew that neither Esther nor Mr. Feroz ate ham. She supposed she should get a small turkey if there were any left.

The stores would be open tomorrow. It was the day everyone makes a mad rush to exchange unwanted gifts and buy leftover Christmas gift items and decorations at huge discounts.

Loraine recoiled from the thought in horror. *I'm not doing any shopping or decorating!* she vowed. There would be no holly on the mantel, no ivy entwining the stair rail. She would simply fix an easy-to-prepare dinner for casual acquaintances with whom she hoped to share a belated Christmas and, perhaps, subtly, the reasons she kept it.

Suddenly, the image of a wide smile lighting brown eyes came into her mind. Well, it really wouldn't take any more effort to prepare for four rather than three, she reasoned—one more place setting at the table, an extra spoonful or two of everything.

"But I'm ordering the turkey baked!" she stated firmly. "And I'm having it sliced!"

O Little Town of Progress

by Wanda Luttrell

Chapter 1

The little town of Progress had made no progress at all in the past twenty years, unless one counted the new stoplight at the intersection of Main and Broadway and the McDonald's at the edge of town. Even the big red and white wooden candy canes hanging from the iron posts below the round white globes of the streetlights were the same ones that had decorated the downtown area at Christmas for as long as Mary Martha Sims could remember.

None of that bothered Mary Martha. She hadn't changed much in the past twenty years either, except that she found it somewhat harder now to see where to step off the curb and a great deal more difficult to maneuver the two steps up to Hanley's Drugstore. But she supposed that was to be expected when a body had been on this earth for eighty-three years. *Yes, eighty-three last September,* she calculated.

Mary Martha stopped in front of Hanley's to catch her breath and try to remember where it was she had intended to go. Absently, she considered the familiar Christmas village displayed in the window and framed by a string of twinkling clear Christmas lights. She couldn't think of anything she needed from the drugstore. After all, the pastor's wife had taken her shopping at the grocery just yesterday—or perhaps it had been the day before. Anyway, it wasn't the drugstore or Kroger's that she needed to visit today. She looked around uncertainly, trying her best to remember, as a gust of December wind blustered around her.

Mary Martha drew her sweater closer, annoyed that she had come out once again without her coat. "Good thing I wore my heavy blue sweater rather than that thin pink one," she muttered to herself. *But enough complaining,* she chided herself. *Except for the wind, it's not all that cold. In fact, this is a lovely, sunny day right in the middle of December.*

Mary Martha waved in the general direction of Jayne's Beauty Shop, just in case Jayne was watching from behind the waving Santa in her front window and the blinking colored lights all around it. She made a mental note to tell Jayne how many compliments her new silver hair rinse had brought her at church the Sunday before. She thought the silver gave her dark eyes the bright, sassy look of a bird. A blue jay, she supposed, in this blue dress and sweater.

Sometimes, living in the Sims house, she had felt like a blue jay trying to live in someone else's nest. Jays are usurpers, though. Mary Martha meekly shared what space she had to and retreated to her bedroom or the garden whenever she could do so politely. She and Mother Sims had always been polite to each other.

As she stood watching, the wind whipped the folded awnings over Hanley's front windows and chased a discarded newspaper into the gutter. Then suddenly, her memory clicked into place. She was headed for the newspaper office with the ad written out exactly the way she wanted it and tucked away in her purse. At least that had been her intention.

I hope I didn't leave it on the kitchen table, she thought as she opened her purse and began to rummage around inside. But it was there, sandwiched between her billfold and her *Pocket Promise Book,* which made her wonder if she had remembered to read her Bible that morning.

"You okay, Mrs. Sims?" A voice interrupted her thoughts. She turned to find the pharmacist in his cream-colored coat peering at her from the doorway of his shop—actually it was his father's shop. Bill Hanley Jr. now ran the town's only drugstore. Once she had called him Billy, but since the day he came home from college and put on that cream-colored coat, she had been careful to call him Mr. Hanley.

"I'm fine, thank you, Mr. Hanley," she assured him, but she could feel his eyes following her as she slowly made her way down the street. *He needn't worry about me,* she fussed to herself. She was sure if she'd come this far, she could make it two blocks more to the building that housed *The Progress.* She wanted the ad in this week's paper—before she changed her mind.

It would be easy to sell her mother-in-law's cherry dining room suite. Truthfully, she never used it anyway. Olivia couldn't come home except in dire emergencies, and P.T. was too busy with his bank and his wife's social affairs. And even if they were to come, she wondered if she could still put a company meal together at her age.

P.T. and Eleanor always invited her to have dinner at their house on Christmas, the only time she might see her granddaughter and great-grandchildren, if they were able to make the long trip home. This year none of them were coming—her great-grandson and his wife were expecting a baby any day.

Parker wouldn't want her to sell his mother's furniture. He had always insisted that it stay just as she had it arranged in the years before her death in 1994. Of course, he really couldn't insist on anything anymore. He'd had a heart attack and died while sitting at his desk at the bank.

"Mama liked the sofa against that wall," or "Mama always kept that table under the living room window," he would admonish, easing the disturbed item back into its original grooves in the flowered carpet. The memory made her smile.

Parker had been gone three years now. She missed him. But that had not kept her from moving the small, walnut drop-leaf table from the living room to a spot under the kitchen window where it would better meet her needs.

She didn't really mind selling her big black grand piano, either. She rubbed her right hand with the left one. The cold just seemed to gnaw at that bone she had broken sledding in the moonlight on the night Parker had asked her to marry him. Now arthritis had set in, making it impossible for her to play the piano.

Her mind returned to the starlit hill behind Mason's house, to the joy of young voices calling to each other across the sparkling snow, to the breathtaking thrill of flying down the hill behind Parker on the sled she had borrowed from her brother, Ben.

Even if Parker had admitted to her that his search for a bride had been motivated by the bank's policy of promoting only settled family men, it would have made no difference. She had been certain that her love could melt his cool reserve and make those icy blue eyes sparkle with shared happiness.

Mary Martha thought again of that night on Mason's hill. It had been the last time Parker had ever gone sledding with her, though she had taken the children many times.

She plodded on, thinking about the ad in her purse. She

didn't *have* to sell her granny's rocking chair. It didn't take up much room, and she didn't need the money. But if she intended to sell Parker's things, she felt she should be willing to part with something of her own, something that mattered.

How many babies has that chair rocked? she wondered. *Mama and her five brothers. Me and Ben. . .*

Her brother, Ben, was gone now, too, she remembered. It had been a year now—no, maybe two—since the cancer had been discovered. He had lasted barely three weeks. It was the same year locusts killed the Damson plum tree. Ben had so loved climbing that tree, her rag doll under one arm and that mischievous, teasing grin on his face.

Mary Martha hadn't been back to the home place since Ben's funeral. His boys had called to see if she wanted anything from the house, but she had declined. It seemed to be time to get rid of possessions rather than add to them. Her mind went back to the rocking chair and the precious hours she had spent in it rocking Parker Thomas and little Olivia.

She had intended to call her daughter Mary Olivia—after herself and Mother Sims, whose middle name was Olivia. But Parker had insisted on Olivia only. Now she understood Olivia used both names at the convent.

Mary Martha stopped in front of Baker's Ice Cream Parlour, struck by the recollection of sitting with her papa in those same wire-backed chairs at one of those little round tables. *When I finish my errand,* she promised herself, *I'll go into Baker's and treat myself to a strawberry soda.*

She couldn't help chuckling as she thought about how little had changed in the little town. "Progress" really hadn't lived up to its name! *But,* she thought as she stepped carefully off the curb, looked both ways, and crossed the alley, *maybe that's not such a bad thing. Over in Olde Towne everybody's in a hurry to pave paradise and put in a parking lot!* Mary Martha felt for the curb with her foot and stepped up onto the sidewalk.

Chapter 2

Nearby Olde Towne had progressed in the past few years until it was bursting its seams. Charlie Justice liked the changes. The new Chrysler plant and all the related growth—restaurants, schools, subdivisions, and the new hotel right in the middle of downtown—made it an exciting place to be. She and Rick, as owners of the town's first daily newspaper, had been quickly welcomed into the Council for the Arts. They had even been invited to the biggest social event of the year—the Mayor's Christmas Ball at the town's newest and most elegant hotel.

Charlie picked up a paper and began leafing through it. Rick insisted that they subscribe to all the locals and urged her to scan every one of them. He felt this would help them keep track of what was happening in the area, even though the news in the weeklies was too old to be of much value.

Once *The Chronicle* was established, Rick and Charlie planned to buy out the weekly in town. It might take all their combined business and journalistic skills, but Charlie saw no reason why their plan to become *the* newspaper in the area could not succeed.

What they hadn't planned on was Charlie getting pregnant,

at least not for a long, long time. She and Rick liked working at the paper together long after their employees went home. A baby simply wouldn't fit well into their busy lives. It was too late to think about that, though. The test was positive; she'd taken it three times. Now she had to find a way to tell Rick.

She didn't have to go through with it, of course. *This is the twenty-first century. Women have control over their own bodies now,* she thought. But the idea repulsed her. The baby growing inside her was part of her, part of Rick, their own flesh and blood—no way could she deliberately destroy their child.

It wasn't a religious thing. She'd been raised by devout Baptist parents who had taken her to every service, but once she left for college, she put all that behind her. Now there was no time in her busy life for religion. It was just—

Will Rick want to get rid of the baby? she wondered. *What if he insists on it?* Charlie felt an unexpected protectiveness rising up inside her. He had made it very clear from the beginning of their relationship that he did not want children for a very long time, if ever. Rick was an only child, born and reared in a staid, affluent section of Philadelphia. Charlie knew he hadn't grown up like she had in a rambling farmhouse with brothers and sisters, knowing the rambunctious joy of pillow fights and the give-and-take of growing up.

Charlie had two of each. Her older brother had been killed in an automobile accident when she was a teenager. It was an old grief but a close one. Bobby, the sibling closest to her own age, had completed law school and joined a big firm in Louisville. She saw him a couple of times a year. One of Charlie's sisters lived on a ranch in Wyoming with her husband and three boys. The other, still single, had moved to Chicago to seek a career in advertising.

Charlie hadn't seen her sisters since the first Christmas after their parents had died—her mom from cancer and her dad, she was convinced, of a broken heart. They had gathered at the home place for Christmas, made plans to sell the farm, and then gone their separate ways. They kept in touch by phone and e-mail but rarely saw each other.

I really wouldn't mind having several children, she thought, *someday.* In the crowded years of sharing everything, wearing hand-me-downs, she never thought she would someday miss being part of a big family. Now she wished they all lived close enough to gather for holidays and share the special events in all their lives—the graduations, weddings, births.

Quickly, Charlie pushed her chair back from the desk and put her head between her knees. If only this miserable nausea, this tendency to faint would pass! She wondered if this disoriented feeling was something like what her mother described as "a swimming in the head." Toward the last, when she was on strong pain medication for the cancer, she had commented, "My head feels just like it did when I was pregnant."

Charlie supposed she really should make an appointment with her doctor. But then she would have to face the fact that this was real—she was going to be a mother. She pictured the life her own mother had lived, staying at home to raise her family. Her mother had seemed happy, never complaining, but it made Charlie feel tied down just thinking about it.

Were they doomed to become the kind of parents whose crying baby disrupts an important meeting or much-anticipated performance? She'd seen that happen many times to parents who had no close family or friends to babysit. They certainly didn't have anyone. And they couldn't afford to hire a sitter very often.

Then a new thought hit her. How could they afford to hire someone to do the countless tasks she performed each day for the paper? She was responsible for all the bookkeeping: the payroll, the taxes, the accounts receivable and payable. She did the social page, the obits, and the editorials. Then there were the interviews, the pictures, and the writing of features.

Would she end up interviewing celebrities with a baby strapped to her back like a papoose? Would her crowded office be forced to accommodate a playpen and toys? Would her concentration be interrupted every few minutes by the demands of a fretful baby?

This so-called morning sickness seems to last all day some days, and this appears to be one of those days, she thought wearily, reaching for another paper.

Chapter 3

The chimes of the tall stone church behind her reminded Mary Martha Sims that it was eleven o'clock and she only had a block to go. She couldn't help letting her eyes wander across the street to the small brick church where she and Ben had gone to Sunday school and she and Parker had said their wedding vows. After that, they had attended Parker's cold stone church every Sunday morning. Eventually, he had insisted that she move her membership there.

Parker would be upset if he knew she was thinking about moving her membership again, this time to the little church down the street from their house, the one he had called "holy roller" because they clapped their hands and accompanied their singing with a lively piano and bass guitar.

On those frequent Sunday evenings when Parker had been too busy with his accounts to attend church, she had taken the children there. And, though she never asked them not to, neither of them ever said a word to their father or grandmother about where they had been. She knew her son's loyalty likely had been to youth group festivities, but Olivia had loved the worship services and had not wanted her father to forbid them to go. When Mary Martha had accepted Jesus Christ as her Savior during one of the summer revivals, Olivia had gone forward, too.

Mary Martha had always suspected that it was Collin Davis marrying the oldest Harris girl that sent Olivia into the convent when she was nineteen years old. It was hard to imagine that Olivia had been at the convent for more than forty years. Thankfully, her letters indicated that she was content with the life she had chosen.

P.T. had his bank in Suttonville. She was grateful for the phone call she received every Sunday afternoon at 3:30—as punctual as an alarm clock. P.T. was fifty-nine years old and definitely his father's son, but he didn't want the Sims house or its furnishings. Perhaps that was because of the somber childhood he'd spent there. Or perhaps it was because of his wife, Eleanor, who wanted a newer and finer house every few years.

Mary Martha sighed again. She had lived in the same house for more than sixty years, ever since she and Parker had come back from their weekend honeymoon and moved in with his mother.

She had dreamed of a place of their own, perhaps a small Cape Cod cottage with an apple tree for climbing out back and a white fence around the yard to protect the children. She had pictured holly bushes under the windows, with their red berries lending joy to the place when winter had drained all color from the yard. Instead, she got Mother Sims who managed to drain all the color from their lives. She had mentioned her dream to Parker only once.

"My grandfather built this house," he had responded in that tone his mother used when Mary Martha was straining her patience to the limit. "My dear, we always use the crystal vase with the roses!" or "Oh, no, dear! The white linen cloth, please!"

Finally, she had resigned herself to life in the tall, dark house under the ever-watchful eyes of her mother-in-law. Later her faith had enabled her to endure without resentment, though she often longed for a better atmosphere in which to bring up her children.

Even Christmas in that house had been a cold, formal affair, she recalled, though she had tried her best to make it a pleasant time for the children. She had insisted on P.T. and Olivia being allowed to hang their homemade ornaments on the tree, though at some point during the holidays she would find that they had been moved to the back where they wouldn't show.

Mary Martha sat down to rest for a minute on the green wooden bench at the bus stop. Suddenly smiling, she recalled the pleasant trips she and the children had made on the city bus to the park. They went often to give the children a chance to laugh aloud without giving Grandmother Sims a headache or to run and play without endangering her formal garden. In bad weather, they sometimes opted to ride the bus along its entire route and back again just to escape the cold, dark house and the watching eyes for a while.

A few days after Parker's funeral, she had replaced Mother Sims's portrait over the piano with a Paul Sawyier print of sheep gracing peacefully along a country lane. She had kept the picture in her bedroom since Ben had given it to her for her birthday one year. He had framed it himself. She never had said a word to Ben against her husband or his mother, but Ben had known.

She didn't hate Mother Sims. She really didn't. She never believed the woman meant to be unkind to her and her children. It was just that Mother Sims had been raised as an only child by austere parents and had been widowed young. She had raised her son the same way, with strong moral values and rigid conformity to propriety. As the years passed, Mary Martha had grown to understand her mother-in-law, but that hadn't made living with her any easier.

Parker would not have liked her relegating Mother Sims to the attic with her face to the wall. But Parker was gone, and now when she dusted or ran the sweeper, she no longer felt those condemning eyes following her every movement.

Mary Martha glanced across the street at the First National Bank where Parker had spent his days. She could almost see him emerging from the wide front door, with its tasteful real pine wreath tied with a deep red velvet bow to mark the season. His black umbrella would be over his arm, and he would stop to center his hat firmly on his head before walking home.

Parker's bank. Parker's house. Parker's family heritage. These were the things that had given her husband his identity and had engulfed hers. Sometimes she had felt that, if she hadn't stood where his shadow gave her substance, she might fade away completely.

Progress was a part of her identity as well. She had memories of her childhood and family that went beyond the years of her marriage.

Mary Martha had lived in the little town since the day she was born, and she had no intention of living anywhere else. P.T. and Eleanor had asked her to "come stay awhile" with them in Suttonville. But she had already decided to move into one of the senior citizen apartments when she could no longer get by on her own. They were bright and attractive, and the church ran a bus over there. They weren't cheap; the added expense would strain her part of Parker's pension and her social security allotment. But Mary Martha was sure she could manage. Her friend Dolly Farney had lived in the senior apartments for four or five years now, and she liked it just fine.

Mary Martha stopped outside the double wooden doors that bore the inscription THE PROGRESS, ESTABLISHED 1892. She pushed into the newspaper office.

Chapter 4

C harlie Justice pulled her small white sports car into one of the parking spaces around the center square of new town houses. She got out, picked up the stack of newspapers she had brought home to read, and locked the car. She inserted her house key into the door of the one she and Rick had made a down payment on nearly a year ago and opened the door.

This will be our first Christmas in our new home, she thought. She could see almost the entire space from the entry, except, of course, the master bedroom and bath hidden around a landing at the top of the stairs on her left. To her right was the galley-type kitchen, and straight ahead was the L-shaped living room that wrapped around into a dining space that backed into the serving bar of the kitchen. *Neat, compact, practical, yet attractive,* she approved. *The place has shaped up rather nicely, if I do say so myself,* she thought with satisfaction, taking in the muted blues and grays of the carpet, wallpaper, and paint with unexpected accents of green.

A green marble fireplace surrounded by overflowing floor-to-ceiling bookshelves dominated the far wall, shared by both living and dining space. It had been one of the deciding factors in their buying this place. They both had so many books! On the few occasions when they had entertained, even with candles on cloth-draped card tables, the space had looked charming in the soft light.

With the moving expenses, down payment on the town house, and costs of setting up the paper, they had little money left for furniture. They had the necessities covered, but the rest would have to wait. They were determined not to go back to Rick's dad for help until they could repay the loan he had given them to get started. The dining area would remain empty until they could afford something nice on their own.

At least that had been the plan—until lately. Rick was saying that they really needed to entertain some influential people during the coming holidays. Their makeshift tables, even with the best white cloths and napkins, wouldn't do for a dinner like that.

Charlie needed dining room furniture, and she needed it quickly. But where would she find something nice for a price they could afford?

Suddenly, for the first time, she felt smothered, trapped by the small space. *There is not enough room here for the kind of dinner Rick would like to give this Christmas,* she thought. *There's not enough room for a dining room suite like the one we need.*

Charlie tossed the papers onto the coffee table, went to the refrigerator, and poured a glass of orange juice. Then she came back to sit on the sofa, sipping the juice and leafing through the papers she had brought home with her. She had read through the dailies at the office, but the nausea had been overwhelming. Finally, she'd given up and headed home, bringing the weeklies with her.

It was while she was looking through the classifieds that she saw the ad from the nearby town of Progress. The ad described a cherry table, eight chairs, buffet, and china cabinet—all for a very reasonable price. Charlie circled the ad with red marker. But would all that furniture fit into their space? She really needed to see it and do some measuring before she got her hopes up.

Even if the furniture fit, there was certainly not enough room in their little town house for a baby! "What am I going to do?" she whispered, tossing the paper on top of the stack on the table. She was sure that Rick would be appalled by the prospect of moving again so soon. And what about their purchase agreement? They were locked in. Unless they could sell the property quickly, they would be stuck with two house payments for longer than they could afford.

The sound of a key in the front door scattered her thoughts. She looked up to see Rick come into the entry.

"Hey, sweetheart!" His smile began at his wide mouth, just above the neat honey blond beard, and traveled to light up his deep blue eyes. *Rick's not really a handsome man,* she thought for surely the thousandth time since she had met him in the research section of the college library, *but what eyes!*

"I've been trying to reach you. You didn't have your phone turned on again, Toots," he said, using the nickname he had given her in college. She had always found it amusing—until today. She really didn't feel like a "Toots" right now.

"What are you doing home in the middle of the day?" he asked. "Shirking your responsibilities as co-owner of the best and busiest newspaper in town?" Then his smile disappeared. "Are you all right?"

"I'm okay, Rick," she answered, averting her eyes from his piercing gaze. What she wanted to say was, *"No, I'm not all right! I'm pregnant, and all our plans are ruined!*" She wanted to feel his comforting arms around her, to hear him say, "*A baby? Hey, sweetheart, don't worry! We'll make it. Everything's going to be all right.*"

"Rick, I. . . ," she began.

"What's this?" he interrupted, picking up the paper with the circled ad from the coffee table. He read the part she had marked, then gave a low whistle. "Good price! I think we might even be able to swing it with the way ad sales have been going. That Jason is a real go-getter! I am eternally grateful that we hired him." He read the ad again. "It sounds huge! Will it fit? I'd love to have it here before the holidays, but you'd better do a little measuring before you make any commitments."

He walked to the bookshelves, opened one of the doors that hid the bottom two shelves, and took out a camera bag. "Well, furniture placement is your department," he said cheerfully. "I just dropped by to get this camera with the zoom lens. I have to cover the swearing in of the new city council this afternoon." He dropped a kiss on the top of her head and was out the door before she could organize her thoughts.

Charlie drew a shaky breath, fighting another bout of nausea. She had been so close to telling him! Now he was expecting her to check out that dining room suite. They needed it for the Christmas entertaining, but if they bought it, there would be even less room for all the paraphernalia a baby required.

She could understand Rick's reluctance to start a family so soon. She agreed with him. He still had at least a semester of school to finish before he had his master's degree in hand. She hadn't even started hers. The plan had been for her to enroll once he finished. Would she ever get it done once she was bogged down in diapers and formula and potty training?

Would she become a copy of her own mother, living her life for her children, never having a life of her own?

Charlie snatched up the discarded paper, rummaged in a kitchen drawer for a tape measure, stuffed it into her shoulder bag, and grabbed her car keys.

Chapter 5

Mary Martha Sims set the teakettle on the stove and then stopped to listen. Was that the doorbell? The tinny sound of the old manual bell hardly penetrated all the way back to the kitchen anymore. Or was her hearing beginning to go?

Turning on the burner, she headed down the hall toward the front door and peeked through the clear petals of a tulip etched into the frosted glass. All she could see was the lower half of a pair of legs in blue pants that ended with navy, low-heeled shoes. The toe of one shoe was impatiently patting the concrete porch.

Mary Martha unlocked the door and narrowed her eyes as she scrutinized the young woman before her. With her matching pants and sweater, dark hair cut almost like a man's, and faintly lipsticked mouth set in an impersonal smile, Mary Martha doubted that she would be the type to need or even want Granny's rocker. She glanced at the short, square hands. Not likely the hands of a pianist. She must have come for the dining room suite. Mary Martha opened the door.

"I'm here about your ad," Charlie explained, holding up the paper with Mary Martha's ad circled in red. "Would it be convenient for me to see the cherry dining suite?"

Mary Martha stared at her for a moment, then extended her right hand. "Mary Martha Sims," she said.

"Sorry! Charlie Justice," the young woman responded, taking Mary Martha's hand, her grin this time wide and infectious.

"Come in," Mary Martha invited, leading the way down the hall to the dining room, then stepping aside for Charlie to enter.

"Why, it's exquisite!" Charlie breathed, reaching out to touch the polished wood, which glowed in the soft afternoon light slanting through tall, lace-covered windows. Then she added, "It may be a bit large for our space. May I measure?"

Mary Martha nodded as Charlie took a measuring tape, a pen, and a notebook from her shoulder bag and began to measure and make notes.

"The piano's in the parlor, if you'd care to measure it," Mary Martha added, a bit sarcastically.

"Thank you," said Charlie. "But neither of us play, and our home is really quite—"

The shrill whistle of the teakettle cut her off. Mary Martha hesitated. She didn't want to leave a stranger prowling about her house while she went to the kitchen. "If you're finished, come with me, please," Mary Martha said, hurrying Charlie down the hall before she could protest. She removed the kettle from the burner and added a teabag. "The rocking chair is there in the corner," she volunteered.

"Oh—I'm sorry—I was only interested in the dining room suite," Charlie answered, looking nervously around the room. Then she put her hand to her face and reached out for the back of a ladder-back chair to steady herself.

Mary Martha was at her side instantly, leading her to the

rocker and easing her into it.

Charlie laughed shakily. "I'm so sorry," she muttered. "I'll be fine now." Her voice trailed off as she sank into the chair. Her face was pale, and perspiration had broken out across her forehead.

Mary Martha pushed Charlie's head down between her knees. "Keep your head down a few minutes. I'll fix you a nice cup of hot tea." Surprisingly, Charlie obeyed. When she finally raised her head, Mary Martha saw that she rested it against the ruffled cushion suspended from the chair's back posts.

"I fainted every time," Mary Martha said, handing her the fragile moss rose saucer holding the steaming teacup. "And the nausea! Oh my!"

Charlie looked up at her, misery plain in the wide blue eyes.

Mary Martha smiled. "I know exactly how you feel, Char—" Mary Martha stopped. The name sounded so ridiculous.

"It's Charlene," the young woman clarified as though she had read Mary Martha's mind, "but I only use it on checks and business papers." She sipped from her cup, then laid her head back against the cushion, closed her eyes, and began to rock gently. "Nice chair," she murmured.

"How far along are you, Charlene?" Mary Martha asked softly.

Charlie opened her eyes, seemed to struggle with a decision, then answered. "Two months, more or less."

"The sickness likely will pass in another month," Mary Martha said. "Mine did." *Except for the last one,* she remembered. She had been sick the whole seven months, and then the baby had been stillborn. Parker had said there must have been something wrong with the baby, and it was for the best.

She was sure that Parker loved their two children, in his

own way. He was proud of their accomplishments and kept their photographs on his desk at the bank. But she had suspected that Parker hadn't wanted this last baby. Babies were a lot of trouble.

She hadn't burdened Parker with her grief, and she certainly wasn't going to worry Charlene with it now! "Drink your tea before it gets cold," she said instead.

Charlie sat up and sipped at the tea. "I'm so sorry to inconvenience you," she apologized again. "And I really must be going." Nevertheless, she made no attempt to move. Instead, she sipped her tea and rocked gently back and forth in Mary Martha's granny's rocker.

Somehow, she looks right in that chair, Mary Martha thought. *Or maybe it's just knowing that she's expecting.* Rocking chairs were made for mothers and babies, after all. There's just something about a rocking chair, something warm and soothing, something eternal to pass on from one generation to the next.

"This is a lovely old house," Charlene commented. "Have you ever considered adding a window, maybe even a skylight, here in the kitchen to brighten things up?"

A skylight? Mary Martha thought, her shoulders tightening with resentment. *Who does she think she is coming in here and telling me how to change my house?* Then she let her shoulders sag with resignation. The house never had been hers, not even during these past three years when she had lived in it alone with her name on the deed. *It always has and always will belong to Mother Sims,* she realized, *at least in my mind.*

"I probably would tear out that wall and open the kitchen right into the dining room, with maybe a serving bar to separate them," Charlene continued, sipping her tea and rocking contentedly. "Or at least join the two rooms with a wide arch.

And I think I'd replace those dark cabinets, or maybe paint them white or a nice sunlight yellow."

Mary Martha looked at her with one raised eyebrow. It was the look Olivia had called her "I've had enough of this nonsense!" look.

Charlene sat up abruptly and placed both feet solidly on the floor to stop the rocker. "I'm so sorry!" she said. "I don't know what got into me! It's a beautiful house just the way it is. It reminds me of my husband's parents' home in Philadelphia—dignified and elegant. I'm not sure why I presumed to remodel it for you!"

Mary Martha smiled. "That's all right, Charlene," she assured her. "I've always thought the house was dark and intimidating. It reflects my mother-in-law's taste, not mine. I've often longed to remodel it myself, but while my husband was alive, he wouldn't hear of it. By the time it came to me, I guess I just felt that it wasn't worth all the trouble for the little time I might have left on this earth."

"I wish we could have bought an old house that I could remodel," Charlie said. "If you ever decide you want to tackle this one, give me a call. I'd love to help." She fumbled in her purse, then handed Mary Martha a business card. "And I'd like to do a feature article on this place sometime in the New Year, if that would be agreeable with you."

Mary Martha looked at the card. "We'll see, dear," she stalled. "And are you interested in the dining set?"

"I like it very much, and I think my husband will, too," Charlie said standing up at last. "I'm just not sure it will fit into our tiny town house. Could you hold it for a couple of days while I take these measurements and work with them? I promise I'll get back with you right away."

Mary Martha nodded and turned to follow Charlie to the front door.

As Mary Martha opened the door, Charlie stuck out her hand. "It was nice meeting you," she said. "And I do hope it will fit—maybe without the china cabinet."

Mary Martha nodded again. "Yes, I could break up the set if necessary. I'm sure the cabinet would sell alone." *If not, I can keep it,* she thought, *or give it to someone.* She didn't think Eleanor would want it, but her granddaughter or one of her great-grandchildren might.

"I'll let you know," Charlie called back as she got into her car.

Mary Martha shut the door and went back to the kitchen. She switched on the overhead lights. *It is dark in here,* she admitted. *But a skylight?* She chuckled then, thinking how Parker would have reacted to the suggestion, or even worse, what Mother Sims would have said. For a moment, the idea was tempting.

Maybe a big picture window there overlooking the back garden, she mused, *where the morning sun can come spilling through onto the golden poplar floor. Or maybe double glass doors opening onto a deck like that lovely one P.T. had built for Eleanor just before she decided they should move again to a more "suitable" neighborhood.*

"I'd love sitting on a deck on sunny mornings, sipping tea, listening to the birds, watching moss roses open in the garden," she said aloud. Mother Sims never would have moss roses in her formal gardens. "An inelegant flower," she had deemed the lovely little blossoms that had always been among Mary Martha's favorites. Once she had tried growing some in a pot in her bedroom upstairs, but they had died for lack of sunlight. *I could have pots of them on a deck without even disturbing Mother Sims's precious formal beds,* she thought longingly.

If her brother were still alive, he'd build her a deck. Perhaps she could get one of his sons or some other carpenter to do it.

Nonsense! she scolded. *I'm eighty-three years old! I've lived in this dark, old house for more than sixty years. It's foolish to think about changing it now.*

She hoped Charlene would be able to use the dining room suite, though. Suddenly, she felt the need to get that big dark furniture out of the house, to make room, to unclutter, to lighten things up.

Chapter 6

Back in her office, Charlie Justice worked furiously for the rest of the afternoon, taking time out only to deal with recurring bouts of nausea and threats of fainting. At 4:00 p.m., she turned off her computer.

"Ellen, I'm going home!" she called to their jack-of-all-trades assistant in the front office. "See you tomorrow!"

Ellen looked up from her cluttered desk, her glasses pushed up into her black curls, a smear of White-Out on her dark skin below her right cheek bone. "Are you okay, Charlie?" she asked, a frown creasing her forehead. "Obviously, you haven't been feeling well lately. Maybe you ought to see a doctor. You know this flu has been going around, and there's a virus. . ."

Charlie read genuine concern in the woman's dark eyes and smiled at her warmly. "You are very astute, Ellen," she said. She had tried her best to hide her symptoms. "I don't think I'm coming down with anything. Maybe it's just fatigue. If I'm not better by next week," she promised, "I'll call the doctor. Have a nice evening!" And, with that, she was out the door, into her car, and heading for home.

Once there, she changed into a comfortable old sweat suit, fixed a hot cup of lemon tea, and took the measuring tape and her notes out of her shoulder bag. She measured the L-shaped room. *L-shaped, upside down,* she thought, scribbling notes, then measuring again.

She thought the table and chairs would fit in the middle of the room, and the buffet along the wall shared by the living and dining areas. *Whether we will have enough room to walk around them, I don't know!* she thought. There definitely wasn't going to be room for the china cabinet, but she could keep her best dishes in the buffet. Mrs. Sims had indicated that she was willing to sell the set without it.

I like Mrs. Sims, she mused. *She must be eighty, and still she appears to be alert and in control of her life. I hope I'm like that when I'm her age!* Then she laughed aloud. *I'm not even in control of my life right now!* she reminded herself.

Rick had said they probably could afford the dining set, and she knew he wanted it in place for the holidays. Should she call Mrs. Sims and say they'd take it? Charlie decided she would feel better if she talked it over with Rick first. And there still was the issue of the baby.

I have to tell him! she thought. The purchase of the dining set—all their decisions from now on—would be impacted by the fact that they were going to have a baby. Certainly, *her* life would be changed completely.

Will I be a good mother? she wondered suddenly. Her own mother had been wonderful, even if, at times, she had felt smothered by her loving concern. Did she have it in her to put the needs of a child above all of her own wants and needs? She didn't know. All she knew for sure was that she wasn't ready for that kind of responsibility, not yet.

A wave of longing swept over her. *If only I could talk it all over with Mom! Would she be shocked by the very unmotherly reactions of her youngest daughter?* She'd never know.

She had been there for all of her sister Sarah's three difficult but much-wanted pregnancies. She supposed she could call her, but Charlie doubted that her oldest sister would be able to identify with someone who didn't want her baby. *She's so like Mom!* she thought. *And it's not that I don't want my baby. I just don't want it yet!*

That didn't change the fact that the baby would arrive in another seven months or so. She would be like all those other mothers at gatherings who could talk of nothing more exciting than how many ounces of formula their little darlings consumed, how many teeth they had cut, how clever they were about learning to talk or to walk or to potty train.

"I will not!" she said aloud. "I will not let this baby rule my life!" As soon as Rick got home, she would tell him. Then she would insist that they go ahead with their plans to buy the dining room suite and entertain for the holidays. The coming baby and its needs would just have to fit in around all that as well as with all the other parts of their busy lives.

At the sound of a key inserted into the front door lock, her heart sank. He was home! It was time. She took a deep breath and swallowed hard, trying to arrange the words of her disturbing announcement on her tongue.

"Get your duds on, Toots!" Rick sang out when he saw her. "We're going to the Mayor's Christmas Ball!"

Charlie was alarmed. She had totally forgotten that the ball was tonight. "But, Rick, I have—"

"No 'buts' about it, babe," he interrupted. "This is one invitation that cannot be turned down. I've worked too hard to get it! And I know you were about to say that you have nothing to wear, but that red velvet dress you wore to Mom and Dad's anniversary party will be perfect. I hope I can still fit into my wedding tux."

Charlie let her breath out in a long sigh, swallowing the news she had been on the verge of sharing. The last thing she wanted to do tonight was go to some formal political affair. She wanted to stay right here and tell her husband they were going to have a baby. She wanted it all behind her. Looking at the excitement shining in her husband's eyes, though, she knew she couldn't spoil it for him. At least the nausea usually bothered her less in the evenings.

"I've got the first shower!" she told him, heading for the stairs.

Chapter 7

W e're so glad you could come to our Senior Saints Christmas dinner, Mrs. Sims!" the pastor's wife said. "Sit down here, and I'll get you a plate."

Mary Martha sat down in a folding chair at a round table covered with a white cloth and decorated with a large pot of poinsettias in its center. Each of the eight places at the table was set with a little basket of candies, a paper napkin of red poinsettias, and silverware.

Stainless ware, she corrected silently. *No one uses silver anymore.* That didn't bother her, though. She had hated polishing Mother Sims's silver. Mother Sims had always done the cooking, assigning Mary Martha the more menial tasks, things she apparently thought her incompetent daughter-in-law could handle. She hadn't even been allowed to wash the good dishes after she broke a soup bowl from the best china early in her marriage. Of course, there was a maid who came in to help with the heavy cleaning two days each week.

Soon after Parker's funeral, Mary Martha had packed up most of the "good" silver and given it to P.T. In addition to the table service for twelve, there had been a lovely tea set she would have given to Olivia had she had a home of her own.

Her daughter-in-law seemed pleased with the gift, for once, oohing and aahing over the elegant pattern and the obvious quality of the silver. She even noted with satisfaction the prestigious name of the manufacturer.

"Here you go!" Mrs. Tanner, the pastor's wife, said, placing a filled plate in front of her. Mary Martha recognized the usual turkey, dressing, and cranberry sauce, with other interesting mixtures heaped around them.

"Would you like iced tea or hot coffee?" Mrs. Tanner asked.

"Tea, please," Mary Martha answered, spearing a bite of dressing with her fork and combining it with cranberry sauce.

The pastor's wife patted her on the shoulder. "I never drink coffee in the evenings, either," she approved. "I'll be right back with your tea."

Mary Martha shrugged off her irritation at the woman's unconscious patronizing. She was a kind woman who was always offering to do some favor for her. When she had taken her to the grocery this week, she had urged her to come tonight, reminding her that the church bus stopped right at the end of her front walk.

Mary Martha often took the bus to church on Sunday and Wednesday nights, when it was too dark outside to walk the short distance to the church. Only recently, though, at her friend Dolly's insistence, had she begun to participate in some of the congregation's social events.

She was glad she and Dolly had become friends. They had known each other in school, but it wasn't until they met up again here at the church, both widows, that they had become real friends. They were as different as two people could possibly be, but she enjoyed Dolly's sarcastic comments on everything around them, her enthusiastic optimism.

She put the dressing and cranberry sauce into her mouth and swallowed. *Delicious!* she thought in surprise. *Almost as good as Mother Sims's corn bread dressing.* Despite her faults, she had to admit that Parker's mother had been an excellent cook.

Finding that she was hungry, she explored other offerings on the plate. *Dolly would love this sweet potato casserole,* she thought, scanning the crowd for her missing friend. *Where is she?*

"Hello, Mrs. Sims!"

Mary Martha looked up into the eager smile of a man she recognized as a local Realtor. He had done business with Parker at the bank and was ten years younger than she. He and his wife had once come for dinner, an evening she had thought would never end. She remembered hearing that his wife had died a few years ago and he had remarried—a considerably younger woman. She couldn't remember his name, but it would come to her. *Probably tomorrow,* she thought wryly, *when I no longer need it.*

"Good evening," she answered casually.

"Tom Winters," he supplied, pulling out the chair beside her and taking a seat. "When are you going to let me sell that big old monstrosity of a house for you?" he asked, cutting right to the purpose for his sudden friendliness. "I could get you a great price! Those old Victorians are in demand again. And no wonder, not too many of them left, originals like yours, anyway."

"Mr. Winters," Mary Martha said, buttering her roll, "I am not interested in selling my house." She knew she used the possessive pronoun loosely. It would never be her house. But she was sure the Realtor knew her name was on the deed. "I've lived there for more than sixty years, and I suppose I'll die there," she added. "Then you and your competitors can fight with my son over it."

Somehow, lately, I've learned to speak my mind, she thought proudly, *and most of the credit for that should go to Dolly.* The woman was about as tactful as the proverbial bull in a china shop but painfully honest. *Perhaps she has rubbed off a little on me,* she thought. *If only I'd had Dolly's influence in my life years ago.*

"But, Mrs. Sims, I could get you a great price!" the Realtor repeated. "You must rattle around in that big old place all by yourself. I could find you something smaller, something cozy and easy to keep. Let me get you an offer, and—"

Mary Martha carefully placed her knife across the edge of her plate and turned to look him squarely in the eyes. She could almost see the dollar signs dancing. "Mr. Winters," she said firmly, as though he were hard of hearing, or maybe a little slow, "let me make this perfectly clear: I—am—not—interested."

He met her unblinking stare for a moment, then dropped his gaze, pushed back his chair, and left the table.

"Merry Christmas!" Mary Martha muttered, taking a bite of the buttered roll.

"Oh, Merry Christmas to you, dear Mrs. Sims!" the pastor's wife gushed, placing a tall glass of tea in front of her. "It's sweetened. I hope that's all right. You're not diabetic, are you?"

Mary Martha shook her head no. *I'm not diabetic, and I'm not completely senile,* she thought. Then, realizing contritely that the woman only meant to be nice, she added, "Happy New Year, my dear."

Mrs. Tanner patted her on the shoulder again and moved away to greet some new arrivals. Among them, Mary Martha spotted Dolly Farney. She waved to her and motioned to the seat beside her. Dolly waved back and started to work her way through the crowd.

"Hey!" she said when she reached the table, removing her coat and neck scarf and draping them over the back of the chair the Realtor had just vacated. "Glad you could make it! Did you ride the bus? Ours was late." She dropped heavily into the chair.

Mary Martha suppressed a shudder as she took in the purple dress encasing Dolly's plump body. *It's exactly the shade of her hair! If only I could convince Dolly to go to Jayne and allow her to create something more suitable!* she thought as someone placed a filled plate in front of Dolly.

"Mmmmm, this is good!" Dolly exclaimed around a mouthful of sweet potato casserole. "Pecans. Cornflakes. Pineapple. What else? If I still cooked, I would want this recipe!"

Mary Martha pushed back her half-empty plate and sipped her tea.

"Aren't you going to finish your food?" Dolly asked. "You're thin as a bird! I know you don't eat right, there in that big old house by yourself. After Mr. Farney died, I got so I hardly bothered to fix a meal. Now I make my own breakfast, and the Senior Center provides lunch and dinner. It's pretty good most of the time." She chuckled, waving one hand at her ample middle. "You can tell I'm not going hungry!"

Mary Martha smiled noncommittally, considering the tray of desserts being offered by a teenage waiter. She selected a small piece of cheesecake topped with cherries and saw Dolly reach for a huge serving of some decadent-looking chocolate concoction.

"What a way to go!" Dolly said, rolling her eyes. Mary Martha laughed aloud. She was glad she had come. Dolly was right. She needed to get out more.

"You really should consider selling that old place and

moving out to the Senior Center with me," Dolly said. "You never liked that house anyway, and it must be hard to keep. At the Senior Center, they do all the heavy cleaning for us. And there's always something going on—games, entertainment, or just visiting with other residents. I haven't been bored or lonely a day since I moved in," she added, poking a forkful of chocolate into her mouth.

Mary Martha took a bite of her cheesecake, chewed, and swallowed, envying, for the first time, the freedom and cama-raderie Dolly had found in her new lifestyle. She and Parker had never had close friends—mostly acquaintances, business associates, people to impress with their formal dinners. Mother Sims had held teas for her garden club and entertained her bridge club.

Once, Mary Martha remembered, she had asked someone home for lunch, a nice girl she had met on the city bus, back before she had children. They had talked several times and had a lot in common. Mother Sims had been polite during the visit, but after the girl left, she had enlightened her errant daughter-in-law about the dangers of picking up strangers. She also mentioned that it was inconsiderate to invite guests to someone else's house. Mary Martha never made that mistake again.

"Of course, I don't own it," Dolly continued, "but we're allowed to furnish our apartments with our own things, except for the stove and refrigerator. My only regret is that I didn't move out there the day after Mr. Farney passed!"

Mary Martha smiled. She never had owned the house she lived in, anyway—no matter what the deed claimed—and few of the furnishings were hers. Everything belonged to Mother Sims.

"If we don't forgive those who trespass against us, God won't forgive us," the pastor had warned in his sermon just last Sunday. She had tried to forgive. She no longer hated Mother Sims, and she had cared for her faithfully those last years after her stroke.

She still had some bitter memories, but she supposed she would have to lose her mind completely to forget those. Long ago she had resigned herself to her jaybird existence in someone else's nest, just as she had resigned herself to living in Parker's shadow. *I married him—and his mother,* she thought wryly. But she had been determined to see it through, no matter how completely that shadow shut out the sun.

Suddenly, Charlene Justice came into her mind, with her suggestions about "brightening up" the house. Mary Martha knew, though, that it would take much more than windows and skylights, even more than a bright sunny deck filled with flowers to brighten up that old house.

"I know you aren't listening to me," Dolly said with a resigned sigh. "But you'd like the Senior Center, Mary Martha. I know you would."

"You make it sound very attractive, Dolly," she answered. "Someday I may just surprise you."

"Yeah, yeah, and I may run for president," Dolly said. "I do want you to come to our Christmas luncheon day after tomorrow. While you're there, you can come up and see my apartment."

"I've seen your apartment, Dolly."

"I know, but you haven't seen the new drapes and bedspread my son got me for Christmas. You've got to see them! All shades of purple."

"Why am I not surprised?" Mary Martha murmured.

"My son would be glad to pick you up," Dolly offered.

"I'll tell you what," Mary Martha said, laughing, "if you will let Jayne do your hair next time, I'll come to your luncheon."

"It's a deal," Dolly agreed, throwing her a high five.

Chapter 8

C harlie Justice drove slowly down Main Street in the little town of Progress. She was early for her assignment to cover the luncheon at the Senior Citizens' Center. Rick thought the innovative home for the elderly would make a good Christmas feature story since there was no place quite like it in Olde Towne or any of the neighboring towns.

"Get lots of photographs!" he had reminded her.

The Senior Center, she recalled from her preliminary research, had been built by a group of doctors seeking a tax break. Then it had been opened up to other investors. Now it was run by a board consisting of representatives of all concerned, including the residents. The one- and two-bedroom apartments—some rented, some purchased like condos—were a bit pricey, but that didn't seem to keep people away. The waiting list was extensive.

Charlie understood that the place was nothing like the typical "rest home," where residents languished in wheelchairs or shuffled listlessly up and down halls that smelled like disinfectant. The residents of the Senior Center were said to be active and happy.

Charlie stopped at the lone stoplight and looked around,

taking in the old-fashioned attempts at honoring the season. She didn't care much for the candy canes on the light posts, but the posts themselves were beautiful wrought iron structures dripping clusters of round, white globes. They reminded her of paintings she had seen of lamplighters igniting the gaslights along tree-lined streets.

In Olde Towne, all the original trees had been replaced with dwarf specimens that were neater and more uniform. They lined up like obedient soldiers between the efficient modern lighting. *Everybody has air-conditioning now,* she thought. *There's no need for shade trees. I'll bet these giant maples and oaks are gorgeous in the fall, though.* They were beautiful even without leaves, their dark branches etched against the gray winter sky.

The light changed, and she moved on, trying to escape the heavy nostalgia that had settled over her. "O little town of Progress," she sang, "how still we see thee lie!" *You've been lying here asleep since you were built back in the early 1900s,* she thought. It was a pretty little old-fashioned village, but she preferred the busy, hectic pace of their more modern town.

The Mayor's Ball had been exciting, and except for one near fainting spell that came on when she, luckily, was near the restroom, she had enjoyed it. She was glad Rick had insisted that they attend. They were carving out a niche for themselves in Olde Towne.

To her right, she noticed the building that housed the town's only newspaper, a weekly. "THE PROGRESS, ESTABLISHED 1892," proclaimed the dignified gold lettering on its double doors.

What would it be like to have only one edition to publish each week? she wondered. The news wouldn't be as fresh, but the pace certainly would be more leisurely than the one she and Rick and their small crew struggled with each day. She imagined having days instead of hours to prepare a feature story, having the luxury of reading it over one last time.

Rick planned to buy the weekly in Olde Towne as soon as they had the money, but working it into their already over-extended schedule certainly would not make their lives more leisurely. She couldn't blame Rick, though. It was what they had planned when they came to Olde Towne. Of course, they had not planned on a baby coming along.

A wave of nausea washed over her, and she pulled the car over to the curb and sat with her head down against the steering wheel until it passed. *I have to see the doctor,* she thought. *What if something is wrong with the baby? And I must find a way to tell Rick.* Right now, though, she had to cover the luncheon, and she really needed something to abate her nausea. Just down the block, she had noticed a pharmacy. Maybe the pharmacist could give her something. She took the keys from the ignition, got out of the car, and locked the door.

Quickly, she retraced her route back to Hanley's Drugstore, climbed the two steps, and went inside. *I might as well be step-ping back a hundred years,* she marveled, crossing the polished wooden floor to where a middle-aged man in a cream-colored pharmacist's coat stood behind a wooden counter.

"Do you have something I can take for nausea?" she asked in a low voice, conscious of a couple seated at a small round table down front.

The man studied her for a moment, then, also in a low voice, asked, "Are you pregnant, ma'am? I can't give you any-thing without a prescription if you are. I'm sorry, but it could harm the baby."

"All right," she answered, feeling a flush creep over her face as the couple turned to stare. She felt sure they thought she was trying to get something illegal. "Thanks, anyway," she murmured, turning and leaving the store, her heels clicking on the old wooden floor.

Still burning with embarrassment, she got back in the car and drove straight to the Senior Citizens' Center. She parked in the parking lot out front, slung her shoulder bag over her shoulder, and picked up the camera. She adjusted the waistband of her pantsuit. *Surely my clothes aren't getting tight already!* she thought in horror, fighting off another wave of nausea. She would get through this luncheon some way, then she would go home, call the doctor, and tell Rick.

As she entered the building's festive dining room, crowded with residents and guests, she saw Mary Martha Sims eating at a small table across from a large woman with purple hair. She decided to go over and speak to her before looking up the Senior Center's director, who was expecting her.

"Why, Charlene! What are you doing at a senior citizens' luncheon?" Mary Martha said with surprise.

"I'm doing a feature for the paper," she explained. "But I didn't expect to find you here!"

"Oh, I'm just visiting a friend. Dolly, this is Charlene—" she began, then stopped.

"Charlie Justice," Charlie said, sticking out her hand. "I'm with *The Chronicle* over at Olde Towne."

"Charlene," Mary Martha said firmly to the purple-haired woman, "is the young woman who answered my ad about the dining room suite the other day. Charlene, this is my friend, Dolly Farney. At least I can remember her name!"

"Nice to meet you," Dolly said, shaking her hand.

"I've done some measuring, Mrs. Sims," Charlie said then, "but I—"

"—you would like to see it again before you make up your mind," Mary Martha finished for her.

It wasn't what she had intended to say, but Charlie let it pass. "I'll see you in a few minutes," she promised. "I've got to do some interviewing, take some photos. Here, you two go first." She raised the camera and snapped a picture of the two women. Then she turned and wandered through the big room taking shots of the huge Christmas tree and seasonal decorations, as well as random shots of the animated diners.

When she came back to the table, she sat down between the women and took her pen and notepad from her purse. "Would you like to tell me how you like living here at the Senior Center, Mrs. Farney?" she asked.

Dolly smiled broadly and began to sing the Senior Center's praises, as she so often had to Mary Martha.

"May I quote you, Mrs. Farney?" Charlie asked as the director led her off on a tour of the facility. When they returned, Mary Martha and Dolly were just finishing dessert.

"If you need to see the dining room suite again, why don't you just drive Mary Martha home?" Dolly suggested. "My son brought her, but he had to leave. She was going to call a cab."

"Why, I'd be glad to," Charlie agreed, relieved that her assignment was finished for now and she hadn't fainted or been sick.

Back at the Sims house, Charlie parked and went around to help her passenger out of the car.

"I've been hoping you would come back," Mary Martha said, leading the way inside and back to the dining room. "The table is large—it seats twelve—but you know that wide middle leaf can be removed."

"It really is exquisite!" Charlie breathed. "That's the only word for it!" Then she reached out to steady herself against the table as a wave of nausea swept over her.

"Oh, dear," Mary Martha said, pulling one of the heavy chairs out from under the table. "Sit here and put your head down."

Charlie sank onto the chair and put her head between her knees. Once the spell had passed, she raised her head. "I'm so sorry!" she said. "You must think I'm a real wimp!"

Mary Martha chuckled. "I know exactly how you feel," she assured her. "Come back to the kitchen and rest for a few minutes. I think we both could do with a good hot cup of tea." She busied herself with the kettle and stove burner. "Have you had lunch? Can I get you something to eat?"

"Oh, no, Mrs. Sims, tea will be fine," Charlie answered, heading straight for Granny's rocker. "This is the most comfortable chair!" she said, rocking gently back and forth.

"That one's held many a mother and baby," Mary Martha said.

The comfortable silence lasted until the kettle whistled and Mary Martha filled two cups with tea. "Is your husband excited about being a father?" she asked, handing Charlie one cup on its saucer.

Charlie looked at her miserably, then dropped her gaze to the cup in her hands. "Mrs. Sims," she confessed, "I haven't even told him yet."

"Oh, my dear, you must tell him! Let him share the joy." Parker hadn't shared her joy over any of their expected babies or her pain when the last one had died. But she saw no reason to go into all that.

"We had such plans!" Charlie blurted. "We have such a tight schedule with the newspaper, and the town house we purchased isn't nearly big enough. There's no room in either of them for a baby. This wasn't supposed to happen, not yet, anyway!"

"Well, babies have a way of choosing their own time," Mary Martha pointed out. "Of course, people have more control over that now than we did in our day."

"That's my fault, Mrs. Sims," Charlie admitted. "I just got so busy I was careless. I'm so afraid of what Rick will say when he finds out. I'm worried that he might even leave me!"

"Oh, pshaw!" Mary Martha snorted. "You love each other, don't you? He won't leave." If Parker hadn't left her. . .but Parker was committed to his image, and divorce wasn't part of it. She reached over and patted Charlene on the shoulder. "Just trust in the Lord, dear," she advised. "He's never let me down."

Charlie ignored that. "I realize this is Rick's responsibility, too, but he's just finishing his master's, and he has plans to buy another paper, a weekly," she said. "We can't afford to hire more help or buy a bigger place to live. We can barely afford this dining room set, and we certainly have no room for both it and all the things a baby requires."

"Tell your husband," Mary Martha urged, "and let him help you make plans. It's his baby, too, though men usually don't recognize that fact until they hold the squirming little bundle in their arms."

Charlie smiled up at her. "I guess you're right. I know you are." She took a deep breath. "I need to get back to the office so I can get away early and get ready for the big announcement. I'll let you know how it goes and what we're going to do about that beautiful cherry dining set." She got up, placed her cup and saucer on the counter, and headed down the hall.

At the door, she turned suddenly and hugged Mary Martha.

"Thank you!" she whispered, tears glistening in her eyes. Then she was out the door and getting into her car. She looked back and waved as she pulled away from the curb.

Chapter 9

Mary Martha stood on the stoop, fighting tears of her own. *What is wrong with me, spilling emotions all over the place?* she scolded. She supposed it was just that it had been a long time since she had seen Olivia, and talking with Charlene about her baby made her realize that she would never share that joy with her own daughter.

P.T.'s daughter and her children always spent more time with Eleanor's mother than they had with Mary Martha. She recalled her small granddaughter telling her one day, "I like you, Grandma, but I don't like this spooky old house. Something is always watching me!"

I hope Charlene will bring the baby by to visit sometime, she thought wistfully, watching a blue sedan pull to the curb and a man get out. Then she recognized the Realtor who had been so set on selling her house the other night at the church. She turned to go back inside.

"Mrs. Sims! Mrs. Sims! Wait!" he called, running toward her. "I've got a buyer for your house!"

Mary Martha gave him her "no more nonsense" look, but it didn't work. Tom Winters held up one hand in a plea for patience while he caught his breath.

"It's a great offer!" he panted, and named a figure that would have widened Mary Martha's eyes had she not trained herself so well at hiding her feelings. It seemed to her a most generous sum, though she was sure P.T. would say it was too low. He and Parker were the money managers. She knew very little about property values.

I don't need that much money, she thought. She had no debts. The house was paid for years ago. Her income from Parker's pension at the bank and her social security was adequate to pay for her homeowner's insurance, property taxes, utilities, and what little food, medicine, and other necessities she bought. *Of course, I could give P.T. a third of it, set up a trust fund for Olivia in case she ever decides to leave the convent, and use my share to pay for an apartment at the Senior Center,* she mused.

Mary Martha banished the plan before it could settle in her mind. Parker would have been outraged at the mere thought of selling the Sims house!

"Mr. Winters, I've told you I am not interested," she said. "What part of that do you *not* understand?"

"But, Mrs. Sims," he protested, "it's such a good offer!"

"There is no good offer, sir, if one does not wish to sell," she said firmly, going into the house and closing the door in his face. She hated to be rude, but the man was as persistent as a cocklebur and just about as irritating! *If I wanted to sell, I'd find some other Realtor!* she thought, watching through the etched tulip in the door glass as Winters turned and walked dejectedly back to his car.

I can't believe how forceful I've become, she thought. *Coaching Charlene in her marriage relationship, sending Winters packing! Dolly certainly has been good for me in that respect.*

What is Dolly doing right now in her cheerful little apartment or down in the common areas where the residents enjoy each other's company? she wondered, walking through the silent, ghost-filled house.

Oh, she didn't believe in haunting spirits, but the house was full of ghosts, just the same. There was Mother Sims forever watching every move she made, even with her portrait stored in the attic. And there was the autocratic Parker, always in agreement with his mother, telling her what she could and could not do.

She recalled the time she had asked him if she could take a part-time job at Hanley's Drugstore—just a few hours each day while the children were at school. His angry response surprised her. "Why would you want to shame me like that? Isn't the allowance I give you enough to spend on frivolous things?" She had to admit that Parker never refused to buy anything she or the children needed, but it really hadn't been about money. She had simply wanted a little something of her own. Nevertheless, she had accepted his decree without argument.

Mary Martha fixed a fresh cup of tea and sat down with it at the small walnut table under the kitchen window. Looking out over the winter garden, she noticed that all was not brown. A fat little chipmunk scurried from its nest under the fountain to the back fence, where the burning bushes painted a deep swath of scarlet across the dark green of the evergreens. The crab apple tree in the center of the yard still held some of its small red fruit, and the hollies were filled with red berries.

Red and green for Christmas, she thought, glancing at the calendar. Only a handful of days remained before the holiday, but she thought she was ready. She rechecked the to-do list in her mind.

She had sent Christmas cards with checks in them to her granddaughter and all the great-grandchildren, who had matured beyond her ability to choose gifts for them. She had ordered a country ham, baked and sliced, for P.T. and Eleanor. She had contributed to the gift fund at church for the pastor and his wife. She had cards with cash in them ready for her hairdresser, the papergirl, and the—what was she supposed to call him now?—the letter carrier.

After Mother Sims had her stroke, Mary Martha had learned to bake the crusty loaves of cinnamon raisin bread they traditionally had given to service people and neighbors. Those neighbors had been gone for years now, though, and she hadn't baked Christmas loaves for at least a decade.

I'm as ready for Christmas as I will ever be, she thought with satisfaction, sipping her tea.

Then she remembered the big grapevine wreath Olivia had made for her in that craft class she took the last year before she went into the convent. Originally, the wreath had held real pinecones, English walnut shells, and bright-colored Indian corn. But when she brought it down from the attic to hang the next year, she found that a mouse had feasted on the corn. Mary Martha had replaced the naked white cobs with artificial holly. Every year since, she had hung the wreath, feeling, somehow, that it gave her a connection with her absent daughter.

Mary Martha knew she would have to subject her arthritic knees and hips to the climb up both long flights of steps to the attic. But she felt it was important to hang the wreath to remember Olivia and to honor the Savior's birth.

She rarely climbed the stairs anymore. After Parker's death, she had asked Ben and his sons to move her bedroom into Mother Sims's front parlor downstairs. She only entered the four upstairs rooms once a year when she called in the cleaning people.

Mary Martha got up, rinsed her cup, turned it upside down in the dish drainer, and headed for the stairway that wound up from the front hall.

I might as well get it done, she thought, placing her foot carefully on the first step and holding tightly to the polished walnut banister. She had fallen more than once on these stairs, so far without major injury, but she didn't want to risk a broken bone or worse, especially during the holidays.

Not that Christmas is so important anymore, she thought, *except for what it represents.* Mary Martha stopped to catch her breath at the second-floor landing. Other than her Christmas Day visit with P.T.'s family, she would spend most of the holidays by herself here in this lonely old house.

Opening the door to the attic stairs, she started to climb the narrow risers, running her hand along the wall for support, since there was no railing here. At last, she was at the top. She took the green garbage bag she had tied around the wreath and turned to retrace her steps to the lower floors.

So far, so good! she thought as she shut the attic stair door and began the easier descent to the first floor. She couldn't see the steps now with the bag in her right hand and her left stretched out to slide along the banister.

She knew the minute she missed the step halfway down, but there was nothing she could do about it. The last thing she remembered was the frantic flailing of her arms and legs and one desperate prayer, "God, help me!"

Chapter 10

harlie Justice sat on the raised hearth staring into the flames of the gas logs, wishing the ordeal ahead of her was over. She counted as the church bells down the street chimed the hour. Any minute now, Rick would come through that door.

What was she going to say? How could she tell him their dreams must be put on hold, maybe abandoned altogether? How could she destroy his well-laid plans? Right or wrong, he had left birth control up to her, and she had failed. Now they would both suffer the consequences.

She got up, walked restlessly to the window, and stood watching the beginnings of snow swirl around the light outside. *Maybe we'll have a white Christmas after all,* she thought. It was too early, though. Any snow that came now would be dirty slush by Christmas Day.

We really ought to get the tree up if we're going to have one, she thought. She felt better this evening, with no nausea and no faintness. Maybe they would go get a tree. It was their first Christmas in their new home. They really should have one.

I want a real one, she thought, *like we always had at the farm.* She remembered the whole family following Dad into the woods to find and cut the perfect tree. Those days were gone, but she had seen that a local club was selling evergreens in the bank's parking lot.

Where had she put that box of decorations—the one they had brought from the apartment in Lexington? Before they moved, she had carefully packed the treasures from her childhood and Rick's, too. She had also included a few new things they had purchased together. She felt sure the box was on that big shelf in the bedroom closet. She would ask Rick to get them down when he came.

Will that be before or after you drop your little bombshell? she asked herself, going to the refrigerator and pouring a glass of orange juice. Since she had been pregnant—there, she had said it!—she hadn't been able to stand the thought of cola. It was a wonder Rick hadn't noticed. It had always been her custom to begin the day with a Coke or Pepsi. Now she drank orange juice, tea, or milk, and she didn't even like milk! The baby was already running her life.

How am I going to tell him? she thought again. She wished she had brought Mrs. Sims's rocking chair home with her. Then she could sit there knitting little booties to ease him into her news. "If I could knit," she added sarcastically.

Hearing Rick's key in the lock, she set the orange juice on the counter and hurried back to the fireplace, her heart pounding in her throat. Her head began to spin, and she dropped quickly to her former seat on the hearth.

"I'm home, Toots!" he called. "Come see what I've got!"

"In here, Rick," she said, afraid to stand. But as he came into the room, she rose to her feet quickly, surprise covering her face.

"It's some kind of fir, like we used to have back home in

Philadelphia. I'd forgotten how good they smell," Rick said, standing the small evergreen tree up on end. He was looking at the tree as her words came pouring out.

"Rick, we're—I'm going to have a baby," she blurted as she burst into tears and covered her eyes with both hands to shut out the frozen look on his face.

She heard the tree hit the floor with a thump, but except for the hissing of the flames beside her, there was no other sound. At least she hadn't heard the door open and shut, so apparently he was still standing there.

Finally, he cleared his throat. "You're having a baby," he repeated. It was a flat statement, not a question.

Charlie knew he was trying to come to terms with her startling announcement. She couldn't blame him for that. Her own acceptance of the fact had been a battle. She removed her hands from her eyes and looked up at him, but he was staring out the window, his back to her. The silence grew until she felt she couldn't stand it any longer.

"I'm so sorry, Rick!" she sobbed. "I didn't mean for it to happen. I just—"

She could sense the effort he was making to adjust to her news. Finally, he turned and crossed the space between them and pulled her up from the hearth and into his arms. He held her against his chest for a few moments until her sobs eased into a quiet sniffling. Then he let her go, just enough to brush the tears from her face with the tips of his fingers.

"Well, Toots, there's no need to cry," he said. "We're having a baby, and that's that. We'll just have to 'drop back and punt,' as my old football coach used to say. You'll need a lighter schedule at the paper, and I guess we'll need to rethink our plans to buy that weekly. Our baby must come first. Is it a 'he' or a 'she'?

What does the doctor say?"

"I don't know what it is, Rick," she answered. "I haven't even been to the doctor yet. But I've taken the test three times, and it is definitely positive. Then there's the nausea and fainting."

Rick drew her close again. "I'm so sorry, Charlie," he whispered into her hair. "You've been miserable, and I've been too self-absorbed to notice."

"You told me from the beginning to make sure we didn't start a family until we were ready!" she cried. "Now all our plans are ruined. Rick, I wouldn't blame you if you walked out," she choked, the tears beginning to overflow again.

"Out?" he repeated. "What are you talking about? We're having a baby. It's mine, too, you know. It's not what I wanted at this stage of the game, but we'll just have to deal with it—together."

Relief swept over her. He was reacting just like Mrs. Sims had said he would. Suddenly, she remembered the dining room suite. "We don't have room here for a baby, Rick, even if we don't buy Mrs. Sims's dining room suite."

He looked around critically. "This open area between the living room and the kitchen is not a good place for a baby's room," he agreed. "There's no way to shut out noise, no way to hide—whatever it is babies need that should be hidden—diaper holders and whatever," he finished lamely. "I suppose we could squeeze a baby bed into our bedroom, but our so-called master bathroom probably won't accommodate even an extra can of baby powder. What do they put on babies nowadays?"

"Rick, what are we going to do?" she asked, swiping impatiently at the tears that wouldn't stop now that they had started.

"Hey, Toots," he admonished, "no more tears! We'll just have to cope until we can sell this place and find something bigger that we can afford. How long before the baby gets here?"

"Maybe seven months," she answered.

"Well, he—or she—can camp out in our bedroom for a while. We'll work it out, sweetheart," he assured her. Then he grinned, and she was glad to see the grin travel upward to sparkle in his eyes. "It might have helped, though, if I'd caught you reading Dr. Spock or knitting baby things. I might have been a little better prepared for your news."

"I thought about it," she said and grinned. "But I can't knit, for one thing, and my sister never used Spock. She's always depended on Dr. James Dobson as her guide in raising children."

"Call your sister," he suggested. "Call Dr. Dobson! We're going to need all the help we can get."

"I'll call Mrs. Sims first and tell her we won't be taking the dining room set," she said, moving toward the phone.

"Charlie, wait. Let's buy the dining room set," he said eagerly. "Let's go on with our plans to entertain. And how about calling my folks and have them come for Christmas dinner so we can make the big announcement. They'll be so excited!"

"But, Rick, where would we put them?" she protested, panic rising at the thought of his parents so closely underfoot while she tried to cope with nausea and all the needs at the paper.

"Charlie, they can afford to stay at the hotel. They won't mind. I'm their only hope for grandchildren, you know."

She leaned against him. "I love you, Richard Justice," she whispered.

"I love you, too," he answered. "Now pick up that phone and tell Mrs. Sims we'll take that dining room set. It will fit, won't it?"

"All but the china cabinet," she said, "but we don't need it."

"Call her!" he insisted.

She got the ad from her purse, picked up the phone, and punched in the numbers. Finally, she hung up. "There's no answer," she informed him.

"It can wait," he said. "Let's decorate this Christmas tree. Then we'll have some eggnog while we admire it."

Her stomach rolled at the thought of eggnog. "Maybe some popcorn," she suggested. "We don't have any eggnog, but I'm pretty sure the ornaments are on that top shelf in the upstairs closet."

As he took the stairs two at a time, she dialed Mrs. Sims's number again, hearing it ring and ring without answer. *Where can she be?* Charlie wondered. "I hope nothing has happened to Mrs. Sims," she told Rick. "She's more than eighty years old and living in that old house alone."

Maybe she's visiting Dolly Farney, she told herself, *or her son.* Charlie thought she recalled Mrs. Sims saying she had a son. *I'll try again later,* she promised, turning to explore the box of decorations Rick had set on the hearth. She was so happy to be here with him, getting ready to decorate their Christmas tree, looking forward to the holidays together.

Chapter 11

Mary Martha Sims could hear the phone ringing in the kitchen, but she couldn't get up from where she lay at the foot of the stairs. Excruciating pain shot through her left hip when she tried to move, and her head throbbed mercilessly.

"What a stupid thing to do!" she scolded aloud. If only she had held more tightly to the banister, been less careless about where she placed her foot, the accident might have been averted. But Mary Martha knew it would do no good to keep going over it in her mind. She was in serious trouble—alone, no way to reach a phone. She folded her arm to cradle her aching head, knowing it might be days before anyone thought to check on her.

What day is it? she wondered. The pastor's wife wouldn't come until next Tuesday to take her to Kroger's. Meanwhile, if she didn't show up at church on Sunday morning, Dolly might try to reach her. Dolly didn't come every Sunday, though. Sometimes, she went with her son to his church. P.T. would call on Sunday afternoon. That was a sure thing, and when she didn't answer the phone, surely he would come to check on her. How many hours of pain and helplessness lay between now and then?

"Mother Sims, I'm so sorry P.T. slid down the banister and fell into your Grecian urn. Yes, I know it cannot be replaced, but aren't you glad he wasn't hurt? Just that little cut on his chin." She held out her hands in a plea for understanding. *"He's just a little boy! He needs space. He needs to be able to make noise sometimes. And Olivia needs to have friends over once in a while. Please, Mother Sims!"*

I must have passed out, she thought, hearing the phone ringing again. She had to get to it! But when she tried to move, the intense pain in her hip made her cry out. Then she felt the blackness closing over her again.

"Parker," she said, *"could we please have a home of our own? It wouldn't have to be new or fancy—just a little cottage somewhere, just us and the children."*

She knew the answer before she heard his words. "This is our home, Mary Martha. My grandfather built this house. It is my heritage. It is our children's heritage."

"But, Parker," she pleaded, *"our children need a place to run and play. Our little boy needs a fenced-in yard where he can have a puppy. Our little girl needs a place to have tea parties with her friends. I need a kitchen where I can make cookies and pot flowers for the windowsill!"*

"What is wrong with you?" Parker asked angrily. *"We have a lovely home here. Mother has bent over backwards to make us welcome, to see that we are well-fed and comfortable."*

"I can't live like this anymore," she burst out, *"with the unreasonable restraints and those condemning eyes watching everything the children and I do! Please, Parker!"*

She flinched at the narrowing of his eyes, though he had never actually hit her. "You are my wife, Mary Martha," he said coldly. *"You will do as I say. And you will not be rude or ungrateful to my mother."*

She knew that was his final answer.

The phone was ringing again. She had to answer it. Parker would be furious if he missed a business call because of her neglect. She tried to get up, then fell back before the fierce onslaught of pain. This time she welcomed the blackness.

Chapter 12

It's nearly ten o'clock, Rick, and Mrs. Sims still isn't answering her phone," Charlie said. "I'm worried about her."

"Do you want me to drive you over there to check on her?" he offered. "I don't think you should go alone. If something is wrong, you could need help."

She didn't argue. Grabbing her jacket, she followed him out to the five-year-old gray Chrysler Rick's father had passed on to them when he bought his new one. She got in on the passenger's side and fastened the seat belt.

"I can't imagine where she could be," Charlie worried as Rick drove the fifteen miles from Olde Towne to Progress. "I'm so afraid she's had a stroke or a heart attack or maybe a fall down those steep, dark stairs."

"Don't borrow trouble, Charlie," he advised. "Maybe she fell asleep and didn't hear the phone. You said she's over eighty. Maybe her hearing isn't so good."

"It seemed fine to me. But she's frail. I'll bet she doesn't weigh ninety pounds. She's bright, though. I really like her, Rick."

"I'm looking forward to meeting her," he said, stopping for the stoplight in Progress.

"Turn left at that next street," Charlie directed. "It's just a few blocks down that way, on the left."

When Rick pulled to the curb in front of the familiar brick house, Charlie hurried out of the car and up the walk. She twisted the old-fashioned doorbell and heard it shrill through the house. "Mrs. Sims!" she called. "Mrs. Sims, are you here? It's Charlie—Charlene!" She listened hopefully for a response but heard nothing except the distant sound of traffic and, a few blocks over, the frenzied barking of a dog. The light was on in the hall, and she bent to peer through the clear spaces of the etched tulip in the front door.

"Oh, Rick!" she cried. "Call 911! She's there on the floor at the foot of the stairs! She's not moving!" She turned the doorknob and pushed against it, but the locked door was thick and strong. She heard Rick talking into his cell phone, asking for an ambulance, giving the address. "Mrs. Sims!" she called again. "Can you hear me? Hang on! We're getting help."

Charlie knew it couldn't have been more than a few minutes before the ambulance came screaming down the street, lights flashing. But it seemed like hours as she stood there praying for some sign of life from the small, crumpled heap beyond the locked door.

Was I praying? she wondered in amazement. Charlie hadn't prayed in years! She had tossed faith into a closet with other outgrown childhood fantasies—Santa Claus, the Easter Bunny, the Tooth Fairy. Like the modern young woman she was, Charlie had learned to depend on her own wits and strength. At this moment, though, she knew they were hopelessly inadequate. She needed something—Someone—more powerful than she was.

Two uniformed EMTs rushed onto the stoop. "Stand back,

ma'am, while we open this door," one of them warned. Then they had the door open and were kneeling over the small, still figure.

"I've got a pulse!" one of them exclaimed. "Let's get her out of here!"

Charlie's breath caught on a sob of relief as she watched the men wheel Mrs. Sims out of the house and lift her into the ambulance. Her head began to swim, and she clutched her husband's arm, but she refused to faint. "I'm going with her," she said so firmly that no one argued with her, not even Rick.

"I'll follow in the car," he said.

Then she was in the ambulance, holding Mrs. Sims's limp hand, pleading silently but earnestly with God for the old woman's life. *I've been arrogant and foolish!* she confessed. *I wouldn't blame you for writing me off, but Mrs. Sims trusts in You. She told me that You have never let her down.*

Charlie swiped futilely at the tears running down her cheeks. *Please, God, don't let her down now!* she begged as the ambulance pulled up to the hospital's emergency entrance and the EMTs whisked Mrs. Sims inside.

Chapter 13

Mary Martha Sims opened her eyes and looked around. "Where am I?" she asked. Then, if her head hadn't hurt so badly, she would have laughed. Wasn't that the classic line of every fainting movie heroine since silent films?

Had she simply fainted? No, she remembered now. She had fallen down the stairs and passed out from the pain. She struggled to see her legs. She was sure she had broken something, probably her hip. That was where the terrible pain had been. It didn't hurt so badly now. Maybe she was drifting on some cloud of medication.

Judging by all the tubes and monitors, I must be in the hospital, Mary Martha thought, *but how did I get here? How on earth did anyone know I was lying there at the foot of the stairs? Did the good Lord send an angel to rescue me?*

"It's about time you woke up," Charlie said, coming into the room. "How do you feel?"

"I've felt better," Mary Martha responded wryly. "How did I get here?"

"I kept trying to call you about the dining room suite. When you didn't answer, Rick and I drove over to check on you," she explained. "When I saw you lying in a heap on the floor, we called 911."

"So you're the angel!" Mary Martha said, giving a weak grin and sinking back against the pillows. "Has anyone called P.T.? Don't bother calling Olivia. It's so hard for her to get away. I'll tell her about it later."

"Your son is on his way," Rick said, joining them. "I'm Rick Justice," he added, "and I'm very glad to meet you, Mrs. Sims."

Mary Martha threw a questioning glance at Charlie and received a reassuring smile in return. Then it came to her. *Charlene must have told him about the baby,* she thought. *I knew it would be all right.* "I'm glad to meet you, too, Mr. Justice. I've heard a lot about you," she said.

"I'll bet you have," he said with a grin, "but I promise to do better."

"Out! Out! Out!" a nurse commanded, bustling around the bed, straightening covers and plumping pillows. "This lady just came back from hip surgery. She doesn't need company! You can come back in the morning."

"Go on," Mary Martha said. "I'll be okay. Thank you so much for rescuing me. I thought I might lie there for hours, maybe even days, but I should have had more faith." She wanted to say more, but her eyes just wouldn't stay open. "Call Dolly," she managed to get out before sleep took over.

She didn't even know when Charlie and Rick left, or when P.T. and Eleanor arrived. She thought she heard the nurse say, "I'll call you if she needs you."

I don't need anybody or anything, she thought, floating in a euphoria of warmth and love. "The eternal God is my refuge," she murmured, "and underneath are the everlasting arms."

Chapter 14

Charlie Justice, holding a magazine and a small pot of pink azaleas, stopped just outside the closed door of the hospital room.

"No, ma'am, you cannot go home by yourself," she heard the doctor say emphatically.

"I will not impose upon my son and daughter-in-law or anybody else for that matter," she heard Mrs. Sims answer just as emphatically.

"Then you will have to go into an extended care facility until you're able to wait on yourself. It could take six to eight weeks, and then you may still have to walk with a walker or a three-pronged cane. You had a clean break, but at your age, Mrs. Sims—"

"I know, doctor," Mary Martha broke in, "old bones take longer to heal."

"Exactly!" the doctor said with a laugh.

I wish I could take care of her, Charlie thought, surprised at the depth of her feelings. She knew, though, with her schedule at the paper, it was impossible. *Maybe I could stay with her at night and someone else could take the day shift,* she thought.

That would leave Rick alone at night, and evening was

about the only time they had together, with their scattered work assignments. Of course, he could come with her, but she doubted that he would want to take on the extra commuting between the towns. Still, she hated to think of Mrs. Sims going to a nursing home.

"I can arrange for the Home Health people to come in once a day to help with baths and meals once you graduate to a walker," the doctor was saying. "Do you have to climb those stairs?"

"What are they talking about?" a voice asked beside her.

Charlie turned to see a plump woman she finally identified as Dolly Farney. Her hair was a dark silver now, the purple nearly gone.

"Mrs. Sims wants to go home, and the doctor is forbidding it," Charlie explained, still fascinated by the change in the woman's looks. "I like your hair," she said. "It's very becoming."

Dolly laughed. "I promised Mary Martha if she came to our luncheon, I would let her beautician do my hair. Mary Martha hates that purple." She chuckled, and Charlie smiled noncommittally. "The color is hard to control when you do it yourself," Dolly added. "I like this silver, though. I can't really afford it, but why not? 'I'm worth it!' " she said haughtily, in such a good imitation of the TV ad that Charlie laughed.

"Anyway, that's what I came to talk with her about," Dolly said, moving on into the room. "Mrs. Sims is going home with me, Doc," she said, "as soon as she can get in and out of bed without me lifting her."

"Dolly, I will not!" Charlie heard Mrs. Sims protest. "I just told this stubborn doctor that I will not impose on anybody. I took care of Mother Sims for several years after she had her stroke, and I know how hard it is to be the caregiver for an invalid."

Dolly snorted. "If you were as mean as that old woman, I wouldn't take you! By the way, how do you like my hair?"

Charlie saw Mrs. Sims eyes widen in disbelief. "It looks great!" she said. "Jayne did it, didn't she?"

Dolly nodded. "When can I take her home, Doc?" she asked.

"We can probably release her before Christmas Eve," he answered. "Nobody likes to hang around a hospital at Christmas."

"Dolly Farney, I am not going to spend two months cooped up in that little cracker box apartment of yours, with you having to wait on me hand and foot!" Mary Martha protested.

"*Hummph!* You are helpless and at my mercy," Dolly said. Then they both burst into giggles.

Just like two little girls, Charlie thought in amazement. It was a side of Mrs. Sims she had not seen, and she doubted that it was allowed to surface very often.

Apparently, Dolly was good for her. Didn't the Bible say something about laughter doing good like a medicine?

"You cranky old woman!" Dolly said, when she could stop laughing.

"You're older than I am!" Mary Martha snapped.

"But I'm not as cranky as you are," Dolly shot back at her. Then they went off into another spasm of giggles.

"Well, ladies, I'll leave you to settle this between you," the doctor said, backing toward the door. "Just remember, Mrs. Sims, you are not going home alone, and that's my final word on it." He turned quickly and left the room.

"She's going home with me, Doc," Dolly called after him.

"I am not!" Charlie thought Mrs. Sims would have stomped her foot if she could. "I am not sleeping with you in that little twin bed when I've got four big empty ones at home."

"Mary Martha Sims, I was planning to sleep on the couch!" Dolly said indignantly. Then she added, "But if you've got all those empty beds, then I'll just go home with you."

"And you'll be the next to fall down the stairs and break something," Mary Martha predicted. "All the beds but mine are upstairs."

"Mrs. Sims," Charlie broke in, "that sounds like a wonderful idea. Maybe Rick and your son could move a bed downstairs. There'll be plenty of room in the dining room when we take out the dining set. And I could come over and stay on Friday nights and Saturdays until I have to go in to work and help with the Sunday edition. That would give Mrs. Farney a chance to go home for a while. It's only for a couple of months."

"Sounds good to me," Dolly agreed eagerly. "How about you, old cranky?" she asked.

Charlie saw Mrs. Sims take a deep breath. "Between the two of you, what choice do I have? But I always pay my way. I won't let either of you do it for nothing," she vowed.

"All right," Dolly agreed quickly. "You can pay Jayne to do my hair for the next two months."

"Gladly!" Mary Martha said. "I couldn't stand being waited on by a purple prune!"

Charlie laughed with them this time. "Well, I need to get back to the newspaper," she said, setting the magazine and the flowers on the bedside table. "Call me if the doctor dismisses you before I get back, and I'll drive you home."

"Thank you, dear," Mary Martha said, "but since I can't bend this monster of a cast, I don't think I could get into that little car of yours. I suppose I'll have to go back the way I came—in an ambulance."

Charlie nodded. "Then I'll follow you and make sure you're all settled in until Mrs. Farney gets there."

As she bent over the bed to give Mary Martha a hug, she was almost sure she saw a glimmer of tears in the woman's dark eyes. She swallowed the lump gathering in her own throat. *It's amazing how much I've come to care for this little old lady in such a short time!* she thought.

Maybe I was meant to get to know Mrs. Sims, she thought as she left the hospital. *With my parents gone and Rick's so far away, our baby is going to need a grandmother.*

Chapter 15

There's been more laughter echoing through this empty old house in the few hours since Dolly's been here than it has known in all its history, Mary Martha Sims thought, carefully maneuvering herself and the burdensome cast from the bed to her new motorized wheelchair. And she certainly hadn't been lonely! *I almost miss the peaceful solitude,* she thought.

Dolly had been so good to come and stay with her. She couldn't imagine how she would have managed without her, and Charlene and Rick had become like her own children. Grandchildren, she supposed she should say. Or maybe great-grandchildren. She wasn't sure that either of them had turned thirty yet.

Soon I'll have a new little great-great-grandchild to rock in Granny's rocker, she thought as she wheeled herself down the hallway and into the kitchen.

"You're getting pretty good with that chariot," Dolly said when she saw her. "Are you ready for lunch? The pastor's wife brought us a pot of brown beans and a salad, and I've made some herb corn bread. A little sage and basil make all the difference." She opened the oven door and peeked inside. "It should be ready in about ten minutes."

"It smells wonderful!" Mary Martha said. "Why didn't Mrs. Tanner come in to see me?"

"You were asleep, and she didn't want to wake you," Dolly answered. "How's the pain?"

"Bearable. I'm not taking any more pain medication until bedtime," she added. "I have to taper off of the drugs sometime. Did Rick and P.T. get your bed moved down here okay?"

"Oh, yes, and a little chest of drawers to hold my things," Dolly said. "Since Charlie and Rick took that huge old dining room set, there's room for three beds in there!"

Mary Martha gave her friend a satisfied smile.

"You had a call about the piano, too," Dolly said. "A man's coming to look at it the day after Christmas," Dolly said, taking the pan of corn bread from the oven. "It's hard to believe it's Christmas Eve already!"

"I don't think I've ever had brown beans and corn bread on Christmas Eve," Mary Martha said.

"Well, it's time you lived a little, girl!" Dolly laughed. "Anyway, we've had turkey and all the trimmings twice this past week, and you'll probably have it again tomorrow at P.T.'s and Eleanor's."

"P.T. and Eleanor have a country ham. I sent it to them. There'll be oysters, too." Mary Martha shuddered. "I never touch those slimy things!"

"I like 'em scalloped," Dolly said, sliding corn bread onto one of Mother Sims's best dessert plates, "but I only eat the dressing around 'em. Bob and Peggy will have both ham and turkey and cranberry sauce made from scratch. What I'm looking forward to, though, is Peggy's jam cake with caramel icing so rich it'll curl your toes! Peggy's a good cook."

"Eleanor always has a raspberry trifle for dessert," Mary

Martha said, "with real whipped cream to top it."

"Are the kids coming in this year?" Dolly asked, ladling beans into two of Mother Sims's best china bowls.

I'm not going to say a word, Mary Martha vowed. *If they get broken, they get broken. Who's left to care?*

"No, one of the great-grandchildren is expecting any minute, so none of them are making the trip," she answered. Dolly placed the bowls on two cheery Christmas placemats that had appeared on the small walnut table under the window.

"Both our grandsons are going to their wives' homes for Christmas," Dolly said, adding two small plates of congealed salad and a dish of green tomato relish to the table. "It will just be Bob and Peggy, Peggy's mother, and me this year. I'll be back over here early, probably before you get back. Do you think you can ride in P.T.'s car with that cast?"

"The backseat of that Lincoln has room for the kitchen sink if I wanted to take it!" Mary Martha said, easing her wheelchair under the table's raised leaf.

Mary Martha bowed her head while Dolly offered thanks. Then they ate hungrily and in silence for several minutes. Dinner was over, and the ladies were sipping their second cup of tea when the doorbell rang. Dolly went to answer it and came back followed by Charlie Justice.

"Merry Christmas, Mrs. Sims!" the young woman said, dropping a kiss on the top of her head. "I brought you two some pecan cake."

"Thank you, dear. Just put it on the counter," Mary Martha suggested, "and we'll eat it later. Right now we're full of beans!"

Charlie laughed. "You two are always full of beans!"

"And corn bread today," Dolly added, dumping dirty dishes into the sink.

Mary Martha's heart sank at the unmistakable sound of something breaking. "Oops!" Dolly said.

Mary Martha closed her eyes, waiting for the expected rebuke. Then, realizing that there was no one to give it, she grinned. "Merry Christmas, Mother Sims!" she said.

"I'm sorry," Dolly offered. "I think I can glue it back together."

"Throw it out," Mary Martha said. "There's plenty more where that came from. Would you like some beans and corn bread, Charlene?" she asked.

She was surprised to see the young woman turn pale and drop into the rocking chair.

"Oh, oh!" Dolly said. "Been there and done that!"

Chapter 16

C harlie Justice felt better now, but she stayed in the rocker, the spell of its ancient rhythm relaxing her taut nerves. She sensed the pleasant memories of mothers and babies past who had taken comfort from its soothing motion.

Suddenly, she felt a quickening inside her. She sat up and placed both feet firmly on the floor. *It can't be the baby!* she thought. *Too early for that!* Charlie sank back against the cushion. Her feet began to push against the floor, rocking the chair of their own volition, and she felt a warmth spreading through her. She knew her baby hadn't moved. But it was there, alive and growing, an infinitesimal but very real little person. Bemused, she looked up at Mary Martha, who was watching her with a soft, remembering smile.

"What did you say you want for this rocker?" Charlie asked.

"I've changed my mind about that," Mary Martha answered curtly. "I'm not going to sell Granny's rocker." She saw Charlie's eager expression melt into disappointment.

"Oh," she said. "Well, I can understand why you wouldn't want to part with it."

"I'm going to part with it," Mary Martha explained. "I'm just not going to sell it." She smiled. "It's yours, dear. I hope you and your little one will spend many happy hours in it."

"But, Mrs. Sims," Charlie began. "I can't—"

"I told you I always pay my way," Mary Martha interrupted. "Of course, its monetary value is little, but that chair is rich in love and tradition. I can't think of anyone I'd rather see have it than you."

"I'll help you get it into your car," Dolly offered. "Take it before the old grouch changes her mind!" she added, smiling fondly at Mary Martha.

A few minutes later, Mary Martha sat in her wheelchair on the front walk, watching her Granny's chair ride down the street under the tied-down trunk lid of Charlie's little white car.

Suddenly, she understood why Parker had felt so strongly about the Sims house. *It had been his anchor to the world, his place mark in the epic of human life,* she thought, feeling a sharp twinge of loneliness as the chair disappeared around the corner.

She couldn't help feeling that some kind of progress had been made here this afternoon, though. She wasn't sure what it was. But at least she no longer felt guilty about getting rid of the things that had belonged to Mother Sims.

She turned quickly and looked at the house, as though fearing it had read her thoughts and would tattle. The house stared back—austere, forbidding. But Mary Martha realized with amazement that it no longer had any power over her, not even to make her feel bitter toward Mother Sims for her unrelenting oppression, not even toward Parker for making her live there all those years.

She moved slowly up the walk, steering the chair carefully around the sunken place. She supposed that she could live in the house for another sixty years without ever spending one comfortable day in it. Truthfully, it was just a dank, dark, old house filled with things that had outlasted those who valued them.

Dolly seems so comfortable in her nice little apartment down at the Senior Citizens' Center, she thought as her friend helped her maneuver the chair up onto the low stoop.

Mary Martha reached for the doorknob, then paused with her hand in midair. Parker never would have wanted her to sell the house.

She smiled, turned the knob, and wheeled into the dimness of the entry. *Parker is gone,* she thought, *and the house really is too big for me.*

WANDA LUTTRELL

Wanda was born and raised in Franklin County, Kentucky, where she lives with her husband, John. She is the mother of five grown children and was employed for nearly thirty years by the Kentucky Association of School Administrators.

Wanda's writing has appeared in various Christian and general publications. Her interest in local Kentucky history eventually led her to write several books with themes from the Bluegrass State, including *The Legacy of Drennan's Crossing*, *In the Shadow of the White Rose*, and the Sarah's Journey series.

My True Love Gave to Me. . .

by Christine Lynxwiler

Dedication

To *my* favorite author, Tracey Bateman, who took time to read this for me every time I revised, even though she was on a killer deadline. I couldn't have made it without you cheering me on, Trace. There's never been a truer friend.

To Kevin, for always helping me find my way home when I'm lost in the dark.

And finally, to everyone who reaches out to others, whether through an organized volunteer program or individually. You're an inspiration to me.

Special thanks and appreciation to: Lynette, Jan, Pam, Susie, Susan, Rachel, Jen, Nancy, and Sandy. What would I do without you all? Hugs to the ACRWers who so readily shared their RVing experiences with me!

*"Command those who are rich in this present world
not to be arrogant nor to put their hope in wealth,
which is so uncertain, but to put their hope in God,
who richly provides us with everything for our enjoyment.
Command them to do good, to be rich in good deeds,
and to be generous and willing to share."*
1 Timothy 6:17–18

Chapter 1

. . . The Key to a Borrowed RV

I gritted my teeth and shifted the cardboard box against the spindly pull-down attic ladder. Whoever invented these contraptions obviously hadn't considered that people would be going up and down the narrow steps with their arms full.

Of course, I could be transferring my aggravation to some nameless inventor instead of placing the blame where it belonged—squarely on the shoulders of my beloved husband with his recent mysterious attitude.

"The—" I pressed the side of my face against the cardboard, clutching my burden tightly, in spite of the dust particles crawling up my nose. "—very—" I lowered one foot, tapping air until I found the next step. It would be a disaster to fall with this box. "—idea!" I jumped off the last step and landed with a thud, gripping my priceless cargo.

For sixteen years, Thanksgiving afternoon at the Lassiters had meant one thing—putting up the Christmas tree.

I set the old box carefully on the hardwood floor in the

den and stared at the words I'd written the year Phillip and I had married—*Fragile: Christmas Ornaments.* On the corner of the box, where I always denoted our storage containers with such titles as *Summer* or *Winter* or *Open When Amanda Turns Ten,* I had printed *Thanksgiving Day.* Even then, at the ripe old age of twenty, I never left anything to chance. Spell it out. No beating around the bush.

No doubt about it; today was the day.

So why had my husband, who loved Christmas as much as I did, announced cryptically at breakfast that instead of putting up the tree this afternoon he had something else planned? Granted, he'd been acting strange for at least a week, but his proclamation had thrown my whole day off-kilter. And then he'd driven off after lunch to take his parents home without another word about it.

"Mom, I can't find today's paper!" The yell from the living room settled my pounding heart some. The kids obviously hadn't paid much attention to their dad's announcement. This very minute fourteen-year-old Amanda and twelve-year-old Seth were scouring the house for catalogs, sales flyers, and every merchandising media they could get their hands on.

I have my traditions. . .they have theirs. While Phillip and I wrangle with the tree, they make long Christmas wish lists.

I smiled, remembering how those lists evolved from a four-year-old's childishly scrawled T-R-U-C-K or D-O-L-L to a certain brand-name DVD/VCR player—right down to the model number, the store that had it on sale, and what day the sale ended. When it came to Christmas, my children were like me. They left nothing to chance.

I grabbed a fluffy towel from the bathroom to lay the

ornaments on while I arranged them for hanging. Phillip always laughed at my ceremonious "spreading of the towel." A twinge of guilt shot through me. *Maybe I should wait and see what he has to say when he gets home.*

No, if I forged ahead and got a jump-start on things, then hopefully whatever Phillip had in mind wouldn't take long. We'd be back on schedule by supper. Never let it be said that Penny Lassiter couldn't compromise.

I settled on my knees and reverently opened the flaps of the box. The slightly musty smell wafted up to me like a comfortable old friend.

Each ornament, wrapped in tissue paper, nestled into its own little section of the eggcrate cardboard dividers I'd long ago modified for this purpose. Just as it did every year on this day, anticipation fluttered in my stomach. My excitement pushed away any lingering doubts about Phillip's strange behavior.

I carefully lifted the first treasure, unwrapped the tissue, and stared at the brittle gingerbread man. A childhood memory leaped into my mind, replaying in video-clip fashion. I ran my finger along the word "Penny" roughly engraved on the tummy above the date.

What a shock it had been to see this homemade clay ornament instead of the collectible one my parents normally bought for my sisters and me. An uneasy feeling had crept into my ten-year-old heart that day, and my mom's pleading smile confirmed that the gingerbread man was a precursor of things to come.

That same uneasy feeling, only slightly more grown-up, had visited me again six weeks ago when Phillip came home with news of his company downsizing. He'd been let go. I didn't doubt he'd find another job. He's a wonderful accountant. But one of the first things I thought of was that if it didn't happen soon, we'd have no money for Christmas.

As he'd checked out the want ads, I'd remembered the year I was ten. There'd been a bad drought, and my parents had almost lost the farm. Of course, I didn't realize that then. All I knew was that I received a homemade ornament instead of the normal store-bought kind, a hand-knitted hat, scarf, and matching gloves instead of the hoped-for alarm clock radio. The new bicycle I'd wanted looked suspiciously like my sister's old one, only with fresh red paint. My sisters hadn't fared any better.

With Phillip's termination notice clutched in my hand, I couldn't keep from fretting. In spite of my best intentions, for the first time in their lives, would our kids have a disappointing Christmas? And, horror of horrors, would I have to learn to knit?

Thankfully, God worked it out. Phillip ended up with a six-month severance pay package, and before his thirty days' notice was up a few days ago, he'd secured an even better job with a new company. Instead of learning to knit, I'd been able to start my shopping early. Then came the most wonderful news of all—Phillip wouldn't begin the new position until January. I'd have him around every day to help make this Christmas the best ever.

Shaking the unhappy might-have-beens from my mind, I removed the tissue paper from the next ornament. A small crystal heart with an etching of a couple in a horse-drawn sleigh proclaimed *Our First Christmas Together.* I held it up to the light. We'd married December 19, and Phillip had given this to me on our honeymoon. We'd just been two crazy kids in love. Ever since that day, this had been my favorite ornament.

"Penny! What are you doing?"

I jerked at the sound of Phillip's voice, and the heart slipped from my fingers. I lunged to catch it. For an agonizing second, my fingertip touched the slick surface, but my hands came together grasping air. The most precious ornament I owned crashed to the hardwood floor and shattered into pieces.

"Oh, no." Phillip rushed over and knelt beside me. "Honey, I'm so sorry." He put his arm around my shoulders, but I didn't move.

I stared at the tiny crystal slivers and blinked back the tears. I'd always taken great pride in my belief that people were more important than possessions. "It's okay."

"No, it's not." He gathered me into his arms.

I relaxed for a minute against him, in an embrace as familiar to me as my own face in the mirror. At least this accident seemed to have chased away the stranger I'd been living with the last few days. My Phillip was back. Snuggled close to his heart, the smell of his soap filled my senses. I'd been right. People *were* more important than things.

I kept my head against his chest. "Will you have time to get the tree down before we do whatever you have planned for this afternoon?" Was it my imagination, or had his heartbeat quickened under my ear?

He pulled me to my feet. "We need to talk." My stomach flip-flopped as I followed him toward the sofa. This bore an eerie resemblance to the scene my friend Kathy had described when her husband had told her he was leaving her for another woman.

"The kids, too?" I nodded toward the thumping around

upstairs, where Seth and Amanda were, no doubt, still gathering catalogs. If he wanted a divorce, he wouldn't want the kids there when he told me.

"I want to talk to you alone first."

Fighting the urge to run screaming from the room, I sat beside him on the sofa. A strange mix of determination and fear lurked in his blue eyes.

"Before you say anything," I stammered, my own heart hammering now, "I know things have been odd around here the last couple of months. You lost your job, and your dad had that heart attack. Thankfully, both ended up okay, but still, it was stressful for all of us. Now, the kids are just getting over their school problems and settling into homeschooling, and we're focused on the holidays. Plus, we're not used to having you home during the day."

I held up my hand and shook my head. That hadn't come out right. "Not that we don't like it. We do."

Fresh tears filled my eyes at the sympathetic look on his face. Phillip knew I babbled when I was nervous, and he'd always been very tenderhearted. If he was feeling sorry for me, it wasn't a good sign. "Phillip Seth Lassiter, don't you dare tell me you've fallen in love with a Peace Corps volunteer and are running away with her to live in a third-world country!"

Phillip burst out laughing. When he leaned across and hugged me, I clung to him like he was the last item on the shelf at Wal-Mart's day-after-Thanksgiving sale.

"My sweet, precious, hilarious Penny. You make it worth getting out of bed every day. Any man would be crazy to leave that."

Relief shot through me, fast and sharp. I grabbed his hand,

squeezing it tight. "You scared me to death! Don't ever do that again."

"Well, my surprise does involve travel."

All this suspense over a vacation? I sighed. From Thanksgiving to Christmas was a busy whirl of parties and activities, but we could squeeze in a short family vacation. A long weekend, for sure. Maybe even a whole week.

"So, tell me! Where are we going?"

"Hmm. . .lots of places." To my amazement, he reached under a home decorating book on the coffee table and pulled out a travel atlas. He flipped the cover open to the big U.S. map and laid it on my lap.

Visions of romantic cruises and weekend getaways fled from my mind. A trail, marked in red, jumped off the page, winding hundreds of miles through the middle of the United States. "How will we do that? Even in a week, there's no way."

"No, but in a little over a month we can."

"A little over a month?" Had he lost his mind?

"Oh, Pen. It's going to be great."

I hadn't seen his eyes sparkle like that in so long, for a minute I had the breathless feeling I used to get when we were dating.

"I borrowed Bob and Sylvia's RV. Since they ended their retirement and bought the shop, they never use it. We'll haul the Mazda behind it for around-town trips." He held up a key with a grin. "We'll leave Monday."

So this is what it's like when your husband has a midlife crisis. That sparkle in his eyes clearly indicated insanity. My breathless feeling edged toward hyperventilation.

"We'll plan to be home right after New Year's Day. That

will give us time to get settled in before I start my new job."

"Are you crazy?" My heart pounded, this time with anger instead of fear. "You expect me to miss Christmas with my folks?" A current of fury, strong enough to furnish power to our whole block, surged through my veins. I slapped the atlas, still open on my lap, and the sound reverberated through the room like a gunshot.

"Isn't that convenient? You wait until after I make Thanksgiving dinner for your parents before you spring this on me. We don't have to worry about letting *your* family down now." Heat flooded my face.

Richard and Janet Lassiter were like a second set of parents to me, and I knew Phillip felt the same way about my mom and dad. But I couldn't stop the hostile words. "Did you plan it that way?"

His face grew taut, but he didn't speak.

"Oh, Phillip." He knew how much I looked forward to Christmas. It wasn't just about spending the actual day with my folks. We'd also miss the weeks that led up to it—the delicious countdown to the big day. Why was he trying to spoil things for us? "What brought this on?"

"What brought this on is feeling like I barely know my kids." His eyes bore into mine. "And that they could care less whether I'm here or not, as long as I'm bringing home a paycheck so they can have the latest video game or the hottest fashion item."

The man who'd always laughingly compared me to a mama tiger with her cubs really should have known better than to insult my kids.

I slammed the atlas shut and threw it on the table, watching through tear-dimmed eyes as it slid off the other side and hit the carpet with a dull thud. "That's not true and you know it!" My voice trembled. Amanda and Seth loved their father, and they were good kids. All of our friends talked about how blessed Phillip and I were to have such well-behaved children.

"It's not just the kids, Pen." He held his hands out in a gesture I recognized as an attempt to soothe me, but his words had the opposite effect. "You don't have time to even look up when I walk in the room. Unless it's to ask me to get something from the attic or run to the store."

"So, you're pouting and ruining Christmas because you feel ignored?" Red-hot anger boiled in my stomach at his childishness.

"No." He shook his head. "You know you're better with words than I am. Maybe I'm not explaining it very well." He reached for my hand, but I brushed away a tear to avoid his touch. "I want us to rediscover Christmas, not ruin it. I want us to rediscover each other. . .and God."

"God?" I laughed, almost a sob. "Phillip, we go to church three times a week. We never miss. When someone dies, I take food. You mow the church lawn when it's your turn. We both teach Bible class. People depend on us. What will God think about that if we go off on your big adventure?" I slapped my palms on my thighs and jumped to my feet. "I don't get this."

"This is important to me, Penny." He shoved to his feet, as well, and looked down at me. His eyes, so sparkly before, just looked sad. Hurt. "How many times have I ever asked you to do something big for me?"

Shaking, I turned and strode to the window where the Christmas tree should be going up right this minute. With my back to my husband, I stared out at our perfectly manicured yard. Phillip took care of it even when he was working fifty hours a week.

Shame mingled with my blinding anger. He was right. In sixteen years, easygoing Phillip had never asked for anything except my love, which I'd always assured him he had. Had the time come for me to put my money where my mouth was?

Chapter 2

...Two Pouting Kids

"What do you say, Pen?"

I kept my back to him, tears stinging my eyes. "What *can* I say? It sounds like you've already decided."

"So you'll go?"

"Do I have a choice?" When we first married and I was learning what it meant for a wife to submit to her husband, every time we disagreed, I'd sarcastically pop off with, "Whatever you say. You're the boss." Phillip, trying to get the hang of loving his exasperating wife like he loved himself, would deflate before my eyes. I promised myself about five years into our marriage (okay, I'm a slow learner) that I'd never use that phrase again. And I hadn't. But, oh, how I wanted to now.

"We all have choices, Penny."

Really? Because, frankly, right now I don't see a plethora of options for me. "I'll go." I turned to face him.

Phillip's emotions were transparent. To me, at least. He

wanted to push me for more, but he was afraid to.

Wise man. But was it too little wisdom, too late?

"Good. When should we tell the kids?"

"No time like the present," I said through gritted teeth.

Apparently deciding again to take my words at face value, he yelled up the stairs, "Seth, Amanda, come down here for a minute. Your mother and I have something to tell you."

"*You* have something to tell them," I whispered fiercely. "I don't."

He just glared at me. We stood in silence by the window, and a minute later, Seth bounded into the room with the limitless energy of a preadolescent boy. His hair stood on end, and he waved an Electronic City sale flyer. "I've found the remote control car I want. It's a real drag racer, and there's a new track out—" Something about our expressions, or the way his dad and I stood, together yet apart, made him stop just inside the doorway. "What's up?"

Before we could reply, Amanda walked in, her arms filled with newspaper advertisements. She looked around the room. "Where's the tree?"

I stared out the window while Phillip told them his plan.

"I'm not going." Amanda threw the papers on the table and crossed her arms. "I'll stay with Emily."

I swung around to face her. Fat chance. Emily's parents thought fourteen was plenty old enough to be left alone at night. And if the girls wanted to go out, Emily's sixteen-year-old brother could drive them.

Before I could respond, Phillip squashed her plan. "This is not negotiable, Amanda. You *are* going."

She stared at him. I could almost see her looking at her

little finger and thinking, *When did my dad come unwrapped?* Then she did what any normal teenage girl does when things go wrong. She shot *me* a venomous look, spun on her heel, and ran up the stairs.

"She's gotten way too big for her britches," Phillip muttered after her dramatic exit.

Seth had been quiet after Phillip's announcement, but he'd apparently learned something by her show of defiance.

"Dad," he said softly, "I'm not sure I'm really up to camping. I haven't been over the flu that long. Maybe I should stay at Grandma's."

Oh! I'm not feeling so great either. Think Grandma could fit us both in? One look at Phillip's red face left little hope that Seth's approach was going to work any better than his sister's. Phillip didn't intend to make this trek alone.

"We're all going," Phillip said. He looked at me like he'd read my mind. "Every one of us."

Seth nodded and trudged up the stairs. Midway, he turned back. "What about our presents?"

What about your presents? What about your grandma and grandpa? And aunts and uncles and cousins? I screamed silently.

"We'll worry about presents when it gets closer to Christmas. There are stores on the road," Phillip answered.

Seth stomped up the stairs to his room and slammed his door.

∽

After the kids were in bed, Phillip came into the kitchen where I was unloading the dishwasher. "Ready for bed?"

I placed a Corelle bowl in the top rack. "Well, you know

I'll be heading out a little after five in the morning for the day-after sales. I thought I'd just sleep in the guest room so I won't wake you."

For a brief second, I wanted him to take me in his arms and tell me that he couldn't sleep without me next to him. We *never* slept apart unless someone was in the hospital.

He nodded.

Ever since he'd told me his crazy plan, he'd been like the little bobble-headed dog Amanda kept on her dresser. No matter what I said, he nodded. What had happened to the man who could charm the lemons off a lemon tree with his caring attitude?

Apparently that man was in hibernation.

Either that or he just didn't care anymore. Maybe he wanted to sleep alone. I slammed a fork into the silverware holder. Then there'd be no one to gripe when he kept his bed-side lamp on studying the travel atlas.

"Do you have an alarm in there?"

"Huh?" I looked up and realized he was still standing by the counter. For a second I thought he meant in the dish-washer. "Oh. In the guest room? Yeah."

"Is Vicky going with you in the morning?"

It was my turn to nod, so I did. Maybe he *was* trying to get up the nerve to ask me not to sleep in the other room. Because that question was a no-brainer. My baby sister (all right, so thirty doesn't exactly qualify as a baby, but in our family it counts) has gone with me to the after-Thanksgiving sales since the year Phillip and I married and Vicky was still in braces.

It was our own special pre-Christmas ritual. One that my mom and my older sister, Sandy, couldn't understand since they thought no early morning bargain was worth leaving a warm bed for, but Vicky and I loved the challenge. Thankfully, we lived in the same suburb of Little Rock, so neither of us had to drive far to keep our tradition.

Since Phillip still stood there silently, I decided to expound. "I'm going to pick her up."

He nodded. In sixteen years, we'd not nodded as much as we had tonight. Was this what couples did when they didn't talk? No wonder my chiropractor's waiting room was always full. Silent arguments had to be a strain on people's necks.

"Okay, y'all be careful. Good night." He swooped in for a kiss just as I put a plate in the bottom rack. He ended up connecting with my hair.

"Good night." When his footsteps faded away, I leaned against the counter. I could count on one hand the number of times we'd ever gone to bed angry. And even in those times, we always woke in the morning in the familiar spoon position. It was hard to stay mad when you were snuggled up against someone.

I reached for my vitamins and admitted something to myself. I *wanted* to stay mad at Phillip. I felt righteous in my anger, and it seemed almost as if getting over it would be wrong. I knew that was silly. *Behold—the convoluted reasoning of Penny Lassiter.*

My righteous anger made a poor bed partner. According to the law of thermostat control, every room in our house should have been the same temperature. But the guest room was like the inside of an ice cube.

When I finally drifted off to sleep, I instinctively scooted over to cuddle up to Phillip. Every time I'd move from my warm spot into the wasteland of cold sheet beside me, I'd wake and the process would start over again.

This exercise in futility went on all night. When the alarm buzzed at four thirty, I was ready for a warm shower.

Driving toward Vicky's house, I decided to pass the whole trip thing off as a lark. Even though I was furious at Phillip, it went against my grain to talk bad about him to someone else.

I'd spent a good ten years training him to be loyal to me. (Oh, I don't mean as in faithful. He had that down pat from the beginning. I mean, as in not talking about me to other people in an unflattering way, even if it was intended as a joke.) The last thing I wanted to be was a hypocrite.

Vicky climbed into the car with the grace of a gazelle, and as usual, I fought a bit of envy. It was a good thing I loved her so much, because I might be tempted to hate her otherwise. She was a natural beauty, and everything seemed to come easy to her. On days like today, that bothered me a little, but most of the time I was glad for her.

"Hi."

"Good morning."

If I were a betting woman, I'd say she'd rolled right out of bed and into her clothes, remembering at the last minute to pull her blond mane up on top of her head in one of those bear-claw clips. She looked incredible.

"Been up long?"

She flashed me a rueful grin. "About three minutes."

"Want to stop at McDonald's?"

"I'm not sure they're open yet. Let's do Wal-Mart first and then drive through Mickey Dee's for breakfast on the way to the mall."

I nodded and smiled as I headed to Wal-Mart. Vicky and I had this conversation every year. At least some things stayed the same. If Phillip were here, we'd probably have to eat breakfast at Taco Bell, just to be different. My smile faded as I remembered the cold guest room bed. That had certainly been different.

"Penny, are you okay?"

I looked over at Vicky. "Sure, I'm fine. Why?"

She snorted. "I asked you if you thought Sandy and Bart would like the DVD player."

I pulled up to a stoplight. Had she lost her mind? Maybe she and Phillip had caught the same mysterious disease. "Vicky, we draw individual names in our family. We have a price limit. Why would you decide to buy Sandy and Bart a DVD player?"

"Penny." Her tone of voice was similar to one she might use with her three-year-old. "I just told you. I drew Sandy's name and Tony got Bart's. That was my question. Should we get them separate gifts like normal, or pool the money we'd spend and get them a DVD player together?"

"Oh. Yeah, that would be fine."

"What's wrong with you?" She crossed her arms, and even in the dim light of early dusk, I recognized the bulldog expression on her face.

"We've had a little change of plans at our house," I said in my most cheerful tone. "About Christmas, I mean." I pulled into one of the few empty parking places in the crowded lot and killed the motor. I could feel Vicky looking at me, so I fumbled in my purse, making a show of counting off the important items—my checkbook, my wallet, and oh, yes, for all those 6:00 a.m. calls I get, my cell phone.

"Pen. What are you talking about?"

Before I could answer, she continued.

"Miss Never-Change-a-Thing Penny has had a change of plans for Christmas?" Her voice squeaked on the last word.

So much for making the trip sound like a lark. I could feel the tears welling, and I was afraid if I made her drag it out of me, the DVD players would be gone when we got in there. Not to mention the things on *my* list. So I spilled the whole story right there in the Wal-Mart parking lot.

"That's not so bad, Penny. It might be fun."

Fun? Didn't she hear the part about us leaving in three days? And missing Christmas at Mom's?

"Yeah, it'll be a blast." I snatched a Kleenex from my purse. "How would you like it if Tony planned a trip during the holidays without asking you?"

"If it meant he was spending time with me and the kids instead of working all the time, I'd be willing to go to the wilds of Africa for Christmas." Her wistful tone cooled my anger quickly. Tony loved her, but he was a workaholic. Even though he'd wanted children, they were completely Vicky's responsibility.

"Won't you miss us?" The squeezing feeling in my chest was back as I thought of them all gathering for Christmas without us.

"Oh, Penny." She hugged me tightly. "You know we will. It'll be awful. What in the world is Phillip thinking?"

That's more like it.

I cried in her arms for a few minutes while she patted my back. Then I thought of the name she'd called me. I jerked away and looked out the window.

"What?" she asked, exasperation creeping into her voice.

We got up at the crack of dawn to make this sale, I could almost hear her thinking.

"Am I really what you said? Miss Never Change—whatever?" I blew my nose.

"Sure, you are, but that's okay." She grabbed her purse. "Come on, it'll all work out. Let's go buy some coffeepots and electric knives. You'll feel better and for five dollars each, how can we go wrong?"

I got out of the car like a good sport, and didn't tell her that, thanks to my unwillingness to break traditions, I still had three coffeepots, one can opener, and two electric knives from last year's after-Thanksgiving sale. Not to mention my stash in the attic from years past.

No sense ruining Vicky's fun.

Chapter 3

...Three Days to Pack

B y Friday night, my resentment had settled. Not settled as in dissipated, but settled as in settled in for a long winter's nap.

I snatched another Christmas sweatshirt from the drawer and tossed it on top of the pile of clothes. The half-full suitcase, open on the bed, was already a sea of red and green. I'd pulled out every holiday shirt I owned to take on *Phillip's* trip. *Let him see if he can skip Christmas with Holly Holiday as a traveling companion.*

Submissive was one thing, but there was nothing that said I had to be nice about it. In my mind's eye, I could see Jiminy Cricket saying something about those scriptures I'd used when I'd taught a ladies' Bible class on submission a few months ago. I grabbed an imaginary flyswatter, and he quickly disappeared. I was going, wasn't I? What more could anyone expect?

Amanda had barely come out of her room since the announcement. Every time I'd passed her door, I could hear her on the phone, whispering to her friends. But when I asked her if she was okay, she just nodded and shut her bedroom door. Not slammed it, of course, but closed it very pointedly, with injured dignity.

Seth wasn't much better. He'd asked a million questions about the RV. They boiled down to one thing. Would he be able to take his electronic stuff with him? I'd used a very sweet tone when I told him to ask his dad. After all, the RV was his department.

"Pen?"

I looked up from my packing to meet Phillip's concerned gaze. He stood in the doorway as if afraid to come into his own bedroom. "Yeah?"

"This trip would be a lot more fun if you weren't mad at me."

Mad? Me, mad? I could feel a vein in my forehead pulsing as I finished folding the shirt. *Could a thirty-five-year-old woman have an anger-induced stroke?* I fixed my gaze on the doorframe to the right of his head. "I agreed to go."

He opened his mouth, then shook his head. "I was hoping for a little more enthusiasm than that."

I didn't speak but went back to my folding and packing as if he weren't still there. He stood for a minute, and I knew he was watching me. Finally, I felt him move on down the hallway.

Still holding a green sweatshirt with a big gold ornament emblazoned on the front, I glanced at the empty doorway. "And *I* was hoping for a normal Christmas," I muttered.

"What?" How could I have forgotten that this was the man who could hear coins jingle in my change purse when I bought a blouse at the mall five miles away?

"Just talking to myself." I held my breath, half afraid, half hopeful he'd come back and insist on having a confrontation.

I heard him tap on Amanda's door instead. *Divide and conquer? Is that his plan now?* My face grew hot at the unjust thought. I tucked the last Christmas shirt in the suitcase and sank down on the bed.

My stomach hadn't stopped burning since the startling announcement yesterday, in spite of the fact that I'd raided the medicine cabinet and taken Phillip's antacids captive. I reached into my cardigan pocket and shook the hostage bottle lightly. He'd need them after the pizza I'd ordered for supper.

I would gladly give them back if he'd call this whole crazy trip off. Maybe I should write a note and tell him that. He used to love it when I made him laugh.

Or maybe I should just take two more antacids. If I didn't find some peace about this, I'd have an ulcer by New Year's.

My prayers didn't seem to be getting anywhere, and I couldn't help but wonder if it was because they all started with, *Dear God, please change Phillip's mind.*

I figured Phillip's were the same, except he inserted my name, of course. I could almost see our prayers colliding headlong in the attic and canceling each other out. Which didn't leave much hope for a happy household.

I didn't want to sleep in the guest room again, but I didn't want to face Phillip either, so, knowing he always watched the ten o'clock news in the den, I slipped up to our room a few minutes before nine and got ready for bed. By nine-thirty, I was lying in the dark.

Unfortunately, I'd never been more wide awake.

My mind whirled with the things that still had to be done before we left. I grabbed a notepad and pen from my nightstand

and, by flashlight, wrote my to-do list.

Cancel the newspaper.
Pay bills.
Call Lynette and tell her I won't be hosting our ladies'
    Bible study ornament exchange this year.
Call Tracey and have her get someone else to make the
    gingerbread hunting lodge for Seth's Boy Scout party.
    Offer recipe from last year.
Call Susan and ask her to organize the mother/daughter
    outlet mall trip. Remind her to be sure everyone has a
    chance to buy a coupon booklet at the mall office.
Call Mom—

Tears stung my eyes. *What will I tell her?* She loved Phillip like a son. How could I say, "Mom, apparently my husband has turned into a pod person and now he doesn't want to be with y'all this year. He'd rather—"? Before I could finish the imaginary, though heartbreaking, conversation, I heard footsteps approaching. I switched off the flashlight and slid the list under my pillow.

"Pen?"

I forced my breathing to even out.

He stood at the foot of the bed for a few seconds, then went on to the bathroom. Just as I finished saying my silent prayers, I heard the bathroom door open and felt his weight on the bed. He turned toward the wall and stayed on his own side. Irrational anger shot through me. The tears that had threatened earlier fell onto my pillow. Within minutes, he was snoring.

I had an overpowering urge to hit him. *Hard.*

Chapter 4

. . .Four Rolling Wheels

Monday came in much the same manner as my thirtieth birthday had five years earlier, like a mischievous little kid forcing me to play when I didn't want to. *"Ready or not, here I come."*

After two nights of going to sleep on the edge of the bed and two mornings of waking up in the curve of Phillip's warm embrace, my anger had waned a little. . .until the gathering rain clouds and my teenage daughter decided to compete to see which could cry the hardest.

Amanda's two closest friends showed up to see her off before they caught the bus to school and she caught the RV to the land of broken dreams. The three of them huddled on the porch, sobbing together. The sky cried with them, and I wanted to but refrained.

I stepped into the house and shook the water from my umbrella just as Phillip came up from the basement. I cast a pointed glance out the window toward Amanda, then gave him a look that spoke volumes.

"Did you see that girl's eyebrow ring?" he asked. "You should be glad to get Amanda away from that for a while."

"Emily will still be here when we get back, Phillip."

"From the way they're carrying on, you'd think we were going to be gone a year," he muttered as he locked the basement door.

"When you're fourteen, there's very little difference between a month and a year." I checked the coffeepot again to be sure it was unplugged. We'd loaded the RV the night before, so all we had to do was go. In theory. In reality, I had to check and double-check everything.

"When I was fourteen, I would have been thrilled if my parents had planned a trip like this. I don't see why Seth and Amanda have to be so obstinate."

"Just for the record, their 'parents' didn't plan this trip. Their 'father' did." I kept meaning to keep my mouth shut so we wouldn't fight, but every time he said something, the words just tumbled out.

"That's right. And they should be thankful."

I snorted. Phillip strode from the room without looking back.

I stepped into the den. I still couldn't believe that, for the first time in the history of our house, it was going to be undecorated until next year. Assuming His Highness allowed us to stay home then. Who knew? We might be going to the moon for the holidays next year.

Tears filled my eyes for the umpteenth time. I despised my bitter anger almost as much as I hated missing Christmas. I'd always been so easygoing. Hadn't I? Or had the going just been easy?

No. We'd had hard times. Like the miscarriage before Amanda was born. And not nearly as bad but still awful, the college days when only a bag of potatoes and a few cans of Campbell's soup stood between us and starvation. But we'd clung together, co-victims of circumstance.

Since Phillip was the perpetrator in the crime of turning our lives upside down, it was difficult to cling to him.

I picked up the fluffy towel from the floor and tossed it over the couch arm. At least, he'd put the Christmas ornaments back in the attic, so I didn't have to face doing that. I tried to be grateful for that crumb of sensitivity on his part, but the spot in front of the window stood out like a missing diamond ring after a broken engagement.

"You ready?" Phillip called from the hall.

Even though he couldn't see me, I nodded and turned off the den light. *Might as well be.* "Are the kids loaded?"

"Amanda's still saying good-bye, but Seth is settling in."

Seth was adapting better than Amanda, partly because his daddy had allowed him to take his handheld electronic game. Technology appealed to Seth more than people did, which was the main reason we'd decided to start homeschooling him.

I'd grown tired of treating black eyes and busted lips from kids who called him a "geek" or worse. *"Grown tired" sounds so long-suffering, and that might be misleading. The truth is, no one will ever know how close I came to ending up the lead story on the six o'clock news: "Vigilante Mama Makes Playground Bullies Eat Dirt."*

"Are you about ready?" Phillip asked from the doorway.

"I guess so."

He must have been encouraged by the sleep-induced snuggling because he put his arms around me and leaned down to kiss me. I slammed my nose against his top button and felt his lips brush the top of my hair.

"Penny, I can't stand this."

It's not too late to call it all off. Before I said it aloud, my heart sank. *Am I really submitting if I manipulate him into doing what I want him to?*

"Can't stand what? We're doing what you wanted," I said to his button.

He didn't speak, but he also didn't push me away in disgust. I rested my ear against his chest, listening to his heartbeat for the second time in a week. I guess I needed reassurance that he hadn't really turned into an alien. I hardly ever got quiet enough or still enough to hear anyone's heart, but this morning I was in no hurry to go anywhere.

The constant *thump, thump, thump* drained away some of the irritation (I know; I'm the queen of understatement) I'd been carrying around the past few days. My husband was as solid and steady as his heartbeat. Why was I worried about giving him a month of my life?

Fine, my inner child whined, *but does it have to be the month that includes Christmas?* As much as her whining got on my nerves, this time I couldn't keep from agreeing with her.

"Penny."

I stepped back to look up at him, but either Phillip was afraid I'd bolt, or he liked me in spite of my. . . ahem. . .irritation, because he kept his hands on my waist. "Yeah?"

"This isn't going to be as bad as you think. Are you sure you don't want to know where we're going and what I have planned for us?"

"I'm sure." I'd made that plain to him as soon as he'd

started waving the travel atlas around and talking about KOA campgrounds. But even though he was acting like a total rat, after sixteen years of enjoying his crooked grin, I couldn't take another second of the worry shadowing his face. I gave him a quick hug and forced a smile. "Surprise me."

He took advantage of my upturned face and swooped in for the first kiss since Thursday afternoon that hadn't landed on my hair.

"I intend to surprise you. . .over and over again," he murmured against my lips.

"Humph. In an RV with the whole family? Fat chance." I pulled away from him and smoothed down my red and green sweatshirt.

He grinned and opened the door, ushering me out. *Is he being gallant, or is he just afraid I'll change my mind and run back to the bedroom and lock myself in?*

The wind had picked up and the rain was blowing on the porch, so Amanda and her friends pressed against the wall. When we came out the door, she sniffed and turned her back on us.

In some bizarre twist of fate, I was bearing the brunt of her displeasure more than Phillip. Tears mingled with the rain hitting my face. Ever since we'd pulled her out of school to homeschool, she'd looked forward to this holiday with her friends so much. Not that she'd told me, but I'd gathered it from bits of conversations I'd heard—usually right before she rolled her eyes at me and closed her door or lowered her voice to a whisper.

Phillip tapped Amanda on the shoulder. "Come on, honey, it's time to go." The firmness in his voice was unmistakable, and Amanda knew better than to argue. She hugged her friends one more time, and they splashed down the driveway to wait for the school bus, huddling together under a piece of black plastic.

I leaned toward Amanda with my umbrella, but she shrugged it off and stomped through the rain to the RV. I knew I should be mad, and I *was* aggravated that she wouldn't give an inch, but a large part of me wanted to hand Phillip the umbrella and stomp right along behind her.

"Don't worry. She'll come around."

I just shook my head and followed Amanda.

Phillip pulled the motor home door shut behind us.

Seth sat in the chair behind the driver's seat playing his GameBoy. Amanda dripped on the welcome mat. Every morning she painstakingly straightened her long blond hair with a blow-dryer. Thanks to her belligerent tromp through the rain, she looked like a combination of Medusa and a teenage Shirley Temple.

Phillip passed her a large towel. She jutted her chin, and for a second I thought she would refuse, but maybe she'd learned from the umbrella incident because she snatched the towel from his hand as forcefully as she dared.

He sank into the captain's chair that served as a driver seat by day and a comfy recliner by night and swiveled to face us. "I thought we'd pray before we start."

Amanda stopped in midtoweling, and for the first time since I'd entered the RV, Seth tore his gaze from his handheld game. Normally, at our house, prayers were reserved for meals and bedtime.

As my own emotions roiled, I looked out the window at the relentless rain and then at Amanda's stormy expression. "I think prayer is a great idea."

Chapter 5

. . .Five Hundred Miles

After the prayer, Amanda plopped down in her chair, buckled in, and used the towel to cover her face. Reality hit me like a punch—we were really doing this. I hadn't been able to talk Phillip out of this mad trip. I sank onto the love seat and fastened my seat belt.

A few minutes later, Phillip breezed merrily onto the I-440 loop, whistling the chorus to "On the Road Again." How I wished I were a fly on the wall of that man's brain. Where had he gotten this sudden determination to do his own thing?

He'd never been exactly passive, but I think I'd imagined that whatever my desires in life were, his were the same. I glanced at the thick portfolio beside him on the console. Maps, sticky notes, and printouts of e-mails bulged out the edges. That notebook may have been the most amazing revelation of all. For the past sixteen years, Phillip couldn't even order pizza without me. How had he gathered all of that information?

Last week, right before I'd thrown the atlas across the

room, I'd noticed a red circle of sorts. I did a mental geography review. We were headed east, so my best guess is that we were on our way to Memphis.

Amanda is a huge Elvis fan. (Okay, I admit it. I'm a little fascinated with the hip-swiveling king myself.) We'd always planned to go to Graceland, and no doubt, Phillip thought he'd start the trip off right by taking us there. I smirked. I'd figured out his first surprise without even breaking a sweat.

Maybe I could pretend for the next few days we were just on a short vacation in Memphis. Who knows? If we got along well and showered him with attention, maybe Phillip would go along with my new plan—thinning out his notebook and heading home ahead of schedule. Like three and a half weeks ahead of schedule.

We'd buzz in, do Graceland, hit the malls, and get home in time to enjoy the Christmas things I'd had to give up. Sounded like a plan.

"Humph," I snorted. Who was I kidding? The nice comfortable man I'd married had turned into a man of steel. I'd have a better chance convincing Superman to let the two trains crash and just spend time with me than I would convincing this new Phillip to change his plans.

"What are you grunting about?" Phillip's blue eyes twinkled in the rearview mirror.

"Nothing, really. Just thinking."

"About what?"

I glanced at the kids. Amanda appeared to be sound asleep, although her wild curls covered her face, so I couldn't be sure. Seth had put on his headphones after I'd objected to the annoying sound on his electronic game.

I waited for a traffic lull, then hurried into the passenger seat and buckled in. "Thinking about you." I could at least try to talk him into the Memphis-then-home idea.

He raised his eyebrows. "What about me?"

"Just wondering why you're doing this. Really."

The twinkle fled from his eyes like a blown-out birthday candle. "You know why. But you won't let yourself really see."

Talking to him was an obvious dead end, so I dug in my bag and got out the Heartsong romances that had come in the mail Friday. I hadn't even had time to look at any of the four since then, but I quickly picked one and lost myself in the pages until we stopped at a roadside park.

I fixed sandwiches, but it was raining too hard to get out of the RV. Seth played his game while he ate, and I didn't have the heart to stop him. Amanda maintained her stoic silence. So I read my book. Phillip tried a couple of conversation starters, but when they fell flat, he picked up his beloved travel atlas.

After lunch, I took my post next to Phillip again, but since I wasn't really speaking to him, I couldn't seem to fight the sleepiness—too many nights of trying to stay on my own side of the bed, I guess.

⟋⟍

"Penny?" Phillip's voice sounded a long way off.

"Hmm?"

"We're about two hours from where we're going to stop for the night. But there's a gas station coming up. Do you need to stop?"

"I don't care." I opened one eye. We weren't on the interstate anymore. Nothing looked familiar. "Are we almost to Memphis?"

Oops. So much for keeping my discovery about our destination a secret. I hate it when I talk before I'm totally awake. *Never a good idea.*

He glanced at me and frowned. "We bypassed Memphis about thirty minutes ago."

Bypassed Memphis? Why would any sane person do that? Oh, I forgot.

I shushed my inner child but not before I heard her wail, *What about the mall? And Graceland? Just when I was dreaming of Elvis in crushed velvet!* "Where are we now?" I asked.

"Almost to Holly Springs."

"Holly Springs what?"

He kept his gaze on the road, but I could see his right eyebrow rise. "Mississippi. Are you sure you don't want to know the itinerary? This is the last time I'm going to offer."

Have you ever heard that expression cutting off your nose to spite your face? Well, in addition to being the queen of understatement, I'm also the duchess of cutting off my nose.

"I told you to surprise me."

"Fine. You can count on it." With his right hand, he slid the bulging black notebook from the console and put it between his seat and the wall.

Phillip knew me too well. When I calmed down, I'd regret not letting him tell me. A surreptitious peek at the contents of that portfolio would be much easier on my ego than asking him to fill me in on the details later.

I drifted back to sleep and didn't rouse until two hours later when we pulled into an RV park.

"We're here," Phillip boomed cheerfully.

I bit back a sarcastic remark. In that drowsy place between

dream and wake that I like to call the land of good intentions, I'd promised myself I was going to start thinking positive about this trip. That included not making sarcastic remarks to the driver.

"It's not raining nearly as hard." Okay, so my comment wasn't exactly exuberant, but it *was* positive.

"Where are we?" Amanda pushed her hair back from her face. She'd slept most of the day. When she had been awake, she'd stared out the window silently like a modern-day Joan of Arc on her way to the stake.

"We're at a campground," Seth answered. He pressed his face against the glass and stared at the little kiosk we'd pulled up next to. A man in a guard uniform stood at the window.

"In Tupelo, Mississippi," Phillip added and then gave the guard at the window his name. "This is where we're going to camp the next few days."

"Why?" Amanda dropped the blinds on her window in disgust. "It doesn't look very exciting."

"Looks can be deceiving." Phillip took the map and papers and drove a few hundred yards. He hopped out, freed the Mazda, and then smoothly backed the RV into its temporary resting place. He beamed like he'd manually hooked us back up with the saucer section of the Enterprise.

"Seth, you and your sister need to help me get things set up outside."

"Great," Amanda said. "Slopping around in the rain is my idea of fun."

"You didn't seem to mind it this morning when you wouldn't take your mom's umbrella."

I cast Phillip a "Hey-leave-me-out-of-it" look.

"Won't we get wet?" Seth asked.

"There are some slickers in the drawer. Get them on and let's get going."

I kicked around the idea of offering to help, but I decided fixing supper by myself was enough of a sacrifice, even if it was just tuna salad sandwiches.

They came in thirty minutes later, hung their dripping ponchos to dry, and dove into the sandwiches like they were a five-course meal. After we finished eating, Phillip rubbed his hands together and smiled. "Who wants to go for a drive around Tupelo?"

I picked at the sleeve of my Christmas tree cardigan. "I think I'll stay here and get our beds ready."

Amanda curled her lip. "Sounds like more excitement than I can stand. I guess I'll just stay here."

"I'll pass." Seth was already engrossed in his game again.

If Phillip was disappointed by our desertion, he hid it well. "Okay. I've got to check on some things for tomorrow, but I'll be back in an hour or so."

Seth looked up. "Tomorrow? What are we doing tomorrow?"

"Oh." Phillip grabbed the car keys from a hook by the door. His grin never faltered, but his blue eyes bore into mine. "It's a surprise."

The next morning, the cell-phone alarm buzzed at six. I think it's safe to say we were all surprised.

Phillip leaped from the bed and pulled on some jogging pants and a T-shirt. "Let's go get a shower."

I blinked. " 'Let's'?"

He grinned. "No, that's not the surprise. Although, now that you mention it. . ." He raised his eyebrow and winked.

I glared at him.

He laughed. "They have a shower house. And thanks to my careful planning, we're parked right next to it. We can all shower at the same time."

"Joy."

Obviously impervious to my sarcasm, he lumbered down the hall to wake the kids. "What should I wear?" I called.

"Whatever you brought will be fine. Forget it, Penny. I'm not giving any hints. You wanted it that way, remember?" He turned his attention back to Seth.

I scrambled to my feet. Now where had he hidden that black notebook?

Chapter 6

. . .Six Hours Working

I didn't find Phillip's itinerary, so I was more than a little shocked Tuesday morning when we parked the Mazda in front of a large, red brick church building on Elm Street. Phillip turned to Seth and Amanda. "You two get to be baby-sitters today."

They groaned.

Phillip held up his hand in a crossing-guard gesture. He very rarely did that, but when he did, the kids both knew there would be no arguments. "They really need you. There are several children coming." He smiled. "Besides, it'll be fun, and you won't be on your own. There'll be an adult around to help you."

He got out of the car and strode to the building. I couldn't even look at Seth and Amanda. I knew they were completely stunned, and I was afraid they'd recognize the same emotion in me. We were going to leave our children with a stranger to look after other strangers' children?

I grabbed Phillip's shirt just as he touched the door handle.

"Can I talk to you for a minute?" I said softly.

He turned to me. "Yes, but before you ask, Tommy's the preacher here. His wife will be with the kids."

Tommy's wife? We'd never met Ronda in person, but Phillip and Tommy had been friends since college, and we'd exchanged Christmas cards for years.

It occurred to me that maybe Phillip's scheming had something to do with wanting to be alone with me for the day. I relaxed.

I was glad Phillip hadn't allowed Seth to bring the GameBoy this morning. He'd have no choice but to talk to the other kids. And maybe a day of babysitting would show Amanda that the world didn't revolve around her.

Phillip stared at me, one eyebrow raised.

What did this man have up his sleeve? "Okay."

His smile drove every cloud from the sky. "Great."

We met Ronda, then left while she showed the kids around the fellowship hall where they would be watching the children.

"Is there a mother's shopping trip planned today?" I asked Phillip on the way out to the car.

"Something like that."

We stopped at McDonald's half a mile from the church and ate a relaxed breakfast. Through unspoken agreement, we didn't mention the road trip, but Phillip amused me with stories of his and Tommy's college antics.

We left the restaurant and had only driven a few blocks when Phillip pulled into a driveway that already held several vehicles. The medium-sized house had partially finished vinyl siding, and I could see two men up on the roof with hammers.

"Umm. . .Phillip?" The bottom dropped out of my stomach. Had he built us a new house in Tupelo, Mississippi, without telling me? These days anything was possible. "What are we doing here?"

"The church is doing a house-raising. And we're just in time to help."

So much for him wanting to spend a day alone with me. "A house what?"

"Like an old-fashioned barn raising. Only this is a house."

"Why?"

"Well, a member had a house fire and no insurance."

I wanted to ask why again, but I didn't. Instead I only asked the more pressing question. "Why do they need us?"

"They have no place to live. The church members are building them a new house. Ronda and our children are babysitting the workers' kids today. I told Tommy we'd help, too." He unfastened his seat belt and touched my hand. "Unless you don't want to?"

Talk about being backed into a corner. If I said I didn't want to, what kind of person—what kind of Christian—would I be? But the truth was, the only thing I really wanted to do right now was throw myself on my bed for a good long cry. Unfortunately, my bed was several hundred miles in the opposite direction. *At least I still have a bed.* "That'll be fine."

Phillip smiled like I'd won the Nobel Peace Prize. "Good. Wonderful."

We were each assigned a partner and a task as soon as we walked in the door. The only bright spot in the day was my tile-laying partner, Donita. She was hilarious. Her self-deprecating humor put me so much at ease that after a short lunch break, I found myself telling her about our trip. . .starting with Phillip's Thanksgiving Day announcement.

She sympathized as we painstakingly cut the peel-and-stick vinyl tiles to fit. After I finished my story, I sat back on my heels. "It could have been worse. At first I thought he was leaving me for another woman."

She nodded. "Been there, done that, got the divorce papers. It was the real deal for me."

"Oh, Donita, I'm so sorry."

She shook her head. "Don't be sorry for me, girl. Be sorry for him. I've always said there wasn't another human being on earth that would be worth me giving up going to sleep in the same house as my children every night. He used to think that, too. But somewhere along the path to 'as long as we both shall live,' he lost his way." She smiled and crow's-feet crinkled at the corners of her eyes. "You pray for him if you get a chance, okay?"

I nodded. *How could any man have left her for someone else? Her beauty is way more than skin-deep.*

Within a minute, she was cracking another joke, and I was laughing.

Six hours after Phillip and I arrived, Donita and I finished. I hugged her tightly and assured her I'd pray for her whole family, including her ex-husband.

"God will bless you for what you did today, Penny. Trust Phillip. He's a good man. He knows what he's doing."

When we were on our way to pick up the kids, Phillip looked over at me. "What do you think?"

"After laying tile all day, I'm so sore I can hardly move.

What about you?"

"I'm tired, too, but it felt good to help."

"Yeah." I thought of the volunteers working so unselfishly. "I just hope the owners appreciate the huge amount of sweat equity that is going into their new home."

He frowned. "Didn't Donita seem appreciative to you?"

"Donita?"

He nodded. "The house is for her and her three kids."

My new friend, Donita, had recently lost her house in a fire? Less than a year after her husband walked out on her?

"I can't believe she didn't tell you."

"Me either." *And all I did was complain.*

As Phillip and I drove to the church building to get the kids, I silently replayed my conversations with Donita. Could someone really be that strong in the face of such adversity?

Um. . .Lord? I'm tired of my selfish heart. Could I get one like Donita's instead?

As soon as I thought the prayer, I started mentally backpedaling. I didn't want to lose my husband in order to get a new heart. Or my house. I sighed. But if those things ever happened, I wanted to face them with the kind of faith Donita seemed to possess.

When Seth and Amanda climbed into the car, they looked as tired as I felt. Phillip grinned. "How did babysitting go?" he asked.

They looked at each other. "It was okay," Seth said. He nodded toward Amanda. "Except *she* wouldn't stop being bossy."

Amanda gasped. "I was not bossy. You were going to let Annie climb up higher than she should have. All I did was tell you not to."

He crossed his arms. "That's what I call bossy."

"Whatever." Amanda shrugged.

"I accept your apology," Seth said.

I looked sideways at Phillip, and he nodded slightly in agreement. Good comeback.

Amanda chose to ignore it. (Or maybe "whatever" *was* the new "I'm sorry." What did I know?) "It was actually harder than I thought it would be. Especially when Jeffie got that extra-large crayon stuck up his nose."

"Mrs. Wilson says he does that all the time. Travis crumbled cookies in Alexis's hair." Seth made a crumbling motion with his hands.

"Oh, gross. How did you get it out?" Amanda asked.

For the rest of the trip to the RV park, they talked about the kids they'd watched. I smiled as they compared notes about who whined the most and who screamed the loudest when it was time to wash their hands. I couldn't remember the last time I'd heard them actually have a conversation. Maybe this had been a great way to start off our trip.

I cast a sideways glance at Phillip. *Kudos to the itinerary planner.* Wonder what else he had scheduled in that elusive notebook of his?

The next day, Phillip gave us a choice. Going back to help on Donita's house another day, which meant babysitting again for Seth and Amanda, or moving on. The kids weren't enthusiastic about either option, but to my amazement, before I could cast my ballot, they voted to stay and help. As sore as my muscles were, I was kind of glad I hadn't had to decide.

The second night, we attended a Bible study at the Elm Street church with the people we'd come to know so well the past couple of days. After we got back to the RV, I fell into bed exhausted. Right before I drifted off, I remembered that if we were at home I would have been hosting the Secret Santa swap for my book group. I would be the proud owner of a new book. (We were predictable. We always gave each other books.) But I wouldn't have been able to help Donita have four newly tiled floors.

∽

The next morning, after a leisurely breakfast, Phillip surprised us with a trip to Elvis's birthplace. It wasn't Graceland, but Amanda and I were thrilled, and even Seth was impressed.

We headed out of Tupelo around noon up the Natchez Trace Parkway. Our tour guide (Phillip) told us a little of the history of the centuries-old road.

"Mom," Amanda asked about half an hour after leaving Elvis's childhood home, "did you know Elvis had a twin who died at birth?"

"I guess I'd heard it a long time ago, but I'd forgotten it." For a change of pace, I'd allowed her to sit with me on the love seat as long as we both wore our seat belts.

"It must have been awful for his mom and dad," Seth offered with surprising insight.

"Yeah, but at least they still had Elvis."

"One baby doesn't take the place of another one, though, sweetie," Phillip spoke from the driver's seat without turning around. "We love you and Seth, but the baby we lost before we had you will always be precious to us."

Amanda stared at me, wide-eyed. "You lost a baby before me?"

I felt a twinge of irritation at Phillip. I'd always thought there was no point in sharing our sorrow with the kids, considering it had happened before they were born.

"Yes. A boy," Phillip answered, keeping his eyes on the road.

"I had a brother?" Seth asked.

"His name was Jared," Phillip volunteered, a regular fount of information.

"Was he stillborn like Elvis's twin?" Amanda asked.

"Actually, I miscarried—" At the look of confusion on Seth's face, I clarified. "He was born way too early, and he was too little to live in the world." Tears edged my eyes and the familiar lump filled my throat. "But we sure did love him."

Amanda leaned her head over on my shoulder. To my amazement, she had tears in her eyes, too. Had I been wrong to protect them from our loss?

We rode in silence for a while, but I noticed Seth didn't pick his game up again.

"Did you see that deer?" he called out.

Amanda and I turned around to look, and sure enough, a big buck stood by the side of the road, almost as if waiting for us to go by so he could cross the parkway.

"Look! He has a family just like us." Amanda pointed to the woods behind the buck, where a doe and two smaller deer eyed our motor home.

"Nobody has a family just like us," I quipped.

Amanda glanced at Seth and her dad and rolled her eyes at me. "That's for sure."

Chapter 7

. . .Seven Wieners Roasting

Traveling the Natchez Trace Parkway was like stepping back in time. No billboards, no neon signs, and slower-than-normal speed limits. We took occasional breaks along the way to walk on the original trail or soak in the view from an overlook. In spite of their grumbling, Seth and Amanda were the first ones out of the RV every time.

Late that afternoon, we stopped at the Meriwether Lewis Burial Site. "Why don't we camp here?" Phillip said while we were reading about the monument.

"Eww! You've got to be kidding!" Amanda shivered. "We're going to spend the night at a burial site?"

Phillip laughed, but frankly, I thought it was a valid question.

"No, at the campground over there."

I gave a small sigh of relief. I'd learned the hard way on this trip never to assume.

After we had the RV set up, Phillip looked around. "Who wants to help me build a fire?"

"Outside?" Seth asked, amazed.

"No. On your bunk," Amanda drawled.

Seth's face turned red.

Amanda stared at her brother. "I was just teasing." She rolled her eyes and punched his arm. "Come on. Might as well."

"How about you, Pen?" Phillip asked.

"I think I'll start supper."

"Hey," Seth yelled from the doorway, "can we roast hot dogs? Like on TV?"

"And marshmallows?" Amanda added as she followed her brother outside.

Roasting hot dogs and marshmallows had been such a large part of my growing up. When had it become easier to just order pizza? I couldn't believe my kids had never experienced a wiener roast.

"There *is* a bag of marshmallows in the cabinet," Phillip said.

I smiled at the thought. "And I have a whole pack of hot dogs in the fridge."

Phillip offered a sheepish grin. "Not quite a whole pack. I ate a cold one for a midnight snack the other night."

I shuddered. Cold hot dogs were not my idea of a culinary delight. "Seven will be plenty. I only want one. Especially if we're having marshmallows for dessert."

I could almost taste the blackened cream puffs. It was a good thing I made it a habit never to diet during the holidays or on trips. Now I had a double reason to eat whatever I wanted. "I'll bring them out when you get the fire going."

"I appreciate you being a good sport." Phillip ran the back of his hand gently across my cheek as if to wipe away an imaginary tear.

A good sport? Is that what you call someone who has to be dragged kicking and screaming on a family trip? Oh, yeah, I should get an award. "No problem."

I knew he could tell I'd mentally rejected the compliment. But he just nodded and walked out to join the kids.

With inexperienced help, it would surely take Phillip half an hour to get the fire going. I grabbed the cell phone and punched in Vicky's number.

"Hello?"

"Hi, Vic. How's everything going there?"

"Penny? Where are you?"

"Through the looking glass?"

"That bad, huh?"

"No. . ." I thought of Donita and her kids having a home for Christmas. "Parts of it aren't bad at all."

"Spill."

"I'd rather hear about what's going on there."

"Well, Patty hosted the book group Christmas thing since you were gone. We laughed so hard, her husband stuck his head in to check on us." She squealed. *"Oh!* Guess what I got from my Secret Santa?"

"A book?" I guessed dryly.

"No! A basket with a mug and some cappuccino mix and a rolled-up fleece blanket. When I pulled the blanket out, there were three Ted Dekker books rolled up in it."

She'd gotten all that extra stuff and three books by my favorite author? And I got to spend the night at a burial site? Where was the fairness in that?

"That's great."

"Are you okay?"

Thankfully, Seth stuck his head in the door before I had to respond. "Mom! Where are the hot dogs?"

"I'm bringing them," I answered. "Vicky, I've got to go. Kiss the kids for me. I'll call you soon."

"Okay. Penny?"

"Yeah."

"I hope you have the best Christmas ever."

"You, too. I'll miss you." I pushed the END button and forced the tears from my eyes with a fake smile. The last thing our first family wiener roast needed was a weepy Willa. Besides I didn't even know what I was crying about. I was glad Vicky had fun at the party. I grabbed the hot dogs and ran out.

An hour later, we'd finished up with a marshmallow-eating contest, and even by the flickering light, I could see that Seth (the champion) had gotten it all over his face. I opened my mouth to tell him to run in and wash it off when Phillip stood.

"I thought we might spend some time with God tonight. . . as a family." Even though he wasn't talking loudly, his voice boomed in the near-deserted campground. "I mean. . ." He cleared his throat. "He's always with us, but He has given us so much, and sometimes I think, in our hurry to get along in the world, we forget to give our time and attention back to Him."

Amanda squirmed beside me. When Phillip produced his Bible from his jacket pocket, she looked at me with a furrowed brow.

I shrugged. Admittedly, Phillip had never talked much about God outside of the church building, but it wasn't that weird. Maybe the open fire reminded him of attending church camp when he was growing up.

Phillip read several verses from Colossians chapter 3 about putting on mercy and kindness and forgiving each other. Then he ended with verses 16 and 17.

" 'Let the word of Christ dwell in you richly in all wisdom; teaching and admonishing one another in psalms and hymns and spiritual songs, singing with grace in your hearts to the Lord. And whatsoever ye do in word or deed, do all in the name of the Lord Jesus, giving thanks to God and the Father by him.' " He put his Bible back into his pocket.

I was so glad he stopped there that I almost said, "Amen." I remembered the next verse of that chapter clearly from the ladies' class I'd just taught on submission. *Wives, submit your-selves unto your own husbands, as it is fit in the Lord.*

Technically, I *had* submitted because I was here at the Meriwether Lewis Burial Site spending the night in an RV instead of at home hosting a party. But had my resentment been keeping me from doing it in a way *fit in the Lord?*

The next evening, Phillip guided the RV into a Wal-Mart parking lot.

"Oh, cool," Amanda said. "Are we going shopping?"

"Yes," Phillip answered. "We can go right now or we can go in the morning."

"Hmm. . ." I wrinkled my forehead. "Wouldn't it be better to just go now since we're here? So we won't have to drive back in the morning?"

Phillip swiveled around to face us. "That's the beauty of it. We're spending the night here tonight."

"You're kidding!" Seth looked out the window again as if to be sure we really were at Wal-Mart.

"Nope. I'm totally serious. I called ahead and asked permission for us to camp here tonight."

I had to choke down an incredulous laugh. "In the Wal-Mart parking lot?" He'd completely lost his mind.

He nodded.

Amanda switched back to the important part of what her dad had said earlier. "But we *are* going shopping?"

"You want to go now?"

She nodded. "There's this new CD. . ."

"I need some batteries," Seth added.

So that's why the handheld game had been *persona non grata* the last leg of the trip. What I'd thought was progress had actually been the untimely death of the Energizer bunny.

"We'll get a few camping supplies, but we're not really shopping for ourselves."

"Oh?" It was my turn to arch a brow. "Who are we shopping for?"

"Well, it's a—"

"—surprise!" Amanda and I finished together.

"How will we know what to buy?" she asked.

That mysterious black notebook appeared in his hands. He pulled out two pieces of paper. "Seth, you're with me. Amanda and Penny, here's yours." He passed one of the sheets to Amanda.

I fought the urge to snatch it from her as my curiosity burgeoned. Instead I looked over her shoulder at the strange list in Phillip's neat handwriting.

40 each of the following items:

Hairbrush with soft bristles
Hand lotion
Talcum powder
White tube socks
Box of stationery
Wall calendar with large numbers
Christmas cards

I gaped at our list. Had Phillip finally flipped his lid? Just as I leaned over to peek at the paper he and Seth were studying, he tucked it in his pocket and grinned.

Amanda and I obviously had more shopping experience than the guys, because we beat them back to the RV with everything on our list.

We laughed about getting there first as we carried the bags in and set them on the dinette table.

"Has Dad gone off the deep end or what?" Amanda asked.

So she'd finally figured out I wasn't to blame. Where was the comfort I should have taken in that?

"He just wants us to spend some time together." I grabbed a soda from the fridge and passed her one.

"Yeah, but right here at Christmas? And in an RV?" She popped the top on the can. "Most people would just institute a family game night."

I snorted cola out my nose. Her dry wit and big vocabulary never ceased to amaze me. Unfortunately I didn't get nearly enough chances to talk to her.

"Your dad's not 'most people.'"

"Is this the part where you tell me that we're on this trip because of some deficiency in his raising?"

I grinned. "I have no idea why we're on this trip."

"But you came anyway."

"It's really important to him." Who was the martyr now?

"So if you care about someone and they want you to do something really important to them, even if you don't want to, you should do it?"

I sat my can on the table, hoping she didn't see my hand tremble. Was this conversation really going where I thought it was? As far as I knew, she didn't even like a particular boy. But no mama in her right mind would brush off a question like that.

"No, that's not necessarily true at all." I weighed every word like my life depended on it. If I ventured too close to her hidden meaning, she'd think I was lecturing and tune me out. *Lord, please give me the words.*

I suddenly remembered Tammy. I hadn't thought of her in years.

"In junior high, my friend Tammy wanted us to become blood sisters."

"Eww! Gross."

"Yeah, well, other kids did it. So, one night when I stayed at her house, she pulled out a knife and insisted that we prick our hands and smear them together."

Amanda shuddered. "You didn't do it, did you?"

"No, even though she was furious at me, I wouldn't go through with it. I loved her, but I knew it was wrong."

"Duh! Mom, you could have gotten AIDS! Or some other disease." The horror on her face made me know she'd remember Tammy for a long time to come.

Before I could respond, the door to the RV burst open, and we both jumped. The top of a small Scotch pine came sliding in the door, followed by the trunk and two proud Lassiter men.

⤔

The three-foot pine looked like the White House Christmas tree in the RV. We were afraid to put ornaments on it since we were pulling out the next morning. (Phillip had volunteered that top-secret information, believe it or not.) But we wrapped it in multicolored lights, and I think all of us watched it twinkle with some satisfaction. It was beginning to look a lot like Christmas.

That night after we were all tucked in bed, I lay in the dark, thinking of Phillip's thoughtful gesture. The tree, though small, had made great strides in breaking through my defenses. I padded over to get a drink, and by the parking lot light filtering in the window, I could see Seth snoring lightly in the overhead bunk. I turned automatically to check on Amanda.

The sofa was empty. I tiptoed back to the bathroom but she wasn't there. Sick fear clutched my stomach. There weren't that many places to hide in an RV.

I ran to the front door. It was unlocked. "Please, God. . . ," I murmured.

As soon as I opened the door I saw her. Clearly illuminated by the guard lights, she had her back to me, and she was talking on the cell phone. "Em, I know you gave me the money for a bus ticket, but I just can't do it. The 'rents would go bananas."

I stood with the door barely open. She was right. This half of the 'rents (short for "parents" in her language) was about to "go bananas." Suddenly our afternoon conversation took on a whole new meaning.

"You *are* my best friend," Amanda practically wailed. She was apparently too upset to worry about keeping her voice down. "And I don't want to miss your birthday party, but I have to."

I didn't know whether to grab the phone from her and throw it as far as I could or step back inside and let her handle things herself. She seemed to be doing a good job. Her next words made the whole world stop.

"I did plan to slip out tonight and catch a bus there, I promise. But I just can't. You have to understand." She sobbed hysterically.

Suddenly I knew what to do. I flung the door open, and in my reindeer flannel pajamas and Rudolph house shoes, I walked out into the Wal-Mart parking lot and touched Amanda's shoulder.

She gasped. "Em, I've got to go. I'm sorry." She ended the call and looked at my face, clearly searching for a clue to how I was feeling.

Good luck, girl. I had so many emotions right then *I* couldn't even sort them out.

She collapsed into my arms. The cold wind sluiced through us, but neither one of us cared. I held her until her sobs subsided.

"Are you okay?"

She nodded. "Am I grounded?"

I motioned toward the RV. "From what?"

"Oh, yeah." She sniffed. "Good point."

Chapter 8

...*Eight Ladies Knitting*

I woke Phillip when I went to bed and told him about the close call with Amanda. But I made him promise not to make a big deal out of it, and he agreed. She'd used her head. But what if she hadn't?

I shuddered again. Phillip pulled me against him and held me close until the sun peeped through the tiny bedroom window.

The next morning, while I fixed coffee, a subdued Amanda shot her daddy a nervous look with her good morning hug.

"I'm proud of you," I heard him say softly.

I was proud of him. A few weeks ago, he would have ranted and raved about Emily being a bad influence. Maybe we were all learning.

After breakfast, we left Wal-Mart and changed direction. We

drove about an hour before we pulled into the far corner of a small nursing home in northwest Tennessee, near the Kentucky line.

"I thought we'd bring the residents a little bit of early Christmas cheer," Phillip said. The mystery of the Wal-Mart lists was solved.

The kids looked like they wanted to refuse to go in, but one look at Phillip's face and I think they knew better.

Thirty minutes later, after we'd given out the gifts, Phillip and Seth went to hang a calendar in each resident's room.

Amanda and I were waiting in the lobby, shooting each other nervous looks, when a group of women streamed into the room.

One of the last ladies to enter grabbed Amanda's hands. "You've got the perfect hands for knitting, sweetie. It's time for our group. Come on and join us."

"Oh. No, thank you," Amanda said and gently extracted her hands from the woman's grasp, her face bright red.

The woman grabbed my hands and quickly dropped them. "Not as good, but maybe they'll do. You'll both come." She took my upper arm in one hand and Amanda's in the other. With surprising strength, she guided us to the couch.

I looked at Amanda and shrugged as the woman sank down between us.

"Essie Mae, help these girls get set up."

I wasn't entirely clear which woman was Essie Mae because they all handed us knitting needles and thread. Maybe she was the one with the red bandanna. . . .

"Mom!" I jerked my attention back to Amanda. She was glaring at me. "If you don't concentrate, we'll never learn."

I nodded.

Within seconds, the sound of knitting needles *click-clacked* in the air. The ladies had split up, and four of them were showing Amanda how to knit while the other four attempted to instruct me.

After twenty minutes of laughing at my own mistakes, I realized the woman had been right. My hands just weren't made for knitting. Amanda had caught on way better than I had. If *her* husband ever lost his job, their kids would have handmade hats, gloves, and scarves for Christmas. I bit back another laugh. Mine would just have to make do with apples and oranges.

"I'm sorry," I said. "I just can't do this."

The *click-clacking* stopped. In the eerie stillness, as eight (nine, if I counted Amanda) pairs of eyes stared at me in dismay, I shrugged. "I think my fingers are too big."

"Maybe if you could stop laughing and be serious. . . ," Amanda scolded from her spot on the couch beside me. I think she'd decided that the sooner we learned to knit, the sooner we could escape.

As soon as she said that, I giggled. I couldn't help it. "Maybe I'm just overwhelmed by being in the presence of so much talent. Thank you so much for sharing with us." I passed the knitting needles and yarn to the woman next to me and stood. "We have to find my husband."

Amanda followed my lead. The women smiled and started knitting again.

"Smooth," Amanda whispered as we hurried away.

"Wonder where your dad and Seth got off to?" I asked.

Amanda looped her arm in mine. "You think a bunch of

old men kidnapped them and are forcing them to learn how to do woodworking?"

I laughed. "That's a distinct possibility."

Just then they came into the lobby.

Seth ran up to us. "We hung calendars in forty rooms."

"Hmm. . .and all I did was learn to knit," Amanda quipped with a wry grin.

When we were back in the RV, Seth cleared his throat. "The place smelled kind of funny, but the whole nursing home thing wasn't half bad, you know it?"

Amanda nodded. "Kind of like you."

"Huh?"

She reached over and mussed his hair. "You're not half bad either once we get past your funny smell."

She started running before the words were completely out of her mouth, but by the time she got out the door, her little brother was less than a foot behind her.

"I really think she teases him because she loves him," I offered.

Phillip grinned. "Dream on."

Just a few miles from Kentucky, Phillip turned down the road leading to the Between the Lakes National Recreation Area. I gaped at the campground, which was almost completely surrounded by a sparkling lake, and for just an instant, I admitted to a tiny element of fun in this whole surprise thing.

Seth and Amanda bounced in their seats. Phillip grinned, looking much younger than he had just a week ago. The worry lines, ever-present in his face—especially during the last few months before he lost his job, had vanished. His blue eyes sparkled constantly now. And I was starting to think it was due to happiness instead of insanity.

After we had the motor home set, Phillip raised an eyebrow. "Who wants to go for a ride?"

"Me!" Seth was already halfway to the car.

"Me, too!" Amanda seconded as she took off like a shot after her brother.

Phillip studied my face. "You going?"

I looked at the sparkling water and the blue sky. God had plunked a brilliant spring day smack dab in the middle of December. And we were in one of the most beautiful places I'd ever seen. "You just try and keep me from it." I ran back in and grabbed my candy cane sweater.

By late afternoon, we'd hiked several trails and driven the length of The Trace, the road that ran between the lakes. Phillip joked that Amanda and I had taken so many pictures of the bison and elk that someday our great-grandkids would think they were their ancestors.

We were soaking in the last bit of daylight while puttering back to the campground when Amanda gasped.

"Daddy!" she yelled. "Stop the car."

Phillip mashed the brake. "What is it?"

She pointed to a tree a few yards off the road. A huge bird perched on a branch.

"A bald eagle," I breathed.

We fixed our gazes on him while I slowly rolled my window down. I snapped several pictures, but the majestic bird sat as still as a statue.

"Let's wait a few minutes," Seth whispered.

Phillip nodded. Just then, the eagle spread its wings and, with princely grace, soared into the sky. My heart ached at the beauty and splendor of his flight.

When the eagle had faded to a tiny speck and blended completely with the horizon, I rolled my window up and we rode back to the campground in silence.

That night around the campfire, it didn't seem odd when Phillip pulled out his Bible.

"I'm going to read tonight from the book of Isaiah, chapter forty, verse thirty-one." The fire crackled in the still night.

" 'But they that wait upon the Lord shall renew their strength; they shall mount up with wings as eagles.' " Just as it had the other night, Phillip's voice rang out. In my mind's eye, I could see the eagle soaring in the sky, so free, so powerful.

" 'They shall run, and not be weary; and they shall walk, and not faint.' "

The familiar verse gave me goose bumps. Patience had never been my strong suit. But I longed with every fiber of my being to soar, unfettered, like the eagle we'd seen that afternoon. Was this road trip part of my learning to wait on the Lord?

After we doused the fire, we sat at the picnic table in the dark and listened to the waves lapping against the shore.

"This is cool," Amanda murmured.

"Yeah, it is," Seth said. I couldn't see their faces very well, but they sounded as contented as I felt.

When the kids went in to get ready for bed, Phillip pulled me to my feet in the moonlight. He held me close and I listened to his heartbeat, not for reassurance that he wasn't an alien, but because I wondered if it, like Phillip himself, had grown stronger.

He tilted my chin to meet his gaze, and I didn't resist. "Forgive me?" he asked softly.

A big part of me wanted to say yes and melt into his arms. Another part wanted to stay irritated or even deny ever being mad in the first place. Plus, I'd realized moments before that Amanda and I had missed the mother/daughter shopping trip already. My emotions spun like a tilt-a-whirl.

The night was made for melting. I settled for standing on my tiptoes and pressing my lips to his and hoped he wouldn't notice I didn't answer.

He pulled away gently and dropped a tender kiss on my forehead. "I really do love you, Penny."

Before I could form a reply around the lump in my throat, he'd slipped into the RV. I put my fingers to my lips. *I think he noticed.*

Chapter 9

. . .Nine Candles Burning

A few miles past Mayfield, Kentucky, Phillip maneuvered the RV into a narrow driveway. Cars and trucks sat willy-nilly in the grassy lot, but the giant oak trees interlocked above the white church house with almost perfect symmetry. Even with no leaves the branches seemed to hold the little structure in a safe embrace.

I snuck a peek at the kitchen clock. We'd made it with five minutes to spare. I always feel like being late on Sunday morning is sort of like being sick. I never want to do it even if I'm at home, but it's something to be avoided at all costs when I'm visiting.

"Wow, it looks like something out of *Little House on the Prairie*," Amanda whispered as we walked up on the porch.

It must have been TV Land day because when we walked in the door, the two elderly ladies who greeted us bore a striking resemblance to the Baldwin sisters from *The Waltons*.

Their suits were identical, one blue, the other lilac. Before I could think much about that, though, they grabbed my husband.

"Phillip? Is that you?"

Phillip nodded and hugged them tightly. While the kids and I stared, the lady in the blue suit pinched Phillip's cheek. It wouldn't have surprised me a bit if she'd said, "My, how you've grown."

Instead she said, "And this is your lovely family?"

Phillip, who had the grace to look embarrassed that he hadn't forewarned us about this particular surprise, nodded. He introduced us to his great-aunts, Earlene and Marla Houston.

I smiled, but if I'd been wearing false teeth I would have swallowed them. I *had* to find that black notebook of Phillip's.

Before we could get further acquainted, it was time for us to take our seats. I did note with pleasure that Aunt Earlene, who sat on the pew next to Phillip, pinched his cheek again and patted his knee several times.

After we were dismissed, both ladies turned to us. "Are y'all ready to go?"

Go?

"Yes, ma'am," Phillip said and cast me a wary glance.

I smiled brightly and nodded. I'm sure it's a pride issue, but I've always hated for people to know that I'm unaware of my family's actions or intentions. Even my kids understand this. They know that if they make a bad grade on a test or get in trouble at school, it's much to their advantage to tell me themselves. Because if they wait and let Trevor's mom or Becky's aunt waylay me in the grocery store to fill my ears with tales of what my child has been up to, there'll be trouble with a capital *T.* Of course, the few times that had happened, I smiled serenely at the tell-you-for-your-own-good woman as if I'd known it for days. So, Phillip knew he was safe from my questions for a while.

But when we climbed into the RV with the door safely closed, I slammed my purse onto the counter and followed Phillip into our room and shut the door. "What were those women talking about?" I took my shoes off and jabbed them one at a time in the bottom of the closet.

As I yanked off my dress and pulled my green and red sweatshirt over my head, Phillip smiled. "Nice shirt. What a surprise that you're wearing it."

I couldn't believe it. All week, he'd been ignoring my constant parade of Christmas clothes. And now he had the nerve to subtly compare his low-down, secret-keeping scheme to keep me in the dark with my harmless game of bringing Christmas to his mind by dressing like Holly Holiday.

"Aargh." I slid into my jeans, and as I tied my tennis shoes, my hands were shaking. "Tell me what your aunts were talking about."

"Oh, the sisters?" he said, like he'd forgotten we'd even seen his great-aunts that morning. "I thought we'd stay with them for a few days and do some work around their place." He grabbed a flannel shirt from the small closet. "Aunt Marla has bad arthritis, and Aunt Earlene is going blind. But they've both got sense enough to know they need some help." He buttoned it slowly. "It's okay with you, isn't it?"

I glared at him. Why didn't he just order me to do it? That way, I could be mad at him and not have to feel guilty for saying no, that wasn't okay. I remembered his aunts, smiling lovingly at our family and both wearing suits that had been around at least thirty years. It was obvious they couldn't afford to hire someone to do the work. "It's fine. I just like to know."

He nodded. "Can you be ready to leave in about ten minutes? They're fixing lunch for us."

He started out the door.

"Phillip?"

"Yeah?"

"What kind of work?"

He shrugged. "Light housekeeping and some odds-and-ends jobs."

I rolled my eyes. "Don't you know there's no such thing as 'light' housekeeping?"

He bent his head and kissed me. "Don't worry. It'll be fun."

⌒

"Fun," I grumbled under my breath when we arrived at the aunts' house. The house resembled a small plantation manor and had undoubtedly been beautiful in its time. But now, in *our* time, shutters hung by a thread and paint had peeled in too many places to count.

When we walked inside, the wonderful aroma made it impossible to think about anything else. Fried chicken? Mashed potatoes and gravy? Homemade rolls? Hadn't these ladies ever heard of counting fat grams?

Thankfully, they hadn't. Ten minutes after the meal (while we were washing dishes, actually), the food-induced haze started to wear off, and I took a good look at the interior of the house. Piles of newspapers and magazines rested on every table. Dust, thick enough to plant a garden, layered most surfaces, and it was almost impossible to see out the windows. And that was just in the kitchen.

After the last dish was put away, Phillip pulled out his black notebook and retrieved some blank pages. He passed them to me with a pen.

"We need to make a to-do list."

I bit back a hysterical giggle. *A to-do list?* We needed to call a demolition company. But I'd already grown attached to Aunt Earlene and Aunt Marla. (Who wouldn't grow attached to ladies who could cook like that?) So I just nodded and poised the pen over the paper.

"Who will volunteer to be my helper while I hang the shutters?"

"I will." Seth's eyes gleamed with excitement. It had been days since I'd seen his electronic friend, even though I knew for a fact that he'd gotten new batteries at Wal-Mart.

"Okay, put Seth and me down for repairing the shutters, honey."

Phillip pushed his chair back and stood, apparently too carried away with his commander-in-chief role to sit. "We have to gather the newspapers and magazines and take them to the recycling center."

"Oh, my," Aunt Earlene gasped.

"Now, Earlie, we promised Phillip on the phone that if he helped us we'd do what he says. And you know we can't see to read those anyway." Marla patted her sister's blue-veined hand.

"I'll handle the reading material," I volunteered, touched by their cooperative spirit. I knew how hard it was to throw out a magazine you hadn't read. Besides, I planned to take the older ones to an antique shop and see if I could get the sisters some extra money.

"I'll help." Amanda smiled shyly at Aunt Marla. For the

first time in her young life, my daughter had discovered that all chocolate pies didn't come from a box marked "instant." She would probably do anything to get another one.

Over the next half hour, we split up the rest of the jobs, and I figured we'd just booked ourselves through New Year's Day, at least. The aunts wanted to sign up for some chores, but we assured them if they would just cook, we'd all be happy.

We agreed to start on Monday, so that afternoon we explored the grounds of the house where Phillip's grandmother had grown up.

Eventually, our exploring turned into the first impromptu family game of tag we'd had since the kids were in preschool. After ten minutes, we'd warmed up to it.

"Tag! You're it!" Seth touched my shoulder, and I froze.

"Mom," he wailed. "We're not playing freeze tag. We're just playing regular tag."

I nodded and put my hand to my side. "I know that, Son."

"You can't rest. You're it!" He was indignant.

"Aw, come on, Seth. Give her a break." Phillip ran up to me. "She can't help it if she's out of shape."

I reached out as if I were going to lean on Phillip for support. Instead I tapped him lightly on the shoulder. "Tag. You're it," I called as I ran off.

For a little while I was an eagle, soaring free and never growing tired.

⌒

The next morning, I landed with a thud.

"I found a wheelbarrow." Phillip greeted me at the door of the RV when I finally stumbled out at six-thirty.

"Good for you."

"You and Amanda can use it to haul the papers and magazines to the car."

"Thanks." I relaxed in his arms for a minute. "Good morning."

He kissed me, then whispered close to my ear. "Are you sore from playing tag?"

I arched an eyebrow. "Like I would admit it."

"I am, too." Phillip grinned. "But we'll work out the soreness today."

For the next three days, I waited to "work out the soreness," but instead it just seemed to multiply. By Thursday morning, though, I could see some difference in the house.

"How long do you plan to stay here?" I asked Phillip as I sipped my coffee. It was 7:00 a.m., but Seth and Amanda had been working so hard we'd decided to let them sleep in.

"Are you ready to leave?"

"No!" My face grew hot. "I. . .well, to be honest, I hate to leave until we finish."

"Me, too. I was thinking we could be ready to paint by the weekend. Then if we paint Saturday, take Sunday off. . ." He smiled, and I knew we were both remembering the meal we'd enjoyed last Sunday.

Though the aunts prepared mouthwatering meals every day, none had been as decadently delicious as that first one. He cleared his throat and took a big sip of coffee. ". . .and paint Monday and Tuesday, we'll be done."

"Three days to paint the whole house?"

"If the four of us work together. Plus, a few people from the church said they'd come help us Saturday." He shrugged.

"We might have to come back this summer and do the second coat. Would you mind?"

"You're asking me about a trip in advance?" The challenge slipped out before I thought.

He turned beet red. "If I'd asked you about this one, what would you have said?"

Before I could answer, the cell phone rang. Phillip looked at the caller ID and frowned. "It's your folks."

I frowned, too, as I reached for it. My mom believed cell phones should only be used in life-and-death circumstances.

"Hello?"

"Penny? Is that you?"

"Hey, Mom. It's me. What's wrong?"

"The presents didn't come."

"What?"

"You told me to call you if the presents you sent didn't come. So I'm calling. We didn't get them."

"Oh, no."

"We don't care one bit about that, Penny. And you know it. But you asked me to call you."

"Okay, Mom. Thanks for calling."

"We'll miss you, honey. Give Phillip and the children our love."

"We love all of y'all, too."

I pushed the END button and stared at the phone. I had a sudden desire to fling it across the room.

Phillip was still frowning. "Penny, what happened? Are your parents okay?"

I nodded. "Remember the presents you mailed that Saturday before we left? They still haven't gotten them."

He just shook his head in what I could only assume was silent sympathy, then got up and headed out the door to work.

༄

That afternoon, Amanda had gone out to take a break, and I was sitting in the den going through the piles of magazines. Not long after we'd started, I'd found the deed to the house between a 1940 *Collier's Weekly* and a 1946 *Saturday Evening Post.* So they all had to be sorted through individually.

I picked up a *Good Housekeeping* magazine from the early '80s, and a stack of photos slid out. When I reached to retrieve them, a small plastic bag with birthday candles in it tumbled to the floor on top of them. I grabbed the bag and dropped it in the shoe box I'd labeled *Keepsakes,* then gathered the photos. Before I could put them in the box for pictures, a familiar face caught my eye.

I held the grainy color snapshot closer to my eyes. A small boy stood between Aunt Marla and Aunt Earlene. It looked just like Phillip, but they were clearly standing in front of this house. He would have mentioned being here before, wouldn't he?

I flipped through the rest of the pictures. The same little boy playing in a sprinkler on the lawn, then eating a slice of watermelon, and next, proudly displaying a green snake. The last picture was a close-up of him blowing out birthday candles. Inscribed in red icing on the cake were the words *Happy 9th Birthday, Phillip.* I glanced at the candles in the Ziploc bag and jumped to my feet, pictures still in my hand.

"Um. . .Aunt Marla. . ."

"Yes, dear?" She hobbled from the kitchen, wiping her hands on the cloth she wore fastened on her apron.

"Did Phillip visit y'all when he was a child?"

She nodded. "What a lovely summer that was. Earlene and I haven't felt that young since." A shadow passed over her face. "Too bad it couldn't have come under better circumstances."

"What do you mean?"

"Well, you know. When Richard left so suddenlike, poor Janet just couldn't handle Phillip. . . ." Her voice trailed off and her eyes grew cloudy.

Phillip's dad had left? What was she talking about?

Chapter 10

...Ten Painters Painting

I cleared my throat.

Aunt Marla jumped slightly. "Where was I? Oh, yes, Janet just couldn't handle little Phillip for a while. So she sent him to stay with us until she got on her feet."

"Oh, I see." *Said the blind woman.* "So he stayed all summer?"

"Uh-huh. By fall, Janet had gotten her nerves under control. She depended on him hard for the next several years, though, so he never did get to come back and see us."

Years? I felt dizzy. She must be mixed-up. Phillip had been twenty when we started dating, and I'd met his parents shortly after. They'd seemed perfectly happy. No one had ever mentioned otherwise.

"I need some air."

"I completely understand, honey. There's so much dust in those magazines."

I held up the pictures. "Is it okay if I take these with me for a while?" I strove to keep my tone casual.

"Oh, sure. Phillip might like to look at them."

"That's just what I was thinking." I walked out to the porch where Phillip worked alone. A quick glance showed Seth and Amanda sitting out by the RV.

"Phillip?"

He spun around and sawdust flew from his hair. "Hey. How's it going in there?"

"Pretty good." I glanced at the house. I had no idea how soundproof the walls were, and I didn't want to be overheard. "Want to go for a walk?"

He glanced at the sandpaper in his hand, then dropped it to the workbench. "Sure."

We walked off the porch and headed down a little lane that led to a long-neglected orchard on the back of the property. He cast me a sideways glance. "What's up?"

"I guess I'm just wondering why you've been keeping secrets from me."

"Oh, come on, Penny." He picked up a dead stick and threw it. "This has just been a game. You and I have both known that anytime you got really ready to know where we were going, I'd have told you. I offered to before we even left."

"So when were you going to tell me about this?" I thrust the pictures at him like a wife confronting her husband with proof of his infidelity.

He took the photos from my hand and stared at them. Red crept up his cheeks. "I spent the summer here the year I turned nine," he mumbled.

"We drove in here Sunday, and you acted for all the world like you'd never been here before. Why didn't you tell me?"

Phillip sank to the ground and pulled his knees up to his

chest. "I just couldn't."

Oh, God, if this is a good time for You, I could really use that new heart right now, because this old selfish one wants to ask him a million questions and demand some answers.

The new carefree Phillip had gone just as quickly as he'd come. As he stared across the desolate orchard, the worry lines creased his face. At the sight of his slumped shoulders, all the anger and resentment of the last few weeks fell away, leaving my soul as bare as the tree branches.

I knelt down beside him and touched his shoulder. "Honey, I'm sorry I've been so awful."

He looked at me like he'd forgotten I was there. Then he shook his head. "You haven't."

I snorted. "Yes, I have, and you know it."

A hint of a grin teased across his face. "Well, okay, maybe a little, but I have, too."

We sat quietly in the dry grass, shoulders touching.

"When I was eight, my dad left. No explanations. He just told my mom he was leaving and he left." He fiddled with a piece of grass and didn't look at me. "Mom sent me here for the summer. I guess she just couldn't take my questions about Dad."

"That must have been tough for you."

He looked up then. "In some ways it was awful. I missed Mom so much, not to mention Dad. But the aunts smothered me with love, and at least here, nobody was crying all the time."

I remembered Aunt Marla's words. "And in the fall, you went home and worked to help your mom."

He nodded. "Then one day when I was sixteen, Dad showed up on our doorstep. He apologized and begged us to take him back. Mom was so happy that I didn't have the heart to stay mad at him."

"That was a lot for a teenager to deal with." I thought of Amanda and her fluctuating emotions.

"It was tough for a while. We moved to another town so we could start over without anyone knowing. We made sort of a silent vow to each other to act like those years had never happened."

I could see why he'd kept it a secret, but how could I have not known that for sixteen years he'd been holding part of himself back?

"I wanted to tell you, Pen. I really did. But I knew my parents desperately wanted to forget it."

"I understand." To my amazement, I really did. Had God moved me to the top of His heart transplant list?

⤴

Six days later, we hugged the aunts and promised to come back next summer to put a second coat of paint on the house. As we pulled out of the driveway, I peeked through the window once more to admire our handiwork. The old house looked like a mansion.

A family from church had helped us paint Saturday, and with the ten of us working, we'd covered a huge amount of ground. . .um. . .board.

The husband and wife were a sweet couple with twin sons Seth's age and a daughter Amanda's age, and we'd all gotten along famously. But the whipped topping on the homemade chocolate pie—in Amanda's eyes anyway—had been their shy, but cute, sixteen-year-old son.

I knew for a fact that he and Amanda had exchanged e-mail addresses. And not because I'd overheard it either, but because she'd told me.

⤳

Two days later, we were rolling merrily across southern Missouri, headed who knew where. Well, Phillip knew, of course, but the rest of us didn't. I was partly watching the scenery fly by, partly dozing. Amanda had developed a sudden interest in Christian romance, so she was reading one of my new Heartsongs. (I had to remind her daddy that she'd be fifteen in two weeks. He'd just cringed.)

"Stop, Dad!" Seth yelled from his post by the window.

I peered out as Phillip obligingly pulled into a circle driveway. I didn't see any wildlife.

"What is it?" Phillip turned to Seth when we were stopped.

"There was a really old man two houses back trying to put up his Christmas lights. I could see him from pretty far off, and he was having a hard time."

Phillip frowned. "And?"

"And we need to go help him."

"Go help him?" Phillip asked. "We don't even know him."

I saw the hurt expression on Seth's face fast enough to swallow my own skeptical response.

"That sounds like a great idea, Seth." I raised an eyebrow at Phillip. "Do good deeds have to be prerecorded in your notebook? Or are we allowed to just do them randomly?"

He gave me a look that said, "You know we can't just go up to a stranger and offer to help with his Christmas lights." And I gave him one right back that said, "That's not any crazier than some of the things you've done."

Seth and Amanda watched the silent interchange between us with apparent interest.

Finally Phillip shrugged. "Okay, but you're going to do the talking, Seth."

Seth nodded and Phillip looped around the circle drive and eased back on the road.

The man was definitely a senior citizen, and from the looks of it, Seth had sized up the situation exactly. We pulled into his driveway, thankfully, another circle.

Phillip had barely stopped when Seth jumped out and ran over to the startled man. We couldn't hear him, but we could see his mouth moving rapidly, and then the man grinned and nodded.

Seth motioned us to come on.

"I don't believe this," Amanda grumbled as we piled out of the RV.

"This is Mr. Reynolds," Seth announced as proudly as a first grader with a big frog for show-and-tell.

Phillip shook hands with the man and introduced Amanda and me.

"So you folks are on a good-deed trip, huh?" Mr. Reynolds's eyes were a little clouded, but a twinkle still lurked in the depths.

I watched the red creep up Phillip's face.

"Yes, sir," he replied. "Something like that."

"Well, bless my bones. I sure wouldn't want to deprive you from doing a good turn, so if you'd help me get these lights up, I'd be mighty obliged."

"We'd be glad to." Phillip took the string of lights from

the old man and climbed the ladder. Seth grabbed the stapler and passed it up to his dad.

"Won't my wife be surprised when I go get her after awhile?" Mr. Reynolds's smile covered his whole face. "She's been in the hospital with the flu, but she's coming home today."

"I'm so glad she's able to come home," I said. And I was so glad that Seth had made us stop.

"Me, too. Me, too. But I'm tempted to call and see if they'll keep her until this evenin' so she can see the lights a-twinkling when we pull into the driveway."

"I. . ." I had no idea what to say to that.

Mr. Reynolds didn't seem to mind my loss for words. He moved closer to where Phillip and Seth were working.

I glanced at Amanda and she raised both eyebrows. "Was he serious?" she mouthed.

I shrugged. I could see the weird logic in waiting until evening. But I doubted Medicare or his wife would agree.

Twenty minutes later, after we'd tested all the lights, Mr. Reynolds shook our hands and thanked us. "I'm going to run on and pick the missus up from the hospital." He winked at Amanda. "I don't think she'd take too kindly to being left there all day for no reason." He smiled. "Y'all have a safe trip."

Amanda and I barely made it inside the RV before we collapsed into giggles.

"Women," Seth said in a disgusted tone.

"Yep." Phillip pulled onto the highway with a grin.

Chapter 11

. . .Eleven Roses Blooming

L

ate one night about a week before Christmas, we pulled into a campground in Springfield, Missouri. Both kids had zonked out hours before.

Phillip looked over at me. "You asleep?"

I shook my head. "Nope. Just thinking." *Wondering what your past has to do with our trip.* I bit my tongue.

He motioned toward the kids. "Think they'll be excited when they wake up in the morning and realize where we are?"

"I'd say that's an understatement." They'd driven Phillip crazy since we crossed the Missouri state line, begging to visit their cousins.

"I guess we'll see your cousin and his family at church tomorrow?"

Phillip leaned across the console. "What would you be willing to exchange for that information?"

"Hmm. . ." I leaned toward him. "Guess you'll just have to tell me and find out."

"Yes, we'll see them in the morning," he whispered against my lips, and I kissed him soundly.

I started to climb back to get the kids settled in bed, but he grabbed my arm. I swung around and he waved his black notebook in front of my nose. "What's this worth to you?"

I giggled softly. "Actually, you can keep it. I think I'm starting to enjoy being surprised."

I remembered those words the following night when just the two of us drove back to the campground from his cousin's house.

"Three days?" I asked. "The kids are going to stay with them for three days?" I had to admit, I'd gotten used to us all being packed in together in the RV like gifts in a stocking.

"Unless you have a problem with it."

"Was this in your notebook?" Could he and the kids have cooked this up after we got here? Nobody had seemed surprised but me. And I'd hidden it well, of course.

He nodded. "I talked to John and Paula about it before we left home. Did you think I'd forgotten that our anniversary is tomorrow?"

"No, but I never dreamed you'd planned anything like this."

"Never underestimate your husband, Mrs. Lassiter."

"Believe me, I'm learning not to."

When I opened my eyes the next morning, a red rose rested on my pillow a few inches away from my nose. *Whoa.* Had a stranger abducted Phillip in the middle of the night and replaced him with a Stepford husband? Phillip was nothing if not pragmatic, and he would never put a rose on my pillow, in case I rolled over and stuck myself on the thorns.

I squinted at the stem and burst out laughing. It had been carefully dethorned. Now that was something Phillip would do.

Now that I was awake, I smelled coffee. "Phillip?"

He stepped to the bedroom door. "Good morning. I thought you were going to sleep all day."

"Happy Anniversary," I said with a smile. "I won." We have a standing game to see which one can tell the other one happy anniversary or Valentine's Day or even Thanksgiving Day first. He'd had the perfect chance to win, but he'd blown it with "Good morning."

"Afraid not. That rose was my 'happy anniversary' to you."

I rolled back over, and sure enough, a little tag on the stem proclaimed "Happy Anniversary." I scrunched up my nose. "Cheater. But thanks for the rose."

"There are eleven more to go with it." He nodded toward the nightstand where an elegant bouquet of a dozen roses, minus one dethorned one, soaked in a crystal vase full of water.

Two days ago, I'd been imagining what it would be like to have our anniversary on this trip. My musings couldn't have been further from reality. "They're beautiful." I stretched and yawned. "How did you get those so early?"

"I got up at the crack of dawn. Unlike somebody I know." He grinned and leaned against the doorframe.

I sat up in bed and stretched again. It had been wonderful to sleep late. All the way across Missouri, Phillip had found volunteer opportunities for us, from caroling in the campground to raking leaves at a senior citizens' center. We teased him about not wanting to make Seth out to be a liar about our "good-deed tour."

"So what do we have planned today?"

"What do you want to do?"

"So suddenly you've lost your notebook?" I grinned to take the sting out of my words.

"No, I've got it all planned, but I thought you might be getting a little sick of that."

"If it doesn't involve volunteering somewhere, I'd just as soon follow your plan."

"In that case, pack enough clothes for two days and two nights."

"Um. . .pack? In case you haven't noticed, we're living in our room already."

He bent down and kissed me. "Are you going to go along with the plan, or are you going to complain all day?"

"I don't know," I teased. "Was that kiss my punishment for complaining or incentive to comply?"

"Incentive."

"Then I'm definitely packing."

He grinned and kissed me again. "I'm going to go up to the office and let them know we'll be gone a couple of days."

I watched him leave, then packed enough for both of us for two days. I included one nice outfit each, just in case. I was getting pretty good at "just in case."

With the suitcases ready, I carried the bouquet of eleven roses into the kitchen and set them on the table. I'd wrapped the single, dethorned bloom in tissue and stashed it in my bag. Nothing said romance like a single rose on your pillow, and tonight *was* our anniversary night.

Finally, I sat down for a cup of coffee and rubbed a soft rose petal between my fingers. Had he bought me roses because he really loved me? Or because it was what he thought

I expected? For the first time I could remember, his motivation was more important to me than his actions.

For our whole married life, I'd treated Phillip like he was an extension of me. We'd had disagreements, and I knew he was the "head" of our household; but I had just never thought that much about his feelings, except in direct relation to my own.

The strength and the vulnerability I'd seen in him these past few weeks had changed my love. Deepened it. And my inner struggle to submit to him willingly, out of love and not out of duty, had made a difference, as well.

He opened the door just as I was dabbing my tears.

"Penny? Are you crying?"

"No." *Not in the last two seconds.*

He sank across from me and took my hand. "Has this trip been so awful?"

I shook my head. "It's been fun, really." And it had. We'd all laughed more together in the last month than we had in the last year.

"But you still wonder why I insisted we do it." He got up and poured himself a cup of coffee.

I chuckled. "Well, now that you mention it. . ."

"You probably know it has something to do with my dad."

"I thought it might."

"You don't miss a trick, do you?" he chided, but I recognized the teasing glint in his eyes.

"Hopefully not anymore. Not if it has to do with you." My early New Year's resolution was to pay way more attention in the future. If I hadn't been so wrapped up in myself, Phillip might have told me about his childhood much earlier.

"A couple of months ago, when Dad had his heart attack,

remember I spent the night with him that first night?"

I nodded.

"We didn't know if he would make it through the night, and he wanted to talk. For the first time, after all these years, he told me why he left."

"Why?" Another woman, no doubt.

"He said he left because he'd spent so much of his time and energy making a living that the people in his house had become strangers to him, and as strangers, it was easy to walk away from them."

"Well, that seems a little oversimplified." I grabbed my tongue between my teeth. *Be still, Penny, and listen.*

"Maybe so, but after he said that and warned me not to make the same mistake, I came home to a house where I felt like an intruder. I didn't feel like I knew you or the kids anymore, and when I tried to turn to God, I found I didn't know Him anymore either, and the realization scared me worse than any horror movie ever could."

I wanted to protest, but I just bit my tongue harder.

Phillip pulled me to my feet and folded me into his arms. "I've still got a long way to go. But I finally know God again—and you and the kids, too—and I'll never let y'all go as long as there is breath in my body. This crazy trip gave that back to me." He kissed me, and I knew he was right. Somehow, out on the open road, we'd all found our way home.

Chapter 12

. . . Twelve Gifts of Love

T was the night before Christmas and in the RV, the Lassiter family curled up by the tree. I took another sip of hot cocoa and surveyed the scene. I almost wished I were a cat so I could purr.

Wrapping paper littered the floor. Amanda sat on the love seat, writing in her new journal, and Seth sorted through the tool set Phillip had bought for him. He was already planning which tools to take to the aunts' house next summer.

Phillip and I had spent our anniversary in Branson, which was what he'd planned all along. It was the first anniversary in years when it hadn't really mattered *what* we did, as long as we were together. It was a good feeling.

After we'd picked up the kids, we went shopping. Working without a list had been a challenge, but I think we had all risen to it. We each bought one gift per family member, so we'd only had twelve gifts under the tree. But the tree was so small that it had looked just right. And it was.

Traditionally, we opened our gifts to each other on Christmas Eve, since we always spent Christmas Day with my parents. Although he hadn't spelled it out (and no, I didn't steal his black notebook—it was almost flat now), I'd surmised that Phillip had a big volunteer gig planned for Christmas Day, so we'd decided to continue our tradition.

Phillip stretched out beside me on the carpet and flipped the pages of the deluxe-version travel atlas I'd gotten him.

"Look, honey. Wouldn't you like to go there?" He pointed to an obscure part of Brazil.

Jungles? my inner child wailed. *What about spiders and snakes?*

I just smiled. "It looks. . .interesting, but it might be hard to do that on a two-week vacation. Maybe we should stick with the States for now."

"I guess you're right." He closed the book suddenly. "Penny, did you open the package from me?"

"No."

"Are you sure? It was small."

"I'm sure." The smallest thing I'd opened had been a new Ted Dekker book from Amanda.

He scrounged around under the wrapping paper and handed me a small square box.

Before I opened it, I looked again at Phillip, Seth, and Amanda all here with me, in body and in spirit. What more could a woman want? *"Girl,"* my inner child corrected me. *What more could a* "girl" *want?* I shook my head at her silliness and tore the box open.

Nestled on soft cotton, a crystal heart ornament shimmered in the light. Below the etching of a couple on a sleigh ride were the words *Our First Christmas Together.*

I couldn't believe it. I'd gotten my new heart.

≈

"Wake up, sleepyhead," Phillip whispered in my ear. I jumped and slammed into my seat belt. Then I remembered. He'd had us sleep buckled in so he could drive through the night to wherever we were volunteering today.

My muscles ached from sleeping in the chair. How could I face a day of cutting up vegetables and handing out soup the way I felt? Heat flushed my face. If hungry people could face standing in line to get it, I could surely face standing in line to hand it out.

"I'm sore." Sometimes my inner child insisted on waking up before me so she could talk out loud.

"Here, let me rub your back." Phillip swiveled his chair toward me, and I leaned forward with my eyes still closed while he kneaded the tired muscles.

"I should be rubbing your back. Where did we have to be today that you had to drive all night to get us there?" I rubbed my bleary eyes and peered out the window.

"Phillip!" My parents' house was directly across the road from where we were parked. Tears streamed down my cheeks. "You didn't have to do this."

"I wanted to surprise you."

Suddenly I remembered Mom's phone call. "Uh-oh." I put my hand to my mouth. "We don't have any gifts." I looked at the familiar house and twisted back around to grin at my amazing husband. "Oh, well, so what? They'll have us. . .and we'll have them." It seemed odd that a year ago, I'd thought carrying in an armload of gaily wrapped packages and steaming covered dishes

343

was the most important thing.

I hugged him again.

He cleared his throat. "But it just so happens we do have presents for them."

I arched a brow. "What do you mean?"

"Well, since this was my scheduled ending to our trip, I didn't mail the packages. I was afraid they might open them before we got here, so I just brought them with us."

I squealed. "You're kidding!"

He shook his head. "They're in the storage underneath."

I couldn't sit still another second. I leaped past the console, my earlier soreness a distant memory.

"Seth! Amanda! Guess where we are!"

I tickled Amanda's bare foot.

"Huh? Mom. Don't." She snuggled farther into her pillow.

"You've got to get up, both of you!" I gave Phillip a pleading look. "Help me! You know my mom comes out to get her newspaper the first thing."

He laughed. "Calm down. They'll get up when they realize where we are."

Ten minutes later, while the kids—finally awake and excited—were dressing, I hurried out to help Phillip get the gifts from the storage. Just as we stepped outside, the front door of the house opened.

Mom stepped onto the porch in her duster and house shoes and scooped up the newspaper. When she straightened, her gaze fell on the RV. She stood frozen for a few seconds. Then, still clutching the paper, she raced toward us.

I ran to meet her and we fell into each other's arms, spinning together like schoolgirls. "Merry Christmas!" I cried.

"Penny! Y'all made it home!"

I looked over her shoulder at the love shining in Phillip's eyes and then to where Seth and Amanda were climbing out of the RV with sleepy smiles. "Yes, Mama, we sure did."

CHRISTINE LYNXWILER

Christine thanks God daily for the joyous life she shares with her husband and two daughters. They work, play, and worship together in a small Arkansas town nestled in the Ozark Mountains. Besides writing and spending time with her family, Christine enjoys reading, kayaking, trout fishing, and going to auctions. She loves to hear from her readers.

A Letter to Our Readers

Dear Readers:

In order that we might better contribute to your reading enjoyment, we would appreciate your taking a few minutes to respond to the following questions. When completed, please return to the following: Fiction Editor, Barbour Publishing, Inc., P.O. Box 719, Uhrichsville, OH 44683.

1. Did you enjoy reading *Simply Christmas*?
   ❑ Very much—I would like to see more books like this.
   ❑ Moderately—I would have enjoyed it more if _____

_____

_____

2. What influenced your decision to purchase this book?
   (Check those that apply.)
   ❑ Cover   ❑ Back cover copy   ❑ Title   ❑ Price
   ❑ Friends   ❑ Publicity   ❑ Other

3. Which story was your favorite?
   ❑ *All Done with the Dashing*   ❑ *O Little Town of Progress*
   ❑ *No Holly, No Ivy*   ❑ *My True Love Gave to Me. . .*

4. Please check your age range:
   ❑ Under 18   ❑ 18–24   ❑ 25–34
   ❑ 35–45   ❑ 46–55   ❑ Over 55

5. How many hours per week do you read? _____

Name _____

Occupation _____

Address _____

City _____ State _____ Zip _____

E-mail _____

If you enjoyed

Simply Christmas

then read:

CHRISTMAS ON THE *Prairie*

FOUR ROMANCE STORIES FULL OF CHRISMAS NOSTALGIA

One Wintry Night by Pamela Griffin
The Christmas Necklace by Maryn Langer
Colder Than Ice by Jill Stengl
Take Me Home by Tracey V. Bateman

If you enjoyed

Simply Christmas

then read:

LONE STAR CHRISTMAS

Someone Is Rustling Up a Little Holiday Matchmaking in Four Delightful Stories

The Marrying Kind by Kathleen Y'Barbo
Here Cooks the Bride by Cathy Marie Hake
Unexpected Blessings by Vickie McDonough
A Christmas Chronicle by Pamela Griffin

If you enjoyed

Simply Christmas

then read:

angels
for christmas

Crafty Little Angels Put Their Charm Into Four Holiday Romances

Strawberry Angel by Pamela Griffin
Angel Charm by Tamela Hancock Murray
Angel on the Doorstep by Sandra Petit
An Angel for Everyone by Gail Sattler

Available wherever books are sold.
Or order from:
Barbour Publishing, Inc.
P.O. Box 721
Uhrichsville, Ohio 44683
www.barbourbooks.com

You may order by mail for $6.97 and add $2.00 to your order for shipping.
Prices subject to change without notice.

If you enjoyed

Simply Christmas

then read:

HOME FOR CHRISTMAS

Love Reunites Four Orphaned Siblings in Interwoven Novellas

Heart Full of Love by Colleen Coble
Ride the Clouds by Carol Cox
Don't Look Back by Terry Fowler
To Keep Me Warm by Gail Gaymer Martin

HEARTSONG
PRESENTS

If you love Christian romance...

$10.⁹⁹

You'll love Heartsong Presents' inspiring and faith-filled romances by today's very best Christian authors...DiAnn Mills, Wanda E. Brunstetter, and Yvonne Lehman, to mention a few!

When you join Heartsong Presents, you'll enjoy 4 brand-new mass market, 176-page books—two contemporary and two historical—that will build you up in your faith when you discover God's role in every relationship you read about!

Imagine...four new romances every four weeks—with men and women like you who long to meet the one God has chosen as the love of their lives...all for the low price of $10.99 postpaid.

Mass Market 176 Pages

To join, simply visit www.heartsongpresents.com or complete the coupon below and mail it to the address provided.

✂ -

YES! Sign me up for Heart♥ng!

NEW MEMBERSHIPS WILL BE SHIPPED IMMEDIATELY!

Send no money now. We'll bill you only $10.99 postpaid with your first shipment of four books. Or for faster action, call 1-740-922-7280.

NAME _____

ADDRESS _____

CITY _____ STATE _____ ZIP _____

**MAIL TO: HEARTSONG PRESENTS, P.O. Box 721, Uhrichsville, Ohio 44683
or sign up at WWW.HEARTSONGPRESENTS.COM**

ADPG05